"I've decided to take you up on your offer.

"But before I say yes, I want you to know that I was engaged once before. My fiancé left town the night before our wedding and broke my heart. I can't take that type of heartbreak again, so know this…I most likely will never love you. At least not the way a wife should love her husband." She breathed out heavily. "There. I've said it, so if you don't want to marry me after hearing this, I understand."

Josiah's heart went out to Anna Mae for her loss. But still it felt as if a huge weight had been lifted off his shoulders. She didn't want a real marriage, either. This was perfect. He laughed.

"You're happy I won't ever love you?"

"Yes. I want to be friends with you, but I can never love you the way I did my first wife."

"Oh, I see." Anna Mae nodded. "But I'd rather no one else knows that this is a marriage of convenience."

He nodded in turn. Anna Mae laughed. "Good, then we can get married whenever you're ready."

Was it his imagination or did her laugh sound forced?

Rhonda Gibson lives in New Mexico with her husband, James. She has two children and three beautiful grandchildren. Reading is something she has enjoyed her whole life and writing stemmed from that love. When she isn't writing or reading, she enjoys gardening, beading and playing with her dog, Sheba. You can visit her at rhondagibson.net. Rhonda hopes her writing will entertain, encourage and bring others closer to God.

Books by Rhonda Gibson

Love Inspired Historical

The Marshal's Promise
Groom by Arrangement
Taming the Texas Rancher
His Chosen Bride
A Pony Express Christmas
The Texan's Twin Blessings
A Convenient Christmas Bride

Visit the Author Profile page at Harlequin.com.

RHONDA GIBSON

A Convenient Christmas Bride

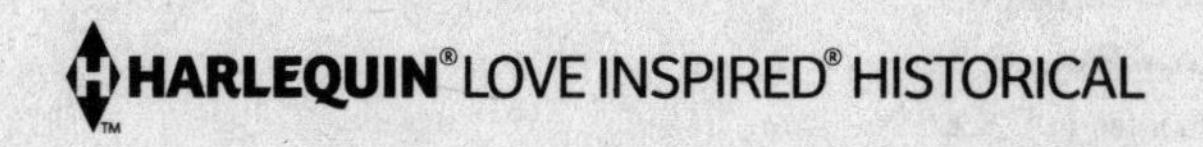

Recycling programs for this product may not exist in your area.

LOVE INSPIRED BOOKS™

ISBN-13: 978-0-373-28340-8

A Convenient Christmas Bride

This edition published by arrangement with Love Inspired Books.

www.Harlequin.com

Printed in U.S.A.

Humble yourselves therefore under the mighty hand
of God, that He may exalt you in due time,
Casting all your care upon Him; for He careth for you.
—*1 Peter* 5:6–7

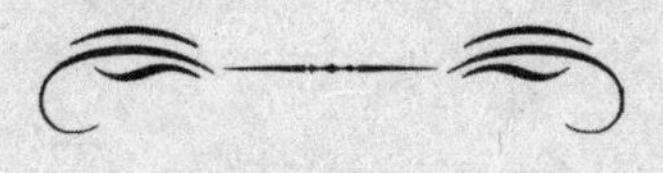

To God be the Glory and to James
who continues to believe in me.

Chapter One

Granite, Texas
October 1887

Sheriff Josiah Miller peered out his cabin window into the darkness, searching for a plausible explanation for the uneasiness shivering down his spine. What had set off the warning bells in his body?

His twin daughters snuggled deeply under their covers, sleeping soundly on this cold winter's night, and for that he was thankful. No worries on that front because he'd just checked on them. So what accounted for the dull disquiet that had him pacing the floor, looking out the window every few seconds?

They were in the midst of a fierce snowstorm and it was only October. Maybe that's what had him skittish as an unbroken mare. Signs pointed to a harsh winter. He dreaded it. Lonely nights out in the cold could work on a man's mind. He shrugged his shoulders in mock resignation.

Dratted snow! He blamed the white stuff for his dismal thoughts.

Josiah stopped pacing midstride and slowly turned back to the window. Snow swirled about, creating almost zero visibility. In spite of the fire that burned in the fireplace, he shivered, not only from the cold pressing against the glass but from the banshee-like wails of the wind.

On nights like this he missed Mary the most. If she were alive, Mary would be humming and the aroma of fresh baked bread would draw him to the kitchen. How often he'd slipped up behind her, slid his arms around her waist, kissing her, tickling her, till she cut him a slice. She'd scold him for his impatience, but always with a twinkle in her eyes that belied her words. She knew how to make a home cozy and warm; a place where he longed to be. Now, when it was too late, Josiah realized how much he missed her and the home they'd shared.

Perhaps he should begin looking for a wife so that his twin daughters wouldn't have to grow up motherless. Raising them alone was hard. Finding a babysitter even harder. They needed a mother's love and he needed help.

Shadowy movement beside the barn caught his attention. Josiah focused intently on the area. There. Right at the front edge by the door something moved again. His eyes weren't deceiving him. What in the world could that be?

He cupped his hands around his face and pressed his nose against the cold windowpane. His breath fogged up the glass. Josiah wiped away the condensation. Could it be an animal? Had his horse gotten out of the barn into the snow and cold? Josiah grunted, tempted to leave the beast to his own devices, but he wasn't a coldhearted man and knew it was a disgruntled thought he'd never act upon. A lawman's horse was as important to him as his right arm.

At the door, he eased his warm feet out of his slippers and into heavy boots. He pulled his fur jacket off the coatrack, thrust his arms inside and then put on gloves. Pulling his hat down tight on his head and wrapping a long woolen scarf around his face, Josiah stepped out into the freezing, swirling snowstorm.

Gripping the rope he'd tied from the rail of the porch to the barn door, Josiah gave a little tug. It held fast. That was reassuring. Some men got lost in a storm like this and died feet away from their barn or house. Josiah had no intentions of dying like that.

After he'd inched away from the house, he glanced over his shoulder. He could barely see the light from his front window. His chest bumped into something and he turned back around. "Well, I'll be."

A small mule waited patiently, head down, nose almost touching the snow. "So it was you instead of my faithful horse that I saw out here." Josiah reached out and touched her nose. Warm air filled his glove. "Poor thing, must be half frozen," he muttered.

A soft thud sounded beside the animal as its rider fell into the snow. Josiah eased around the mule to see who it had been carrying. Yards of dark fabric covered the woman's legs. A scarf much like his own covered her face. He reached down and lifted her out of the snow.

The woman sagged against his chest. In a weak voice that sounded low and scratchy she moaned, "Please, take care of my mule."

He couldn't make out her face, but her voice sounded familiar. Her wet dress, slightly frozen in places, pressed against his coat and he felt no warmth from her whatsoever. Big brown eyes beseeched him, glazed with what he could only assume was a fever. "Now don't you go fretting, ma'am. I'm not one to leave an animal out in this storm."

Josiah looked to the mule. He could take care of only one of them at a time. "Sorry, lil' feller. I'll be back as soon as I get your mistress settled." He weighed his options for a few moments, then decided there was nothing for it but to place the woman over his shoulder like a sack of potatoes. He had to have a hand free to hold on to the line and be guided back to the house. Expecting a fight, he immediately knew her condition to be serious when she only groaned slightly. He grabbed the rope in his gloved hand and headed back to the house.

His thoughts bumped together as he worked to get there. What a night for being out in this weather. Where had she been going? And why couldn't it have waited until after the storm. The woman slumped limply against him as she lost consciousness.

Out of breath from his battle through the snowdrifts, bearing the slight weight of the woman, Josiah gave a sigh of relief to find the bottom step of the porch. He pulled her closer to his chest and carried her the rest of the way to the front door.

Wet clothes added weight to her body. In the light from his window he could see that her hood had fallen back and brown hair spilled out over the fabric. Deep brown eyes fluttered open for a brief moment, causing Josiah to gasp as recognition gripped him.

"Anna Mae?"

"Josiah." His name whispered across her lips as she slipped back into unconsciousness.

His name, spoken in a weak and tremulous whisper, was the sweetest sound he'd heard in a long time. As long as she could speak, he had a chance to save her. His heart leaped in his chest with fear as her breathing became raspy. Josiah pushed the door open and carried her to the couch. He laid her down gently. Now what was he going to do?

"I suppose I should get that wet cloak off of you. I'm sure you'll feel much better once that is removed." Whiskers scratched his palm as he rubbed his jaw.

Carefully, he shifted Anna Mae up and about until he was able to remove the heavy, wet cloak. He lowered her. Brown hair that he'd only seen up in a bun now cascaded about her shoulders in a soft curtain of silk.

Anna Mae Leland was the town's schoolteacher and a good friend of his sister-in-law, Emily Jane Barns. What had she been doing out in this weather? He'd known her only a few months but Josiah believed her to be a sensible woman. So why was she traveling in a blizzard? And where had she been going?

He walked to the door and looked out at the shadow

of the mule. His gaze moved back to Anna Mae. Both of them needed immediate care, both needed warmth.

Josiah tossed more wood on the fire and then went into the bedroom where his girls slept. He pulled blankets from the chest at the foot of the bed and carried them back to her. Should he try to make her more comfortable by getting her into dry clothes? Or leave her in the wet dress? The thought came that she needed another woman, not him. He tucked her tightly within the blankets.

Unsure what to do for her next, Josiah decided to take care of the mule. He opened the door and stepped out into the raging blizzard. He'd been in enough storms in his lifetime to know that this one was going to be long and hard.

His gaze moved back to the window, which offered light and comfort. What on earth was he going to do about the woman resting on his couch?

For the first time since her arrival at the farm, Anna Mae sat at the kitchen table with the Miller family. It had been all she could do to walk the short distance from the bedroom where she'd been for over a week.

The day before, her fever had finally broken, and she'd awakened and explained to the sheriff that she'd been lured out into the storm by Bart, her ten-year-old student. She'd told him it was probably just a prank but still hoped he'd check on the boy. Josiah assured her that the boy was probably home before the storm ever hit. She latched on to that small ray of hope, trying hard to be very thankful.

But now she had other problems. She traced the outline of a knot in the wooden table. "What am I going to do? As soon as word gets out that I've been here throughout the entire storm, the school board will fire me for sure." She rested her arms on the tabletop and dropped her head on them. Weakness overwhelmed her. Her throat still hurt, but not like it had.

"Here, drink this." Josiah placed a hot cup in front of her.

She raised her head. Rose and Ruby, the sheriff's two-year-old twins, sat on their side of the table motionless, watching the adults. Each held a handful of eggs and a piece of bread.

Josiah dished scrambled eggs onto a plate and set it before her. "I don't see what the fuss is about, Annie. We'll just explain what happened and everything will be fine." He returned to the stove.

"Eat?" Rose asked hopefully.

"Not yet. Let me get my plate and we'll be ready," Josiah answered, pouring coffee into another mug and bringing it and his plate to the table.

Anna Mae tried to think of the children as chaperones, but didn't believe the school board would go for that. No, she was doomed.

"Please don't call me Annie, Sheriff Miller. And I really don't think they are going to care what my excuse is. They aren't going to approve of my staying here with you for so long." Anna Mae sighed. She'd asked him not to call her Annie before but it didn't do much good. He seemed to enjoy teasing her.

The big sheriff shrugged his shoulders and sat down

at the table, his plate heaped with eggs, bacon and bread. "I believe you are wrong. All they have to do is take one look at you and know you've been sick."

Did she look that bad? Anna Mae tucked a stringy hank of hair behind her ear. Sadly, he was right. She knew without looking into a mirror that she was a sight.

"Now don't go fussin'. All I meant was that you've lost weight and the luster in your eyes hasn't quite come back. If you add that to your scratchy sounding voice, well there's no mistaken you've been under the weather."

"Eat now?" Rose pleaded, looking from one adult to the other.

Josiah's gaze moved to the girls. They sat poised at the table just as they'd been moments ago. "We best pray before these two get tired of waiting and start throwing those eggs at us to get our attention." A wide grin spread over his face just before he bowed his head to pray.

Anna Mae couldn't concentrate on his prayer. Just like before, she was out of a job and it wasn't even her fault. If Bart hadn't lured her out into the storm, she would be home in her room at the boardinghouse.

As soon as he said amen, Anna Mae asked, "Did you go check on Bart?"

Josiah laid his fork down. "Haven't had a chance to but I'm sure the boy is fine. If he weren't they would have sent out a search party for him, and I'd have been the first one they came to for help. Why don't you tell me how that happened again?"

Anna Mae sighed. "I was at the school grading papers when Bart came running inside. He asked me to go with him into the woods. He said Miles Carter, one of the smaller boys in my class, was hurt and I was the closest adult who could help him." She took a sip of her coffee.

"Go on." Josiah helped the girls with their meals and ate his breakfast at the same time. Her heart went out to him. She would have been dead now if he hadn't helped her. He already had so much to do and he'd stayed with her during the worst of her illness. His eyes were surrounded by dark circles, showing his lack of sleep since her arrival.

She focused on her story. "He'd already brought the little mule to the front of the school so we left almost immediately. At first I believed him, but the deeper we went into the woods the more I began to doubt his story. I knew Bart was still sore that he had to stay in at lunch and sweep up the school, but I really hadn't thought he'd do spite work."

"Spite work?" The sheriff turned quizzical eyes on her.

"That he'd leave me alone." A deep sigh slipped from between her lips. "I was wrong." Anna Mae set her cup down and reached for her fork.

He looked up and smiled. "Well, no matter what brought you here, it's nice to see you up and sitting at my table, Annie." A wicked twinkle entered his eyes.

She almost corrected him again, but he'd saved her life so she decided he could call her whatever he wanted to. "It's nice to be here, Sheriff Miller."

He bent over to pick up the bread Rose had dropped. When he straightened he asked, "Then what happened?"

"Bart distracted me by saying he thought Miles was directly in front of us. While I focused on the spot where he pointed, Bart took off, leaving me alone in the woods. I never even saw him go." Anna Mae felt foolish, but continued on. "The sky had become overcast and I couldn't get my bearings. I think I wandered around at least an hour before it started to rain, and then the rain quickly turned to snow. It got so bad I couldn't see two feet in front of me, so I decided to give the mule her lead, praying she'd take me back to the schoolhouse." Anna Mae shivered. "I was so cold and wet." Just the memory of the sharp pain in her chest as she breathed in the icy air sent another shiver down her spine.

"It's a good thing your mule found my place. I hate to think what would have become of you," Josiah stated, before dishing more food into his mouth.

"Thank you for saving my life."

He held her gaze as he swallowed and then said, "That mule out there saved your life. All I did was keep the fever down and get a little water in ya. Now eat up." He waved his fork toward the plate in front of her. "You tell the school board what you just told me and I'm sure everything will be fine."

The eggs scratched as they went down, and Anna Mae turned her head to cough. The cough seemed to come and go, but at least her chest no longer burned from the pain of it.

Once the coughing subsided, she asked, "Do you think it's safe to go to town today?"

He shook his head, gently wiping eggs off the side of Ruby's mouth. "Not with a wagon. That rainstorm we got right before the snow turned into a layer of ice. Besides, it's best to stay out of the cold air and let that cough heal."

"But the longer I stay here…" She left the words hanging in the air.

"Nothin' to do for it. I can't have you and the girls out in this weather." He sipped his coffee.

He was right. If it were just her safety, Anna Mae felt sure she'd risk going out. But it wasn't just hers, it was the twins', too. She sighed.

"If you need something, I can take Roy and go out."

"Roy?"

A grin split the sheriff's face. "Yeah, my horse."

"You named him Roy?" Anna Mae felt a chuckle rise in her sore throat. The big black gelding Josiah rode looked like anything but a Roy. Her papa had a business associate named Roy who was old, bent over at the waist, and sported a bald spot right in the center of his hair. Other than their names, there were no similarities between the fine-looking horse and the balding old man.

"Now don't go makin' fun of Roy, he's seen me through some rough weather. I believe he could get me to town without too many mishaps."

The thought of Josiah out on ice and snow with his horse slipping and possibly breaking a leg didn't appeal to her at all. She shook her head. "No, I don't need anything. Just wanted to get back before the school board missed me." She spooned another bite of egg into her mouth, worry making the food flavorless. She brushed crumbs from her lap. If the board were to see her wearing Josiah's shirt and long johns, she'd be in more than a heap of trouble. She'd be run out of town on a rail.

Thankfully, his shirt covered her to right below the knees, but still her cheeks flushed every time she remembered struggling into the clothes that belonged to the sheriff.

Shortly after she'd arrived, Josiah had insisted she put on dry clothes. She'd been shaking so badly from the cold and the fever that consumed her body that it had taken much longer than normal for her to change. Concerned, he'd threatened to come in and help her. She'd managed to get them on before he'd made good on his threat, but was so exhausted she'd fallen into a deep sleep. Hopefully, she'd be able to change back into her own dress right after breakfast.

Josiah pushed away from the table, taking his and the twins' plates with him. The little girls were covered in egg and wet crumbs. "Maybe, if the sun comes out full force, we'll be able to get to town in a couple of days." He raked the scraps into the slop bucket and carried it to the back porch to be thrown out later.

Anna Mae offered, "I can help you with that." She pushed away from the table and immediately felt the weakness in her limbs.

"Nope, you are just recovering." He walked over to her and placed a hand under her arm. "I'll help you to the couch and you can rest there until you need to return to bed. I don't want you to come down with another fever."

Tears filled her eyes as he walked beside her into the sitting room. Josiah had been so nice to her. He'd saved her life and then tried to make her comfortable during the worst of her sickness. Anna Mae vowed that during the time she had to stay here, she'd offer her help and make herself useful.

"Why don't you bring the girls in here and I'll read to them," she said, hoping he'd at least let her help out in that way.

"Now that's a right nice idea. Give me a minute to get them cleaned up and I'll put them in the corral." He waited until she seated herself on the sofa, then handed her a small quilt before he returned to the kitchen.

Anna Mae stared into the fire, disturbing thoughts troubling her. Would she have a job when this was all over? If not, where would she go? Would this town be as hard on her as her hometown had been? Fears and past hurts ran deep within her. How she hated this feeling of uncertainty. She'd just lately felt secure enough to put down roots. As if she finally belonged. Now her very livelihood could be decided by others known for judging harshly.

Without warning, Anna Mae remembered the shame she'd felt when her ex-fiancé, Mark Peters, had left her standing at the altar. She'd given up her teaching job to marry him. She'd thought he loved her, but he'd left the night before their wedding and had a note delivered at the hour of the marriage ceremony. Fresh tears filled her eyes, for just thinking of it shattered her. Not because she'd loved Mark to the point of distraction, but because he'd made a laughingstock of her. The whole town had shaken their heads and secretly called her a fool. With her teaching job no longer available, Anna

Mae had done the only thing she felt she could do. She'd answered Levi Westland's ad for a mail-order bride.

But thankfully, God knew that Levi wasn't the man for her, and had sent Millie Hamilton to be his new bride. Anna Mae had breathed a sigh of relief the day Levi announced his intention to marry Millie, confirming in Anna Mae's heart that she was meant to be a schoolteacher and a spinster.

"I wish you'd stop worrying about the school board. Whatever comes, we'll face it together and I'll make sure that they understand." Josiah placed the girls into what he'd called the corral, made of boards and fabric, and stood to smile at her.

Lost in thoughts of the past, Anna Mae needed a moment to reorient herself. She longed to trust in Josiah's assurances, but she was reluctant to place her faith with a man again.

Chapter Two

Josiah stood in the kitchen and listened to Anna Mae's soft voice as she read to the girls from the book of Genesis. He knew the girls didn't understand the story of Adam and Eve, but they looked up at Anna Mae with sincere interest. He dried the last dish and laid the towel to the side.

His boots made a soft clomping sound as he walked across the floor. He knelt down beside her chair and touched her hand. It felt soft under his rough fingers. She turned her big brown eyes upon him. "Would you mind terribly if I go check on Roy and the mule?"

A soft smile graced her chapped lips, reminding him that she needed to drink more water. "Not at all. I'm sure they would enjoy breakfast and a little attention."

He nodded and stood. Josiah reached for Ruby and touched the soft black curls on her head. He glanced between her and Rose. "You girls be good for Annie, ya hear?"

"Go," Ruby said as she worked to stand up.

"Not this time, little one. It's too cold out there for little girls." He leaned over and kissed her soft cheek.

Rose scrambled for him. She smacked her lips, wanting her kisses, too. "Tisses!" she demanded.

He laughed and scooped both girls up into his arms. Kissing them both all over their faces sent them into squeals of delight. Josiah's love for the girls grew stronger every day. They were changing so much as they got older.

Anna Mae's soft laughter joined in. He looked over at her and saw that her face looked a little pale. Had she overdone it this morning? Possibly. Maybe now wasn't a good time to leave her alone with the twins. He stood to his full height and looked down on her.

As if she could read his mind, Anna Mae said, "You better hurry and take care of the animals. We'll be fine until you return."

Josiah nodded and quickly set the girls back into the corral. He pulled on his coat and scarf. Cold air blasted into the house as he hurried out the door.

Snow glistened on the ground and the early morning sun rays added to the brightness. He shielded his eyes and exhaled, his breath forming a cloudy vapor. Thankfully, the snow had stopped falling. He followed the trail to the barn, the cold air stinging his face.

When he opened the door, warmth greeted him along with the scent of hay and dust. Roy snorted from his corner of the barn and the little mule hailed him with a loud bray. "I hear ya, you ornery beasts."

Josiah hurried to give the animals water, grain and hay. As quickly as he could, he mucked out their stalls and laid fresh hay. A glance at his pocket watch told him he'd been out of the house for close to two hours. Giving the horse and mule a final pat, Josiah started the trek back to the house. He glanced up at the sky. In another hour or so the sun would sit directly over the house. That would help heat the place up a bit.

Lord willing, in the spring he could add another fireplace; or maybe he'd just buy one of those new-fangled stoves he'd seen advertised down at the dry goods store. He figured Anna Mae would like that. He reined in his thoughts immediately. What in the world was he thinking? She wouldn't be here in the spring. A woman like Anna Mae was looking for a love relationship, and he wasn't. He didn't want love. It hurt too much when the one you loved died.

For all he knew, he might not be here, either. He'd thought about getting a house in town but didn't want to seem ungrateful to William, his brother-in-law. After all, he'd been the one to buy the orchard. William might not like the idea of him moving to town and leaving it vacant. When he got to the front porch, Josiah stomped as much snow from his boots as possible before entering the house.

His gaze roved around the room and he saw the twins napping in their corral and Anna Mae asleep on the couch. He walked over and gently, so as not to wake her, covered her with a quilt.

Josiah reached out and touched Anna Mae's forehead. Cool. He stared down into her lovely face. Dark lashes rested against her pale cheeks. Her dark hair feathered about the pillow. Anna Mae Leland truly was beautiful.

He grinned as he remembered the first time he'd called her Annie. She'd flared up like a hissing cat. That little bit of spitfire seemed to rouse her to get stronger. Truth be told, he preferred Annie over Anna Mae. The name seemed softer. It suited her better, so he'd continued to tease her with the name. Now it just felt natural.

Josiah made a mental note not to call her Annie once their lives returned to normal. It was a little too informal for the schoolteacher position that she held. Would the school board fire her? He took a deep breath. He'd only wanted to help her, keep her safe, and he may have ruined this sweet woman's life. It couldn't be helped. There was no way that he would have turned her away, sick and in the middle of a blizzard.

Josiah caressed her cheek with the back of his hand. He cared about her. How could he not? For the past week, he'd worried over her health and at times her life. Did Anna Mae realize how close she'd come to death?

He shook off the worry he felt for her even now and, with a sigh, turned to the kitchen for a hot cup of coffee.

If he could save her job and reputation, he would. If not, well, he'd cross that bridge when he got there.

Anna Mae woke to childish giggles and the smell of frying ham. She pushed herself up and looked about. Josiah stood at the stove and the girls played in their corral.

How long had she slept? Her gaze went to the window. The sun still shone through the glass, and she sighed, thankful she hadn't slept the whole day away.

"I see you are awake." Josiah cradled a cup of coffee in his hands and rested a hip against the sturdy kitchen table. "Did you have a good nap?"

Her throat felt so dry, Anna Mae couldn't speak. She tried to swallow but found she couldn't do that, either. She nodded.

He must have sensed her need because Josiah walked to the stove and poured her a cup of coffee. He held it out to her. "Take small sips. It might burn a little going down."

She took the cup and did as he instructed. The warm liquid both felt good and hurt. It was just what she needed to be able to speak. "Thank you." The two words sounded scratchy as she forced them out of her tight throat.

"You're welcome." He sat down beside her on the couch.

"It's kind of early for dinner, isn't it?" she asked. "Or are you making a late lunch?"

Josiah laughed. "Trying to get a head start on dinner tomorrow night. My wife used to make the best ham and beans. I thought I'd try my hand at it, but I think I'm doing something wrong." He sighed dramatically. "Mine never tastes like hers."

"Is that why you're frying ham now?" Anna Mae asked, looking toward the stove.

He nodded. "But for the life of me, I can't seem to get it right."

She grinned. "That's because you don't fry the ham

first. Do you have a ham hock that hasn't been cooked?" she asked.

"I'm sure there is one in the root cellar. Why?"

Anna Mae swung her legs off the couch. "Because that's what you should put into your beans." She croaked hoarsely as she spoke.

"Now, Annie, don't go thinking I wanted you to get up and cook." He stood also. "Because that wasn't my plan."

She smiled over her shoulder. "Go get the ham hock and we can have boiled beans and fresh bread for dinner tomorrow." Anna Mae watched him slip into his coat and scarf, then head out the back door.

In the bedroom she hurried out of his clothes and into her dress. It felt good to be back in her own clothes, and Anna Mae realized that if she must stay with the Millers, she needed to give Josiah his bedroom back.

She eased her feet into her stockings, thankful for their warmth. As she made the bed Anna Mae made a decision. No one she'd ever known liked feeling beholden to someone, and neither did she. If she could pull her weight around here it would benefit them both. She'd look for other ways to help and right now she needed to get the beans on.

She returned to the kitchen, pausing to check on the twins, stealing a kiss from each one. Worn-out from everything she'd done, Anna Mae sat at the kitchen table and began sorting the dry beans, making sure not one black rock remained in the mix. She could almost taste tomorrow's meal.

She heard Josiah before she saw him. He stomped

the snow from his feet, then entered the house, triumphantly waving a ham hock in his hand. "I found it, took a while, but we now have meat." He seemed undecided what to do with it and she stifled a giggle. "Boy, it's cold out there. Brrr."

Anna Mae laughed. "Set the ham hock in that bowl to thaw. I'll put the beans on to soak on the stove as soon as I finish sorting them."

If he noticed she'd changed clothes, Josiah didn't say anything about it. Instead he asked, "Would you mind having fried eggs and ham for dinner tonight?"

"Not at all." Anna Mae set a rock off to the side of her bowl.

"Good. Eggs, bacon, ham and beans are about all I know how to make. Mary was the cook, not me." He pulled a chair out and sat down. "And when I'm on the trail of bad guys, I don't have to cook much." He grinned.

Anna Mae focused on the job at hand. She wondered about his wife, but didn't want to be nosy. She knew that Mary had been killed during a bank robbery and that she was William Barns's sister, but that was all anyone seemed to know about her. "Back when we lived together, Emily Jane did all our cooking, before she married William. I'd gotten used to her fixing all my meals, and now that I'm staying at the boardinghouse and Beth provides my meals, well, I'm a little rusty at cooking myself. But together I think we'll do just fine."

"Well, we won't starve to death, that's for sure. Emily Jane helped me stock the pantry before the storm hit, and the root cellar is full of meats and vegetables." He leaned back and studied her. "But I don't want you to overdo it today."

She smiled. It was nice having someone care about her. Since Emily Jane married, Anna Mae had felt alone. A feeling she was very familiar with, since she'd felt that way most of her life. She couldn't deny that of all the things she longed for in her life, belonging to someone, being important to at least one person, ranked right at the top of her list.

The flames crackled in the fireplace, drawing her back to the present. There was nothing like a fire to give the house a cozy feeling. She raised her eyes to find the sheriff watching her, a glint of concern in his analyzing gaze.

"I won't overdo, I promise." She dumped the clean beans in the pot beside her. "It just feels so good to actually be up and moving about. To be doing something of importance. I am not fond of idleness at all."

Josiah picked up the pot of beans and moved to the counter. He rinsed the beans well before setting the pot on the back of the stove. When he returned to the table Anna Mae asked him, "What do you normally do while the girls have their afternoon nap?"

Josiah shrugged. "Read or clean my guns."

Anna Mae pushed away from the table. "I don't want you to change your routine because of me." She walked back to the couch and sat down.

Josiah followed. He dropped into the rocker beside the fireplace. "All right. What do you normally do midafternoon?" he asked, setting the rocker into motion.

"Well, if I'm at the school I teach math, but if I'm

at home I sew, read or create lessons for the next day." She pulled her legs up onto the couch and slipped them under the quilt she'd left there earlier.

"What made you want to be a teacher?" Josiah asked as he put a cloth ball back into the corral with the girls, who had awakened when the adults started talking.

Her gaze moved to Rose and Ruby. "I loved to read as a child and my teacher had all kinds of books he'd loan me. He told me I was smart enough that I could teach, if I wanted to. So when I got old enough to do so, I did." She paused, watching the twins play together. They rolled the ball back and forth between them and giggled as if each time something new happened. Their enjoyment of such a simple task reminded Anna Mae of her calling.

"Watching children learn new things and the excitement on their faces when they realize they've figured out a math problem, or understand a new word they just read, gives me a thrill that I can't explain." Anna Mae looked up to see Josiah studying her face.

"What made you want to become a farmer?" she asked, feeling a little self-conscious.

He laughed. "I never wanted to be a farmer. William bought this place, and while I'm happy for the home, I never figured to be a farmer." He shook his head as if to shake away funny memories.

"So was your dream to become a sheriff?"

Josiah set the rocker into motion again with his foot. "I'm not sure I'd call it a dream. When I was a boy, I was accused of stealing my neighbor's puppy." He chuckled. "I didn't take the pup, but since it was the doctor's dog and his son was pitching a fit, the sheriff came to 'talk' to me about it. Well, I tried to convince him I hadn't taken the puppy, but he didn't believe me. So after he left our house, I set out to find out where the little dog had gone." He closed his eyes and rocked.

When it became apparent he wasn't going to continue, Anna Mae leaned forward and asked, "Did you find the puppy?"

His eyes flittered open. "Sure did. It was at the meat market, trapped under the boardwalk with a bone too big to get out." Josiah chuckled. "I enjoyed looking for that pup and proving to the sheriff that I hadn't stolen it. It was then that I decided I wanted to be a lawman when I grew up." He glanced at the girls, who continued to crawl about the corral like playful puppies.

"I imagine it's an exciting job." Anna Mae sat back against the cushions.

"It can be, but it's also dangerous and stressful when you have a family to consider."

Her gaze moved to the girls once more and narrowed speculatively. "Have you ever considered a different line of work?"

"Yes and no." He sighed. "Right after Mary died, while I searched for the bank robbers who shot her, I thought a lot about quitting. But what can a seasoned lawman do besides upkeep the law?"

Anna Mae grinned at him. "Farm?"

He chuckled. "I know little to nothing about farming."

She tucked the thin quilt closer around her legs. Even

covered as she was, she felt the chill in the air. "So I take it you grew up in town?"

Again he nodded. "Yep, I was known as a street rat. My mother had died when I was a baby and my father… he hadn't taken her death well. So to my way of thinking, when the doctor's kid accused me of stealing his puppy, he did me a great favor."

"Gave you a direction to follow?"

"You could say that. I went to Sheriff Grady and told him I wanted to work for him. He took a twelve-year-old boy under his wing and helped me grow to manhood." For a moment Josiah seemed to travel back in time.

Anna Mae could barely stifle a yawn. "I'm glad. We were both fortunate to have someone mentor us." She covered her mouth to conceal another yawn.

"You look like a woman who needs more rest. Why don't you go on back to bed for a little while? I will call you for dinner."

She shook her head. "No, it's time I started sleeping out here and let you have your room back."

"Now, Annie. You aren't fully well yet and I can't allow you to do that." He stood and pulled the rifle down from over the fireplace.

"I appreciate all the help you've given me, Sheriff Miller, but I am well enough now to take care of myself." It was a weak protest that came from a still scratchy throat.

He grinned at her and said. "Sheriff Grady used to say, 'Young man, as long as you live under my roof, you'll abide by my rules.' I think I'll use those words on you. So no more protesting, go get some rest." Josiah set the gun down and reached for her hand.

Anna Mae wanted to argue but didn't have the strength. She took his hand and allowed him to pull her up. "All right, but as soon as I'm feeling better, I will be moving to the couch."

He laughed at her weak words. "We'll see."

Anna Mae went into the bedroom and shut the door. If truth were told, she liked him being in charge. But Anna Mae refused to allow herself the luxury of depending on a man. The last man she'd depended on to keep his word had failed miserably. No, she wasn't going to get close enough to Josiah or his girls to depend on them for happiness or anything else.

A few days later, Josiah inhaled the hearty fragrance of fresh, hot bread mingled with a pork stew cooking on the stove. His gaze moved to the woman who sat reading with his girls.

She was amazing.

Over the past few days, she'd managed to clean the house and at the same time keep the girls happy. He'd helped her with a lot of the cleaning, but still she seemed to be able to spot just what needed to be done. She'd also allowed the girls more freedom from the corral. They'd wobbled about the house and seemed happy just to explore and play.

Unfortunately, the storm had picked up once more, and as the snow fell, Anna Mae became quieter and quieter. Josiah assumed she worried over what the school board would say once she did make it back to town. He noticed little Rose releasing a mighty big yawn.

"Looks like these two are ready for a nap," Josiah said, taking Rose from Anna Mae's lap.

"Yes, it is that time," she answered, swinging her legs off the couch.

"You stay put. I'll come back for Ruby," he instructed as he carried the little girl into the bedroom he shared with the two children. He glanced over his shoulder.

"No nap," Ruby muttered, tucking her head under Anna Mae's chin. Her chubby little thumb found her mouth and her eyes began to close.

Josiah slipped Rose into her crib and then returned for Ruby.

Anna Mae yawned, too, as she met him halfway to the bedroom. She offered him a gentle smile as he took Ruby from her arms.

"Go lie down. You could use some rest, too, after all you've done this morning." He turned to the bedroom before she could protest.

Ruby was already asleep as he tucked her little blanket about her small shoulders. His gaze moved to her twin, who also breathed in a steady, slow manner. His girls were freshly bathed, wore clean dresses and smelled of talc powder. If only they had a mother to keep them smelling and looking like sweet little girls.

Josiah walked back to the sitting room. Anna Mae rested on the couch with the quilt over her. Her steady breathing told him that she, too, had settled in for a nap. Had she overdone it? He'd noticed she grew tired after each task, but would take a short break and then start back to cleaning or doing something with the girls. Maybe he should have made her relax more.

She'd been at the cabin now well over a week. It was time she had her own bedroom. When he and the girls had first moved into the house, he'd started using the extra two rooms as storage rooms. Now his guest needed one of them.

As he cleaned and straightened it up, his thoughts turned to Anna Mae's future. Would the school board fire her for being at his place for so long? Josiah sighed. Even he knew that they weren't going to approve of her extended stay.

Maybe Levi Westland would be able to help her. Levi was the reason Anna Mae was in Granite in the first place. He'd invited her to their small town as a mail-order bride. Then when he'd chosen to marry Millie Hamilton, Levi had made sure that Anna Mae got the teacher's position when it became available.

But if Levi couldn't persuade the school board, what in the world was Josiah going to do about her? He had no idea what would become of Anna Mae should she lose her job. Would he be able to help her? And if so, how?

Chapter Three

Three days later, the sun came out and melted most of the snow and ice, making it possible for Anna Mae to return to town. Mud squished under Josiah's boots as he hitched his horse to the wagon. He'd decided to leave the mule in the barn. It would be hard enough driving the wagon through the mud without trying to pull a cankerous mule behind it. Josiah had assured Anna Mae he'd bring it back to town as soon as the ground hardened up a bit.

Anna Mae remained inside, preparing the kids for the trip. Her illness had taken its toll on her body and she appeared much slimmer than she'd been when she'd arrived two weeks earlier. He wasn't sure if the weight loss was due to her being sick or from worrying about her job. She'd lost her appetite but had kept up her good nature.

He watched as Anna Mae stepped out onto the porch, holding a child in each arm. What he could see of her dress looked clean and pressed. She also wore her green cloak and gloves. She'd drawn her hair into a tight knot at the nape of her neck, giving her pale face a pinched look.

Josiah guided the horse up to the porch and reached for Rose.

"Thank you, Sheriff Miller." She passed the child to him and waited as he placed Rose upon the seat and then handed the child a small rope attached to the bench for her to hold on to. Next, he took Ruby from Anna Mae's arms and did the same. The twins looked at each other and grinned happily as they clung to the rope. The word *go* was about the only recognizable thing they said to each other. The rest of the sounds they made were not real words, but the twins seemed to have no problem understanding each other as they nodded and smiled.

Anna Mae turned back to the open door and retrieved a picnic basket. "I packed a lunch for you and the girls' return trip." She offered him the hamper.

"That was very nice of you, Annie." He took the basket and placed it in the bed of the wagon. He checked that the girls were comfortable and covered with a thick blanket before turning to assist Anna Mae.

"Please, Sheriff Miller, don't call me Annie while we are in town." Anna Mae twisted her hands in the folds of her dress.

He gave her a gentle smile. "I'll be on my best behavior."

Anna Mae gave him a doubtful look, then took his hand while she pulled herself up onto the seat beside the girls. "See that you are."

"I promise." Josiah planned on being the perfect

gentleman once they entered town. He had to admit, though, that he felt a sense of loss already with her leaving. He shook his head regretfully. He sure was going to miss Anna Mae.

When he seated himself on the other side of the twins, she asked, "Is it very far to the Bradshaws' place?"

"No, just across the pasture." Widow Bradshaw lived a little too close for his comfort. True, she supplied him with fresh bread each week, but her constant hinting that she'd make a good mother for the girls was becoming a nuisance.

"Good. I know you think I'm being silly, but I want to make sure that Bart is doing all right," Anna Mae said, smoothing the wrinkles from her skirts.

Josiah raised the reins and was about to gently slap them over the horse's back when he heard another wagon pulling onto his property. He looked behind him and saw Mrs. Bradshaw and Bart. "It looks like Bart made it home," he said matter-of-factly.

Anna Mae nodded. "Yes, it would appear so."

The widow called out as their wagon drew closer. "Yoo-hoo! Sheriff Miller! I see you are able to get out today, too. I've been so worried about you and the girls."

Josiah put a smile on his face, praying that it looked sincere. "Yes, ma'am, we were just heading to town."

The wagon stopped beside them and Mrs. Bradshaw's smile faded away. "Why, Miss Leland, what are you doing out here?"

"Uh…"

The widow's face slowly began to turn red. Whether she was angry or embarrassed, Josiah wasn't sure.

"We were just headed to your house, Mrs. Bradshaw. It seems that Bart thought it funny to strand Miss Leland out in the snowstorm last week."

She looked to her son. "Bart, darling, what is he talking about?"

The boy glanced down at his feet. "It was just a joke."

"A joke that could have cost your teacher her life," Josiah answered in a firm voice.

"What was just a joke?" Bart's mother demanded.

Bart sank deeper onto the wagon seat and refused to answer. His brown hair was tousled. And his deep brown eyes focused on his feet.

Mrs. Bradshaw turned her attention back to Josiah. "I don't understand."

He nodded toward the boy. "Bart told his teacher that one of the younger boys was hurt, and led her into the woods right before the storm. Then he disappeared, leaving her lost. When the freezing rain and snow hit, Miss Leland almost froze to death before she arrived here at my farm."

The boy looked up as if shocked by his words. Had Bart not realized the danger he'd put his teacher in? Probably not. Josiah held Bart's gaze with his own.

The widow looked to Anna Mae. "Are you saying she's been here for over two weeks?" When no one answered, she crossed her arms and huffed. "She doesn't look injured to me."

Josiah cleared his throat and then said with quiet emphasis, "Regardless of how she looks now, Miss Leland has been very sick due to your son's deceitfulness. The facts are, he lured her into the woods, then left her in the middle of a fierce storm." Josiah so badly wanted to add that all of the above were offenses against the law.

"I don't believe it." Mrs. Bradshaw glared at Anna Mae.

Still sounding a little hoarse, Anna Mae answered, "I'm afraid it's true, Mrs. Bradshaw. Isn't it, Bart?" Her gaze moved to the little boy.

"Yes, ma'am," he answered, before ducking his head once more. "I didn't think about you getting caught in the storm," Bart admitted.

"I believe you owe your teacher an apology. She's been very worried about you and whether or not you made it home safely," Josiah told him.

Bart looked up. "I'm sorry, Miss Leland." His young voice sounded hopeful as he asked, "Were you really worried about me?"

A tender smile touched Anna Mae's lips. "Of course I was."

His young cheeks turned a bright pink and once more he looked away.

Mrs. Bradshaw's voice sounded colder than the icicles that had been hanging from the roof a few days ago. "Well, it's done and over and the boy has apologized. Since you've had a woman to cook and bake for you, I don't suppose you need fresh bread."

"No, we don't, but thank you for offering," Josiah answered, still looking at the boy. Bart had been doing lots of mischievous things over the last few weeks. Josiah wondered if the boy simply craved attention. "Now, back to Bart." He let his words hang between the two wagons.

"What about him?" his mother demanded.

"I think the boy needs to be punished for leaving his teacher out in the woods to freeze. Don't you?" Josiah asked, fearing what she'd say.

"No, I don't." She sputtered. "I think you are—"

Bart's young voice interrupted her. "He's right, Ma." The boy turned to look at him. "I could chop your wood for you, Sheriff, if you think that would be a good punishment," he offered.

"What do you think, Miss Leland?" Josiah asked.

Anna Mae nodded. "I think that would be good for the boy. Plus, he could cut some for the school, as well."

Mrs. Bradshaw sat on the wagon bench with her mouth hanging open. "You are seriously going to punish my boy for a childish trick?" She shook her head.

Bart looked to his mother. "I shouldn't have deceived her and then left her in the woods, Ma." He turned his attention back to Josiah and lifted his chin. "I'll cut the wood."

Mrs. Bradshaw slapped the reins over her horse's back. "Good day to the both of you," she said, turning the horse back in the direction of town. Josiah watched her leave, utterly mystified.

Anna Mae leaned back and sighed. Her fears had been realized, and they hadn't even left the Miller property. Mrs. Bradshaw would be knocking on the door of every school board member as soon as she got to town. It was as plain as the nose on her face that the other woman was interested in the sheriff and that she'd assumed the worst when she'd learned that Anna Mae had been staying with him.

She turned to look at the little girls, who up to this point had sat quietly listening to the adults talk. Rose pulled at her left ear and puckered her little face into a frown. Was she coming down with an ear infection? Anna Mae reached across and touched her forehead.

"Something wrong?" Josiah asked.

"I'm not sure. You might have Doc look at the girls' ears when we get to town. Rose acts as if hers might be hurting." Anna Mae turned back around on the hard seat.

Josiah nodded. "I'll do that as soon as I drop you off at the boardinghouse." He snapped the reins over the horse's back and the wheels made a sucking noise as they pulled free of the mud.

Anna Mae wanted to bring up Mrs. Bradshaw, but didn't know how to go about it. She couldn't come right out and say that the other woman hadn't been happy to see her with Josiah. Did he realize that the widow was sweet on him?

That didn't matter. What did concern Anna Mae was that the widow would tell the whole town that she'd been out at the Miller farm for over two weeks. She feared the other women in town would think ill of her. Anna Mae chewed the inside of her cheek as she worried about what would be waiting for her in Granite.

Would the school board demand her resignation? Or simply fire her on the spot? Would the women avoid her? Would she ever be able to look anyone in the eyes again?

She'd gone through this before, but at least when her fiancé had left her at the altar, the women knew that she'd done no wrong. He simply hadn't loved her enough to keep his word or take her with him when he left town. This would be different. The women would talk. Everyone would talk. She was sure to be fired from her job and looked upon as a wayward woman.

As they pulled up in front of the boardinghouse Josiah said, "It looks like the good widow has gotten here before us."

Anna Mae saw three of the board members' buggies already parked in front of the boardinghouse. She offered a wobbly smile. "Well, she did have a head start." Anna Mae climbed down from the wagon and took Ruby from Josiah.

Levi Westland stood on the porch waiting for them as they walked up to the front door, hands shoved in his pockets, shoulders hunched forward. He tipped his hat to Anna Mae and nodded to Josiah. "Glad to see you are safe, Miss Leland." His voice was calm, his gaze steady. Icy fingers of fear seeped into every pore of her being.

"Thank you, Mr. Westland," she answered, her voice shakier than she would have liked, fully aware that he was a member of the school board.

His mouth spread into a thin-lipped smile. "So the rumor is true."

"Rumor?" Josiah repeated the word, but Anna Mae watched him tighten his hold on Rose. His vexation was evident.

The talk had already begun. Anna Mae hugged Ruby to her and inhaled the baby smell. It had a calming effect on her and she looked to Levi. With a slight smile of defiance, she responded, "If the rumor is that I've been out at the Miller farm waiting out the storm, then yes, the rumor is true." She pulled her shoulders back and raised her head. Anna Mae knew she had nothing to be ashamed of, but if Levi's manner and tone of questioning mirrored the rest of the town, then she didn't stand a chance.

Levi sighed in resignation. "I hoped it wasn't. We've been worried about you, but with the weather the way it was, none of us could come looking for you. We searched the school and about town, but weren't sure where to look from there." His handsome face twisted in regret. "I'd intended to come out and get Josiah to help round up a search party, but Mrs. Bradshaw just arrived in town and said there was no need." He paused, the silence stretching between them as the severity of the situation became clearer. Finally Levi offered her a sad smile. "I truly am glad you are safe."

Josiah placed his hand at the small of her back and gently urged her toward the door. "Let's go inside and talk where it's warmer."

Levi nodded and held the door open for them.

Anna Mae slipped inside. Her heart raced in her chest. She felt her face flush with humiliation. She didn't want to lose her job or reputation, but deep down felt as if she probably had already lost both. Anna Mae just couldn't accept the dull ache of foreboding. And once again in her young life, she experienced the nauseating, sinking feeling of despair.

A terrible sense of bitterness threatened to overwhelm her. She glanced at Josiah and found his expression grim as he watched her. He'd said he'd stand beside her, but what good would that do? Would his being there only make things worse?

Tears filled her eyes, but she refused to release them as the questions roared through her mind, one more insistent than the others. What was she going to do now?

Chapter Four

As Anna Mae had expected, within minutes of her arrival the last remaining two board members miraculously showed up at Beth's Boardinghouse.

They whispered among themselves, argued a bit, then called her into the sitting room and invited her to sit. Mrs. Anderson, the bank president's wife and head of the school board, pointed to a chair placed in the center of the room, and it was not lost on Anna Mae that her back was to the door. The board was in full intimidation mode and wanted no interruptions or distractions. She sat in the chair, her fingers tensed in her lap.

Josiah slipped into the room and sat off to her right, with his cowboy hat resting on his knee. Anna Mae could only assume that he'd left his girls with Emily Jane. Having him there made her feel somewhat better, but not much.

Mr. Holiday, the newly elected town mayor, leaned forward and lowered his voice as if the charges against her were too vile to speak out loud. In a soft, yet firm tone he said, “Miss Leland, it has come to our attention that you were out past dark on the night the storm hit. That you ended up at the Miller farm, where you have resided for over two weeks. Would you say that these statements are true?”

He was a large man, with a walrus-type body and face. His mustache twitched when he spoke and his normal voice came out loud and robust. But not today. Now his dark eyes searched her face as he waited for an answer.

“Yes, that is true but—”

Mrs. Thelma Anderson, the bank president’s wife, interrupted with a sharp tone. “There are no excuses for such conduct. It is very plain in your contract that we will not tolerate this type of behavior.”

Anna Mae’s breath caught in her throat, her heart pounded, and her eyes widened in astonishment. The suddenness of the attack took her breath away. Surely they would give her a fair hearing before pronouncing her guilty and firing her. “If you will just let me explain,” she pleaded. She couldn’t accept the dull ache of foreboding.

Levi Westland nodded. “Yes, I believe we should allow her to explain.”

“I don’t see the point. The evidence is here for all to view. Miss Leland admits she spent many nights at the Miller farm.” The bank president’s wife spoke with a contempt that forbade any further argument.

“Now, dear, let her speak.” Mr. Anderson patted his wife’s hand.

The woman looked ready to argue further, then took

a deep breath and sighed. "I don't see the point, but if she must."

"I believe she must." Josiah's low voice reminded Anna Mae of his presence. She hated that he was here to witness her shame.

Mr. Anderson waved his hand in her direction. "Go ahead, Miss Leland. Tell us what happened."

Anna Mae remembered Josiah's words, *"Just tell them what you told me."* She took a deep, calming breath and did just that. Her hands shook in her lap as Mrs. Anderson studied her with impassive coldness. The woman's mouth twisted wryly as Anna Mae recounted how she'd followed Bart out into the woods.

Levi nodded his head as if agreeing with her choice to go search for the little boy, as did a couple of the other men.

She assured them of the innocence of her stay and that she'd been very ill. Anna Mae finished by explaining that she and Mr. Miller had returned to town the moment it was safe to travel with the girls.

Josiah stood. His hands worked the rim of his hat while he spoke. "I can vouch for Miss Leland. Everything she has told you is the truth. When she arrived at the farm, Miss Leland was very ill. It wasn't until the last few days that she's felt well enough to get up and eat."

Mrs. Anderson gasped, but he pressed on. "I'd like to add that Miss Leland behaved like a perfect lady, watching over the girls as best she could, being sick and all, while I handled the care of the horse and mule. She has done nothing wrong and I request that you allow her to keep her teaching position."

Anna Mae knew that in his own way Josiah thought to help her, but she feared his words caused more damage than good. He must have felt so, too, as the tensing of his jaw betrayed his deep frustration. Her heart warmed at the thought that at least he'd tried to help her. She watched the play of emotions on his face and realized he felt the same hopelessness that tore through her.

For a moment she allowed bitterness to slip in. He would walk away with no repercussions. His job wasn't threatened. He would suffer no embarrassment, no aftermaths, yet she stood to lose everything. Where was the fairness in that?

Then she realized how unfair her thoughts were. He'd been nothing but kind to her. Even in front of these people, Josiah had tried to help her. They'd become friends during her stay with him. If truth be known, it was a friendship she wouldn't have minded cultivating, if the circumstances were different.

She imposed an iron control on herself, stifling any warmth she felt toward the sheriff. Josiah simply felt guilty for her predicament. It wasn't his fault, but she knew he felt as if part of it were. Either way, Anna Mae refused to allow herself to soften toward him. She couldn't afford to let another man break her heart. Besides, by the way things looked, after today she wouldn't be staying in Granite.

She raised her eyes to find the board members watching her, gauging her reaction to Josiah's words. Her gaze shifted from one person to the other, the majority of them staring back in accusation. Thoughtfully, she searched each man and woman's face. Several of the men looked at her with what appeared to be sympathy, while Mrs. Anderson's features showed nothing but scorn. Levi Westland held her gaze as if to say he was on her side.

Mrs. Anderson spoke once more. "As honorable as Miss Leland's tale sounds, she still broke several of the rules of her contract. Gentlemen, I realize you think she did the right thing by going out for the boy, but that doesn't take away from the fact that she signed a contract. What good is the contract if we do not hold our schoolteachers to it?"

When no one answered, Anna Mae was assailed by a terrible sense of bitterness. She knit her fingers together and rested them in her lap. Her throat ached with defeat. *Lord, why?* In desperation her heart cried out to her creator. *Have You forgotten me? Is there a purpose in allowing this to happen a second time? Did I not learn the lesson You wanted me to through the humiliation of being stranded at the altar? Must I be humiliated again through no fault of my own?* Bitter tears burned the backs of her eyes. She lowered her head so that they couldn't see them.

The woman's voice droned on. "I move that we dismiss Miss Leland as our schoolteacher. She broke the contract when she left town with Bart Bradshaw and stayed out after dark. As for what happened at the Miller farm, that is between Sheriff Miller, Miss Leland and the good Lord."

Anna Mae raised her head and boldly looked Mrs. Anderson straight in the eyes. She might stand accused, but she most definitely was not guilty, and she refused to cower in front of them as if she were. God knew that she had done no wrong and therefore had nothing to be ashamed of.

Mr. Anderson spoke up. "I second the motion."

Mrs. Anderson continued with the ruling. "All in favor raise your right hands."

Three of the men raised their hands. Levi Westland sat staring at them with hard eyes.

"All opposed." Mrs. Anderson continued as if daring Levi to raise his hand.

He did so and said, "This is wrong, Thelma Anderson, and you know it."

She ignored him as if he hadn't spoken. "Miss Leland, you are hereby removed as the schoolteacher of Granite, Texas, for your unladylike conduct."

"Now hold on just a moment." Josiah's voice boomed about the room. "Miss Leland never once misbehaved as a lady. And if I hear such words bantered about town, I may just lock you up for slander."

Anna Mae stood. "Sheriff Miller. Thank you for your kind words, but the school board has spoken." She smoothed out her skirt and walked to the door. Just before exiting, she added, "I'm sure Mrs. Anderson is too much of a Christian to go speaking falsehoods about me. Now, if you all will excuse me, I will be retiring to my room." Her chin quivered but she managed to hold her head high as she exited the room.

Josiah looked at each of the school board members. He ought to arrest every one of them. They'd just delivered a verdict without any evidence. A court of law would have thrown them out of the courthouse. He could think of any number of things to charge them with. Slander, destruction of character and illegal firing from a job. And the unfairness of it—now that cut the cake. All in the name of moral correctness.

"Well, now, what will we do for a schoolteacher?" he asked, noting that none of them would meet his eyes.

Mrs. Anderson raised her head and sighed dramatically. "I suppose I shall have to fill in until another teacher can be found. I suggest we advertise for a male teacher this time."

He looked at the older woman, her actions finally making sense. "Ah…" He deliberately drew the word out. "I see." Everyone knew the bank president's wife was bored, but Josiah wouldn't have thought she'd fire Anna Mae to give herself a job to do.

She glared at him, but a telling flush crept into her cheeks and deepened to crimson.

Josiah shook his head, distaste curling the edges of his mouth into a grimace, which he allowed the board members to see. To their credit a few of them had the grace to look ashamed, and dropped their heads. He slapped his hat back on his head and left.

He made his way to Emily Jane, who sat with the twins just outside the door. "Thank you for watching the girls," he said in greeting.

"It didn't go well for Anna Mae, did it?"

"I'm afraid not." Josiah took Rose from Emily Jane and looked about for Ruby.

The little girl sat at the foot of the stairs, looking up.

Ruby held a soft spot for the young schoolteacher. She pulled herself up on the bottom step and began to climb.

"Oh, no, you don't, little lady." Josiah scooped her into his free arm and held her tight. His gaze moved up the stairs, where he knew Anna Mae had fled.

Poor woman. She'd lost her job and her reputation today. When word got out that the school board was looking for a new teacher, everyone would want to know why, and even though he'd threatened to toss Mrs. Anderson in jail if she bad-mouthed Anna Mae, he knew the older woman would tell everyone what had happened. And if she didn't, Mrs. Bradshaw would. He sighed heavily.

"I think I'll go up and see if I can make her feel any better." His sister-in-law pushed herself up from the bench.

Josiah nodded. "Thank you again for taking care of the girls."

"You're welcome. They were good." She walked past him and headed up the stairs, then stopped and said, "I hope you and the girls can come into town for Sunday lunch. I'll fry up a chicken if you do."

He grinned at her. "If the weather stays clear, we'll be there."

She nodded and then continued up the stairs.

Josiah carried the girls out to his wagon and put them onto the seat. He handed them the rope to hold on to and then tucked several blankets around them. The wagon tipped slightly as he pulled himself up and sat down beside Rose. As long as he was in town with the wagon he might as well go to the general store for supplies.

Mentally he ticked off what he needed—coffee, salt and beans. Thanks to Anna Mae, he now knew how to cook ham and beans that didn't taste plain and hard. He guided the horse to the store.

Once inside, he sat the girls down and took each one by the hand. They were old enough now to toddle along with him. Carolyn Moore came out of the back room.

"Josiah, how good to see you. Did you get a lot of snow out at your place?" she asked, coming around and kneeling in front of the girls.

"We got our share, that's for sure." He laughed as he watched Carolyn give both twins a big hug.

"You girls don't look too frostbitten," she teased.

They giggled and tucked their faces into his legs.

It always amazed him that the girls could turn shy in an instant. He stroked their curls and grinned like the proud papa he was.

"What can I help you with today?" Carolyn asked. She wiped at a thin layer of flour on her apron, reminding him that he should get some more of that, too.

"It seems I'm in need of coffee, beans, flour and something else." For the life of him Josiah couldn't remember the other item. Anna Mae would know what he needed at the house.

Would she be all right? Now that she'd lost her teaching job, what would she do? Maybe instead of denying that the school board would release her, he should have helped Annie plan a new future.

"I'll gather the coffee, beans and flour for you. As for the something else, as soon as you remember what it is, let me know and I'll add it to your pile." Carolyn went to measure out his requests.

A heaviness centered in his chest and there was a sour feeling in the pit of his stomach that caused him to rub the affected area. He should have stood up for her better. But what more could he have said to help her keep her job? As it was, he thought he might have made the situation worse. He could still see the look of tiredness that had passed over her features, and hear the strained tone of her voice.

"Have you remembered what the other something was that you needed?" Carolyn asked as she placed a brown paper bag full of beans onto the counter.

Josiah looked about the store. His gaze landed where the spices were and he remembered. "Salt."

Rose and Ruby pulled at his hands. He didn't understand their babble, but looked toward where they were straining. They seemed to have spotted a section of toys and wanted to get closer to them. "When did you start carrying toys?" he asked, as he allowed the girls to pull him forward.

Carolyn grinned. "We got a shipment in right before the storm hit. Wilson thought it would be good to carry toys, since Christmas is right around the corner."

"If these girls are any indication, I believe your husband was right," Josiah said, releasing their little hands so that the girls could get to the toys. It wouldn't hurt to see what they might be interested in. As Carolyn had said, Christmas was right around the corner. He watched as Ruby grabbed a stuffed brown horse with a white mane and white spots, and Rose pulled at an ugly gray toy elephant.

What would Anna Mae do about the upcoming holidays? With no job and no income, she certainly wouldn't have much of a Christmas. He sighed and let his gaze move about the store. A dress hung in the dry goods area. The pretty fabric would look nice on the schoolteacher.

Josiah shook his head. His thoughts refused to stop bringing Anna Mae to mind. He felt responsible for her. Hadn't he said that no matter what happened he'd stand beside her?

"Is there anything else I can get you, Sheriff?" Carolyn asked, placing the salt into a box for him.

"Do you think the twins will remember the toys they're playing with now, if I buy and hide them until Christmas morning?" he asked, picking up each of the girls, who held tightly to the toys. Josiah carried them to the counter.

"I doubt it. They are still pretty young," Carolyn said, tickling Rose and taking the toy from her at the same time.

"Then go ahead and wrap them up for me, if you will."

"Be my pleasure to do so." Carolyn handed Rose a peppermint stick to replace the toy.

Josiah grinned at the ease with which the shopkeeper distracted the girls with candy. She took Ruby's toy also and replaced it likewise. The twins smiled and smacked their lips as they sucked on the candy. They were so, oh what was that word Anna Mae described them with? Oh yes, adorable. They had a double dose of it.

"You do have a way with children," he said.

Carolyn wrapped the toys in brown paper and placed them in the box. "I've had lots of experience." She smiled at him and then added the cost of the toys to the list she'd been tallying for him.

Josiah paid for his supplies and the toys and then carried them out to the wagon, while Carolyn watched the girls. As he placed the box in the back, he froze, his hand clenched on the sideboard. Suddenly, with crystal clarity, he knew what he had to do to make things right with Anna Mae.

The girls needed a mother and Anna Mae needed a home and her reputation restored. And he needed someone he could trust to take care of his girls while he worked. His sister-in-law could no longer watch his girls and run a bakery with a newborn to take care of as well.

With courage and determination settling like a rock inside him, he girded himself with resolve. He would marry her.

His mind went through a thorough deliberation process before he allowed himself to act. Would this benefit them both or were his motives selfish? If she agreed to this harebrained scheme, what would her motives be? Would a marriage between them benefit them each?

He already knew that marriage would solve both their problems. She would have a home and the girls would have a mother. But would it produce positive results like he pictured in his mind, or bring regrets further down the road?

Josiah stood still and listened to his gut. In the few years he'd been sheriff, it had never steered him wrong. He turned his head sideways to hear better. Not a word; not even a growl.

He fell back on the evidence. She cooked better than he did. She'd been sick the entire time she was with him, yet his house looked cleaner. The most persuasive piece of evidence won the case. She loved his girls and she tolerated him pretty well.

Now all he had to do was convince her that marrying him would solve both their problems. He'd have to be up front with her and tell her that he could never offer her a husband's love, but that he would happily and freely supply her basic needs for the rest of her life. Surely she'd understand that he'd already lost the love of his life and that he couldn't risk losing another person that he loved that deeply.

Would Anna Mae agree to such a proposition? The future looked so vague and shadowy. Why, he didn't know what would take place in his own life, so how could he expect her to join up with him? He had a farm, yet wasn't a farmer; he was a sheriff.

But could he keep being a sheriff and possibly leave his daughters without a daddy? If he married Anna Mae, and something did happen to him, he knew she'd take care of the girls. Yes, the girls needed a mother. A stable woman they could depend on to take care of them. They needed Anna Mae.

Chapter Five

"How could I have been so stupid?" Anna Mae folded another dress and placed it in her satchel. She might as well get this over with; there was no way she could survive another smirch against her character. If she left before the entire town knew, which should be in about an hour, give or take a few minutes, she'd avoid the pitying glances and censuring looks.

She plopped down on the bed, a green shawl clutched in her hands. How could this keep happening to her? It would be different if she engaged in bad behavior. But she didn't; never had, never planned to.

All her loneliness and confusion welded together in one upsurge of yearning, and she bent over, her hands clutched against her stomach, a groan pushing through her gritted teeth. Would she ever belong? She thought she'd found a place to call home, but now she'd have to move on.

Without warning, Emily Jane rushed through her door and knelt in front of her. "Oh, Anna Mae, I'm so sorry. Please don't cry."

Anna Mae collapsed into her friend's arms, yielding to the compulsive sobs that shook her. She wept aloud, as Emily Jane rocked her back and forth.

Little by little Anna Mae gained control of her emotions, and with a hiccup or two accepted a hanky from Emily Jane. She mopped up her face, but the compassionate, caring look in her friend's eyes almost undid her all over again.

"Why are you packing, Anna Mae?" Emily Jane spoke in an odd, yet gentle voice, as if she were afraid she'd cause the waterworks to start again. "We're not letting you leave. Why, where would you go?" Emily Jane's eyes grew large and liquid. "I couldn't bear it if you weren't around to talk to. We've lived together since we both arrived here." She took one of the dresses from the valise and hung it back on the hanger. "Plus, I need you around so my baby will have an aunt to spoil it rotten and let it do things that as its mother I can't." She rubbed her rounded belly and offered a genuine smile.

"How can I stay, Emily Jane? Everyone thinks the worst of me." Anna Mae shivered, uncertain if it was from the fear taking root in her heart or from the cold that crept through the window.

Emily Jane lifted the shawl off the bed where it had fallen during their embrace, and wrapped it around Anna Mae's shoulders. "Come. Let's get out of this cold room and go sit in the dining room." She turned her toward the door with a slight nudge.

Moments later, a sigh shuddered through Anna Mae as she took a deep drink of her cream-and-sugar-laden hot coffee. “I can’t believe I acted so stupidly and placed my employment in jeopardy.”

“It wasn’t stupid to want to help one of your students,” Emily Jane said, patting her hand in comfort.

Anna Mae looked about the room. Thankfully, the noon lunch rush hadn’t begun and she and Emily Jane were the only occupants. “Thank you, Emily Jane, but I knew better than to believe a student as mischievous as Bart.”

“Then why did you go with him?”

Anna Mae’s breath caught in her throat and tears filled her eyes again. Did Emily Jane realize her voice sounded accusatory?

“No, no. Don’t look at me like that. I meant, was there a reason beyond what you’ve said so far? Did he act scared or was he crying?”

Anna Mae thought back to the day Bart had lured her into the woods with his lie. Maybe she had still wanted to help him, to win him over. She didn’t know. Her stomach growled and she wished suddenly she’d taken Emily Jane up on her offer of cake. It was probably for the best. Anna Mae didn’t think she’d be able to get food down her tight throat, anyway.

“Anna Mae?” Emily Jane’s voice was infinitely compassionate, but probing, snatching Anna Mae back to reality. She realized she’d been quiet for too long.

“Oh, I’m sorry. I went because he seemed so upset and he rushed me so that I didn’t take the time to think it through. If I had, I would have realized that he was lying.” She took another sip of coffee, the sweet taste mingling with the sourness in her stomach. "Well, it can't be helped now."

"What are you going to do?" Emily Jane nibbled on the applesauce cake she'd ordered.

Anna Mae set her cup down. "There's nothing else for it, Emily Jane. I'll have to leave town."

"But why?" Her friend dropped her fork, creating a clatter that sounded loudly in the room. "I don't understand that way of thinking. Why would you leave town?" She scrambled to retrieve her fork.

"I have no job, and as soon as word gets out that I spent two weeks out at the Miller farm, my reputation will be ruined." Fresh sorrow filled her at the truth of her words. "I have to leave." Her sense of loss was beyond tears. Everything had been going well. She'd had a job, a home and friends.

Emily Jane shook her head. She lowered her voice so that the few people who had filtered into the dining room wouldn't hear her. "The only ones who will think ill of you are the ladies who are jealous of you, like Mrs. Bradshaw. Why don't you give it a few days and see what happens? I'll check with William and see if I have enough money to hire you to work at the bakery. I'm sure I'll need the extra help with the arrival of our new baby." She rested her hands protectively around her rounded tummy with a small grin.

"Thank you, dear friend, but I can't ask you to create a job for me. I love you for wanting to, but I can't accept it."

A pair of boot tips appeared in her line of vision and then a man cleared his throat. Anna Mae looked up to find Josiah standing beside the table. She took a quick sharp breath. What was he doing back at the boardinghouse? Had he come to tell her what the doctor had said about Rose's ear?

"Ladies, mind if I join you?" He twisted his hat in his hands as he waited for an answer.

Emily Jane responded first. "Of course, please do." She indicated he should take the seat between them.

Beth Winters hurried over to take his order. "What would you like, Sheriff?"

He pulled the chair out and sat down. "Coffee and a piece of whatever kind of cake my sister-in-law is having."

She nodded and hurried off to get them.

Anna Mae nervously fingered the handle of her cup. Where were the twins? Didn't he know it would add fuel to the fodder if they were seen together?

"Where are the girls?" Emily Jane asked.

He hung his hat on the back of his chair. "I left them with Carolyn Moore for a few minutes."

"Did you take Rose to the doctor?" Anna Mae asked, drawing his attention back to her.

"Yep. He said her ear is a little red and to put a few drops of oil in it this evening before putting her down for the night." He grinned at Anna Mae.

As their eyes met the tenderness in his expression amazed her. But there was something more. She couldn't put her finger on it, but he almost seemed pleased with himself; as if he'd just confirmed something that had been on his mind. Good for him, she thought sarcastically, irked by his easy manner.

Beth returned with his coffee and cake. "Here you go, Sheriff, it's on the house."

"That's right nice of you, Mrs. Winters." He tipped his head in her direction.

A soft pink filled Beth's cheeks as she turned to go. Was Beth sweet on him? Anna Mae realized that first Mrs. Bradshaw and now Beth seemed to be interested in the sheriff. She crossed her arms protectively across her chest and studied him thoroughly.

He was handsome, with wavy black hair that touched the back of his collar, and deep blue eyes. His nose was a little crooked, as if it had been broken at one time or another. When he smiled his eyes seemed to hold an inner light that drew a person, much like a bee to a honeycomb, but was that any reason to fall over oneself around him?

Josiah glanced up from his dessert to catch her staring at him. He measured her with a cool, appraising look. "I've been worried about you, Annie."

She peered about to see if anyone had heard him use his pet name for her. Assured that no other diners sat close by, she returned her attention to him. "I'm fine, Sheriff Miller." She stressed his last name, reminding him they were no longer at his cabin and not to call her by her given name.

"Anna Mae just told me she's thinking about leaving town," Emily Jane interjected, taking a big bite of her cake and carefully observing both of them.

Anna Mae felt more than saw Josiah's posture stiffen. She would have liked to be the one to tell him that she was leaving. Not that it mattered, but she wanted him to know that it wasn't his fault. He couldn't help it that Bart had led her into the woods on a stormy night, or that her mule had chosen Josiah's farm to take her to. Anna Mae hadn't decided when or how she would tell him, but she had hoped to do so herself.

"So you're thinking about leaving?"

She nodded. "I planned to tell you before I left." She became aware of Emily Jane watching them with acute interest. "Because I wanted to thank you for all that you did for me when I was sick."

Josiah looked to his sister-in-law. As if he'd silently asked her to leave, Emily Jane picked up her purse and said, "Well, I hate to eat and run, but I need to get back to the bakery and start tomorrow's bread."

She hugged Anna Mae and whispered in her ear, "Don't make any rash decisions today." Then she waved, leaving the two of them sitting silently.

Without Emily Jane's presence, Josiah suddenly felt tongue-tied. How did one propose a marriage of convenience? He didn't want Anna Mae leaving Granite. She seemed to sincerely care about his daughters and they needed a mother. Josiah knew deep down, though, that she'd never capture his heart the way Mary had. It was impossible that any woman would truly take her place. Because he felt so sure of this, Anna Mae would never be a true wife to him. However, for the girls' sake, and to save Anna Mae's reputation, he had to ask her to marry him. He might as well jump in with both feet. As casually as he could, he said, "You don't have to leave, you know."

She looked at him over her coffee cup. Clear brown eyes rimmed with pink puffiness regarded him curiously. He could tell she'd been crying earlier, and an emotion he hadn't felt in a long time swept through him. He wanted to take away all her pain and embarrassment.

Her sigh tore at him. "Yes, I do. I don't want my friends feeling sorry for me, and I can't face the shame of having to impose on them for my livelihood."

Josiah knew that feeling. Maybe not for his means of support, but didn't he have to impose on others to watch his children so he could work? It felt like the same thing. Maybe he could convince her that he knew the feeling, and that if she'd permit it he'd make certain neither of them would feel that way again. But even a small-town sheriff like himself knew this was a delicate situation and should be handled with care.

He reconsidered that tack. One wrong word or move and he could push her in the opposite direction. "Maybe you don't have to impose on your friends for your livelihood." He said the words tentatively, as if testing the idea.

"I know I don't. And I won't. That's why I'm leaving. My room is paid here until the first of November. Emily Jane asked me not to make any rash decisions, so I suppose I'll stay until then. Hopefully, by the first I will know where I'm going and what I must do when I get there. I'll simply have to endure the gossip until I leave." She set her cup on the table and squared her shoulders. Determination tightened her jawline.

He admired her fortitude. It would serve her well in the days ahead. But right now he didn't need her stubborn and unwilling; he wanted to be her knight in shining armor and rescue her from distress. He breathed a plea heavenward. *Lord, a little help here, please. Can You make her receptive and sensible?*

Half in anticipation, half in dread, Josiah pushed his plate back and reached for her hands. "What I mean, sweet Annie, is that maybe we can help each other."

Her fingers shook against his palm so he tightened his grip. "How?" Confusion laced her pretty features as she held his gaze.

"You could marry me," he blurted, scarcely aware of his own voice.

Anna Mae snatched her hands back and shook her head. "What did you say?" She pushed stray tendrils of hair away from her cheek.

Josiah felt a curious, swooping pull inside him, surprising him to stillness. Why had he never noticed how incredibly beautiful Annie was? Her features were dainty, her wrists small and her waist curving and regal.

He forced himself to focus on the statement he'd just made. All right, it probably wasn't the best proposal she'd ever heard. She must think him an insensitive clod. Josiah cleared his throat and tried again. "We could get married. I need someone to take care of the girls, and you wouldn't have to find another job or leave." To his annoyance he felt heat climb up his neck and into his face. His aggravation increased when he noticed his hands were shaking. What was wrong with him? This was how a man in love acted; and he certainly wasn't in love. He made a gesture with his right hand. "This is not how I rehearsed this in my head on the way over here."

She leaned closer and whispered, "You want to marry me so you'll have a babysitter for the girls?"

He ran a hand behind his neck and rubbed. "Well, yes, but it would benefit you, too."

Anna Mae crossed her arms over her chest once more. "Explain to me how that would work exactly?" At his puzzled look, she pressed on. "How marrying you and taking care of the girls will help me?"

"You wouldn't have to leave your friends."

She laughed bitterly and wagged the tip of her finger at him. "Believe it or not, I am capable of making new friends, Sheriff."

He dropped his head and stared at the checkered tablecloth. "I'm sorry. This isn't coming out right." Josiah sighed heavily, and without looking up at her, he continued. "All I'm proposing is a marriage of convenience. It wouldn't be a real marriage." He lowered his voice as she had done. "I don't expect us to share a bedroom, only the responsibilities of the children, the farm and the house."

How could he explain to her that he only wanted to help? He'd been partially responsible for her job loss and the town thinking they'd been intimate. He just wanted to make up for that. Maybe this had been a bad idea. She was right. How would marrying him help her face the women in town who were probably gossiping over their luncheons right now? Still, he gave an impatient shrug. The idea had merit and he'd be foolish not to realize how much it would benefit him. *Lord, if You're of a mind to, I could use that help right about now.*

Her soft hand covered his and he looked up quickly, so surprised his mouth dropped open. He merely stared, tongue-tied. Tears filled the beautiful milk-chocolate orbs regarding him with tenderness. Her voice, when she spoke, still held a touch of hoarseness. "I know you're trying to help me, and what you said is right; the girls do need someone to take care of them. In a real sense, it's a lovely suggestion. As my grandmother used to say, it would kill two birds with one stone."

Josiah watched as she fought some inner battle before speaking again. What an honorable woman she was. Even in distress, she managed to consider the feelings of others. She was three times a lady compared to her accusers.

"I can't give you my answer right now, Josiah, but I'll pray about it." She lifted her hand from his and stood up. She touched his shoulder briefly. "Thank you."

She walked away with stiff dignity, the long skirt of her dress swaying gently. She paused just inside the door and looked back at him. For a moment she studied him intently and then she was gone.

She'd said thank you? What on earth did that mean? He hadn't done anything that she had to be thankful for. Had she been referring to him nursing her while she was sick? For proposing marriage to her? What? He gritted his teeth and barely suppressed a groan of frustration.

If he lived to be a hundred, he'd never understand women. *And why, Lord, didn't You give me a more ele-*

gant way of speaking and expressing myself? One thing was for certain; Josiah hadn't the foggiest idea what Anna Mae's answer would be, nor when she'd tell him.

Chapter Six

Anna Mae took one more look at her reflection in the mirror, then gathered her Bible and shawl in preparation for church. Today, sink, swim or drown, she'd face the gossipmongers and learn if her friends were true or not.

Almost a week had passed since Josiah's proposal. She'd cowered in her room as much as possible, coming down for meals only after everyone else had left.

Miserable without the twins, she'd worried over Rose. Had Josiah remembered to administer the sweet oil twice a day? Were the girls wondering where she was? Did they cry for her at night? She'd shared their bedroom, many nights placing them in bed with her if they seemed distressed after she diapered them. Their mother had died when they were just babies, then their uncle and Emily Jane had cared for them. Finally their daddy had shown up and taken them. At least with Anna Mae at the farm they'd had the sense of stability of a mother for a brief few days.

Needless to say, the twins needed her, and she needed

them. They filled a void she hadn't recognized she had. That still small voice she'd grown to recognize as the Lord's asked if she could just walk away from them.

Her friends, Emily Jane and Susanna had visited her. She'd shared Josiah's proposal with them, purposefully leaving out the marriage-of-convenience part. They'd both been thrilled that he'd offered marriage and that she would be staying if she accepted his proposal.

When she finally wrapped her mind around that Josiah was offering "a marriage of convenience only," she found it lacking to say the least. Josiah was another man who didn't see her as a true wife. What was wrong with her? Did men see something she didn't? Why couldn't someone love her?

She arrived late at the church but still beat Josiah and the girls there by mere seconds. Josiah pulled the wagon to a stop at the boardwalk. The twins spotted her and both scrambled to get out of the box in the back. Anna Mae could no more stop herself from reaching for them than she could stop breathing. They fell over the side into her arms, causing her Bible to fall to the ground. Both chattered a mile a minute, though most of their words were unintelligible.

"Girls, girls. Calm down," Josiah chided, but his eyes were lit with laughter and he seemed as pleased to see her as the twins. He recovered her Bible and reached for Rose. She fussed but finally released her hold on Anna Mae.

"Shall we go in?" he asked.

A wave of anxiety swept through her. "Maybe you should go first and I will sit near the back." She started to hand Ruby over, but two little hands pressed against Anna Mae's cheeks and Ruby's lips quivered. "Ruby go you." The little head shook up and down positively, a question in the depths of her eyes.

Anna Mae placed her forehead against the little girl's. To turn this baby away could possibly relay that she wasn't loved enough, that she somehow lacked the ability to be loved. Anna Mae knew all about those feelings. No way would she ever make this child feel unloved or unimportant. "We'll all go together." Bolstering her courage, she shifted Ruby to her side and walked up the church steps.

Josiah rushed ahead and pulled the door open. Anna Mae was happy to see that no one else waited on the steps or in the entryway as they entered. She slipped into the back pew and made room for Josiah and Rose. The piano began playing the moment they were seated. She breathed a sigh of relief, realizing that no one would be able to speak openly to her or about her until after the service.

When it was finished, Anna Mae hurriedly gathered her things. *Please, Lord, don't let anyone speak to me. Just this once, please, can I be selfish and make it out of here without embarrassment? Please, Lord? Just this once?*

It seemed as if the Lord had too many people at that moment to listen to because Mrs. Harvey, a sweet older woman, immediately turned in her seat. "Anna Mae, I am so glad to see you this morning. I'd heard you were sick. Are you feeling better now?"

Anna Mae smiled at her. "Much better, thank you."

The woman motioned for her to sit back down. She did and then Mrs. Harvey leaned against the pew and whispered, “You won’t have any more trouble from Thelma. I told her that if she breathed one word as to why you chose to quit teaching, I’d tell some of her secrets.” The sweet woman chuckled. “Don’t expect to hear her ever speak of it again.” She patted Anna Mae’s hand.

Could it be true? Had Mrs. Harvey really stood up to the bank president’s wife? Anna Mae lifted her hands in utter disbelief before exhaling loudly. “How can I ever thank you, Mrs. Harvey?”

Ruby tugged at her. Anna Mae pulled the little girl into her lap, her mind searching frantically for words to express her relief. She came up empty. She simply didn’t know what else to say to Mrs. Harvey. Such kindness seemed to render her speechless.

“Nonsense, no one hurts one of my kids and gets away with it. Not even my best friend.” Mrs. Harvey stood slowly. “Well, I best be getting back to the house. I understand we’re having meat loaf for lunch.” She looked down and winked at Anna Mae. “It’s my favorite, you know.”

As the older woman walked away, Anna Mae felt blessed. She hadn’t realized how much she’d meant to Mrs. Harvey.

In the spring, when they’d all lost their homes to a tornado, Mrs. Harvey had become a dear friend. When William had left the girls in Emily Jane’s care while he worked, Anna Mae became close to them as she assisted with some of their daily care. Mrs. Harvey had helped them with the girls and had been there to support everyone after the tornado. The older woman called Anna Mae one of her kids. It felt good.

Thank You, Lord, for answering my prayer. It's not exactly what I expected but You do work in mysterious ways, don't You? She smiled secretly, knowing the Lord had heard her and answered in His own way.

"Anna Mae? Would you join us for lunch? I've fried a chicken and made potato salad."

She turned to find Emily Jane and William standing beside Josiah and Rose. Still a little befuddled by Mrs. Harvey's kindness, Anna Mae nodded.

"Ruby go you, too."

Anna Mae grinned at the little girl in her arms. She'd missed her so much.

"You're coming, too." Emily Jane tickled Ruby's tummy, sending childish squeals throughout the church.

Several women and men stopped to shake hands with them and wish Anna Mae well. She had thought they'd all turn on her. How foolish she felt now. Her true friends stood faithfully beside her.

Anna Mae looked at Josiah; a dark figure of a man, big and powerful, yet the blue eyes intent upon her brimmed with tenderness. She felt weak in the knees. She thought again of his proposal. Did he still want to marry her? Or had he changed his mind?

"I do believe that's the best fried chicken I've had in a long time," Josiah said, wiping potato salad out of Rose's hair.

Emily Jane picked up his empty plate and carried

it to the kitchen. "Thank you, Josiah. I'm glad you enjoyed it."

Anna Mae had been quiet during lunch. She'd hardly eaten anything and her brown eyes seemed glued to her plate. Was she nervous around him and the girls? Or did she fear he'd ask what she'd decided regarding his proposal?

Her sweet voice filled his ears. "Yes, I think you outdid yourself this time, Emily Jane."

"If you think that was good, just wait until you taste her fruitcake. She's been working on this recipe for weeks and has finally perfected it." William rubbed his tummy and licked his lips.

Josiah shook his head. His brother-in-law had always been a ham, but since he'd married Emily Jane he seemed to have gotten worse at overacting.

"If you haven't noticed, Anna Mae, I think my husband's saying he's tired of eating fruitcake." Emily Jane carried what looked like more of a fruit loaf than a fruitcake into the dining area.

William put on his shocked face. "I didn't say that."

"No, you implied it. No cake for you." Emily Jane handed each of the girls a cookie and then sliced the moist cake. She passed a piece to Josiah.

Josiah laughed. "Serves him right." He took the dish and passed it to Anna Mae.

"It looks wonderful, Emily Jane." Anna Mae set the dessert down and stood. "Who would like a cup of fresh coffee?"

Both Josiah and William answered, "I would."

Her blue skirt swished about her ankles as she walked.

Today her hair wasn't up in its normal teacher-style bun but hung in long graceful curves over her shoulders. She carried herself confidently. Josiah's admiration grew. Anna Mae had a strength and stamina at odds with the slenderness of her body.

He watched her fill everyone's cup and return the pot to the stove. She sat back down and lifted the fork to her lips. He noticed that Emily Jane closely watched for Anna Mae's reaction. What did his sister-in-law expect? He held his own fork midair, preparing to taste the cake, but decided to see what Anna Mae thought first.

Josiah sat mesmerized as she took a bite, chewed slowly and then sighed. Anna Mae took a sip of coffee before saying, "I believe William is right. This is the best fruitcake I've ever tasted. You will have to give me your recipe." Her brown eyes met his as if she realized that he was staring.

He quickly lowered his gaze.

"I'll give it to you, but you have to promise not to share with any of the other ladies. I'm going to start serving it in the bakery and then take orders for Thanksgiving and Christmas." Emily Jane sat down and smiled at Anna Mae. "I've missed having meals with you," she said before digging into her own slice of cake. "You were a great sampler."

Anna Mae teased. "I miss you, too, as well as a couple of pounds." She smoothed her hands over her waist. "I could never turn down your desserts."

Women were so strange. Men never gushed over each other like they did. Josiah felt relieved that his brother-in-law's wife liked Anna Mae, since he'd asked her to marry him. A question she hadn't yet given him an answer to.

He ate his dessert in silence. Josiah didn't really care for fruitcake, but Emily Jane's was probably the best he'd tasted. He didn't tell her of his dislike for fruitcake in general, not wanting to appear ungrateful.

His gaze moved to his silent daughters. They each held part of a cookie in their chubby hands, but were fast asleep, leaning into each other like kittens in a basket. He'd missed Anna Mae over the past few days. *Lord, for the girls' sake, please let her say yes to my proposal.*

As if Emily Jane had heard his prayer, she said, "William, why don't you and I take our nieces to the bedroom and lay them down for a nap? I believe Anna Mae and Josiah would like to catch up."

"Catch up?" William looked from one to the other. "Catch up on what?"

Emily Jane laughed. "You'll find out soon enough." She gently lifted Rose into her arms and carried her to the bedroom.

With one last look at both of them, William carefully scooped Ruby from her chair and followed his wife. He patted the fussing little girl's back as he left.

Josiah reached out and took Anna Mae's hand in his. "The girls missed you, Annie."

Her big brown eyes looked overly large in her pale face. "They did?"

He stroked the back of her hand with his thumb. "Of course they did."

"I missed you and the girls, too," she quietly replied.

Josiah released her hand. He didn't want her to miss

him, just the girls. The last thing he needed was for her to have deeper feelings for him than friendship. He rubbed the back of his neck and cleared his throat. "Have you given any thought to the question I asked you?"

She nodded. "Yes, and I've decided to take you up on your offer. But…" Anna Mae paused. Her big brown eyes searched his intently.

What was she going to say? That she'd decided she wanted a real marriage? That she expected him to fall in love with her? He held his breath and waited. After several long moments he couldn't stand it any longer and asked, "But what?"

"Before I say yes, I want you to know that I was engaged once before I came here. My fiancé left town the night before our wedding and broke my heart. I can't take that type of heartbreak again, so know this… I most likely will never love you. At least not the way a wife should love her husband." She breathed out heavily. "There. I've said it, so if you don't want to marry me after hearing this, I understand."

Josiah's heart went out to Anna Mae for her loss. But still it felt as if a huge weight had been lifted off his shoulders. She didn't want a real marriage, either. This was perfect. He felt laughter bubble up in his stomach and exit his lips.

Anna Mae sat looking at him as if he'd grown horns. He was sure she wondered what had overcome him. "You're happy I won't ever love you?"

He forced himself to stop smiling. "Yes. I want to be friends with you, but I can never love you the way I did my first wife, Mary."

"Oh, I see." Anna Mae nodded. "But I'd rather no one else knows that this is a marriage of convenience."

He turned up his smile a notch and nodded in turn. Anna Mae laughed. "Good, then we can get married whenever you're ready."

Was it his imagination or did her laugh sound forced? He searched her face but saw no sorrow in it. Was it possible they were making a mistake they both would regret in the near future? Should they allow a bunch of townspeople to dictate to them how they should behave? What they should do?

Chapter Seven

When Josiah had said he didn't think he could ever love her as he did Mary, something inside Anna Mae felt crushed. She continued to smile and forced herself to laugh with him, but actually, she wanted to cry. Deep down she had hoped to find love someday.

"Do I hear laughter in here? Does that mean what I think it does?" Emily Jane asked, pulling William behind her.

Josiah stood up and smiled. "I've asked Anna Mae to marry me and she's agreed."

"Marry you?"

William looked as if someone had gut punched him. Anna Mae should have seen this coming; after all, Mary had been William's sister. He sank into one of the chairs.

Josiah nodded, "Yes."

Anna Mae watched realization of the impact this would have on his brother-in-law cross Josiah's features. His expression turned somber. "I'm sorry, William. I didn't consider how you would feel about it. I just assumed you'd be happy for me. For us." He reached down and took Anna Mae's hand, pulling her to her feet.

"I didn't figure you'd get married so soon." William shook his head as if to clear it. "But of course you'd want to get married. You have the girls to consider." He stood and then walked over and slapped a hand on Josiah's shoulder. "I'm sure Mary would understand, too."

Anna Mae watched the two men, surprised that William chose to believe that his brother-in-law was marrying her only for the girls' sake. Josiah's confirming nod bore witness that sadly, it was true.

Seemingly unaware of the truth, Emily Jane ran over and hugged Anna Mae. "I can't wait to tell Susanna. You know she's going to want to make your dress, like she did mine. Oh, you are going to have the most beautiful wedding. I think you should make it a Christmas wedding. Think how pretty the church will look." It was as if the woman couldn't contain her joy. "And I will make your cake. Oh, I am so excited for you!" She clapped her hands happily.

"Emily Jane, we aren't having a big wedding. I want a simple ceremony. And I think the sooner the better, don't you agree, Josiah?" She prayed he'd give the correct answer.

As if they were a loving couple, Josiah lifted her hand and kissed the backs of her fingers. "Anything you want, Annie."

"See?" Emily Jane pressed. "He doesn't mind waiting until Christmas."

Anna Mae pulled her hand from his. Her skin tingled

where his warm lips had touched. She stood. Her voice came out as electrified as her hand felt. "Well, I don't want to wait until Christmas. That's almost two full months away. I'm ready to get married now."

The room grew silent as all three adults stared at her, various degrees of questioning in each expression. Josiah seemed pleased as punch and William looked as if he'd suffered another punch. Emily Jane appeared ready to hit someone if she didn't get her way. Anna Mae stifled a giggle, then sobered.

They each had their own thoughts, but she was the one who had to prepare for the worst. The worst being that Mrs. Bradshaw still might spread rumors. Mrs. Harvey had put a stop to Mrs. Anderson's meddling, but that might not stop Mrs. Bradshaw.

Anna Mae knew her friends would ignore the widow's lies, but what if Josiah started thinking she wasn't good enough to be a stand-in mother for his girls? Then what? She would be left stranded again.

Until she said her vows, Anna Mae knew she had to be on her toes, ready for anything. So to her way of thinking, the sooner the better.

"She's right." Josiah placed his strong arm around her waist. "We don't want to take the chance of being separated should another storm arrive, with me and the girls stranded at the farm and Annie here in town."

His arm about her waist gave her a sense of protection, a feeling that they would stand together against anything or any person that came between them. She leaned lightly into him, tilting her face up to his, wishing there was a way to express how she felt about their united stance.

She felt rather than saw his shocked reaction. Had he thought she wanted to kiss him? She stepped out of the circle of his arm, her face flushed with humiliation and anger at herself. She'd only wanted his protection.

Just when she started to put distance between them, he caught her elbow, gently turning her to face him. "So how soon will you do me the honor of becoming my bride?

Anna Mae couldn't believe she was married. The last three days had felt like a Texas twister. She was blown about preparing for the big day that just didn't seem real.

As Emily Jane had predicted, Susanna created a dress just for her wedding. It was a soft peach with lace ruffles around the long sleeves and neck. Her friend had fussed that it wasn't enough, but Anna Mae thought it was perfect.

Emily Jane baked a two-tiered cake much too large for the handful of friends and family who were present at the church. It seemed extravagant for a marriage of convenience, but then again, her friends didn't know it was just that.

Josiah stood with the minister in a black suit, black boots, and his black hat in his hands as she'd walked down the aisle. They hadn't spent much time together since having Sunday lunch at William and Emily Jane's house. Anna Mae had questioned her decision several times, but when she saw him standing there, a pillar of strength and security, she felt the Lord's peace wash over her and knew she was doing the right thing.

The twins had walked in front of her, throwing colorful ribbon bows onto the hardwood floor and giggling. Their little legs were slow moving and it had seemed like an eternity before she'd arrived at Josiah's side.

They'd said their vows, he'd kissed her lightly on the cheek and the minister had pronounced them husband and wife. What had taken three days to prepare for was over in less than five minutes.

Josiah helped her up into the wagon and then turned to take Rose and Ruby from Emily Jane and William. As he reached for Rose, his sister-in-law said, "We could keep the girls tonight, Josiah. They wouldn't be any trouble."

"Thank you, but those clouds look like they might contain snow and I'd just as soon have the twins with us if we get another storm." He handed Rose up to Anna Mae.

She released the breath she'd unintentionally held, relieved that he'd declined to leave the girls. Even though they were now married, Anna Mae wasn't prepared to spend an entire evening alone with her husband. She set her new daughter into the wooden box that Josiah used to keep them safe when it was just him and the twins riding in the wagon. She knew the crowd of well-wishers would expect her to sit beside her new husband.

William gave Ruby to Josiah, who handed the second little girl up to her. Then he hurried around to pull himself up beside Anna Mae.

She set Ruby beside Rose and then turned to wave

at the small crowd of people as he pulled away from the church. She turned back around in her seat to find them heading toward the farm. Now her home.

When they were far enough away from the church so that no one would hear him, Josiah said, "That went well." He smiled over at her. "Did I tell you how pretty you look?"

She eased farther across the seat from him and smoothed out the wrinkles in her dress. "No, I believe you were too busy getting married," she teased.

"True, but you do look very pretty. I like the way you're wearing your hair." He clicked his tongue, causing his horse to pick up the pace.

"Thank you." Anna Mae reached up and touched the silky strands and ringlets that Mrs. Harvey had declared was her gift to Anna Mae. The older woman had insisted that she leave it down, flowing sleekly over her shoulders with wisps curled in ringlets about her face. It had taken a long time to get the curls to hold. They would be out by tomorrow morning and Anna Mae's hair would be back to its old mousy-looking style.

She turned to check on the girls, who had grown quiet and found they had slumped down in the box and fallen asleep against each other. Their little faces shone with sweet dreams. Anna Mae tucked a thick blanket around them and then took another and placed it over the top of the box to help lock in their warmth.

Knowing they were safe, she turned back on the seat just as large fluffy snowflakes began to fall. She pulled her cloak tighter around her body and looked up at the sky. If the truth were truly to be known, aside from worrying about her job and the reaction of the townspeople, she had enjoyed being snowed in at the farm. It had seemed as if they were alone in their own little world, snug, cozy and warm. Now it looked as if it would happen again. Her silent prayers of thanks winged up to the Lord, for the small addition of snow on her wedding day and especially for her new family.

She and Josiah may not have married for love, but Anna Mae felt she'd done the right thing by marrying him. She felt an inner peace, as if she finally belonged somewhere. Josiah might not need her, but his girls did, and she planned to be the best mother she could be.

They rode for several minutes before he glanced her way again. "Why so quiet? Do you regret marrying me?"

"No." She grinned. "But I am glad the service is over. I'm not a fan of being in front of everybody."

His brows drew together. "Really? I figured it wouldn't bother you, since you stand in front of a classroom full of children every day." Josiah lifted one hand and lightly slapped the reins against the horse's back to speed him up a bit. The blowing snow came against their faces in a cold, wet kiss.

"They're children. Not adults. Besides, kids really don't pay attention to the way I'm dressed or the way I walk and talk. Today I felt like an ugly ink blot on a fresh piece of paper."

Josiah pulled the wagon to a halt.

Why had he stopped? She looked about but didn't see anything amiss. The snow wasn't falling at an alarming rate, so there was no reason for him to stop and turn them around. When she looked at him to inquire, Anna Mae found him turned in the seat, studying her face. "You really do feel that way, don't you?"

She nodded. "Yes. But it's no reason to concern yourself. I've always felt like that." Anna Mae offered him what she hoped was a cheery smile. She hadn't been looking for sympathy, just stating how she felt. How she'd always felt.

He picked up her hands. "You are far from ugly. Next to my Mary, you're the most beautiful woman I've ever seen. Your hair looks silky soft, and your brown eyes have a mysterious, captivating glint in them. Your smile…well, it warms a person right up, and the shape of your face is beautiful."

She didn't know what to say. His gloved hands holding hers made her feel as if he truly meant every word. "Thank you. I believe that's the nicest thing anyone has ever said to me." Her face flushed right to the tips of her burning ears.

Josiah nodded and then released her hands. He quickly got the horse moving toward home once more. "You're welcome. I hope you never believe such negative things about yourself again."

Anna Mae didn't answer him. She'd been told all her life that she was plain. It was sweet of him to tell her differently, but she knew the truth. Once the wedding day came to an end, Josiah would see her for who she truly was—simple, plain Anna Mae.

Half an hour later he pulled up to the front of the house and stopped. Josiah jumped from the wagon and hurried to her side to help her down.

"The girls are still napping. I'll bring them in as soon as I get the horse taken care of." He smiled down at her.

"Are you sure they will be all right? It's pretty cold out here." She gnawed at her lower lip.

He gently touched her cheek. "Thank you for worrying about them, but this is the way we have done it the last few months." He dropped his hand and climbed back onto the wagon. "As long as they are covered up in that box, they are toasty warm."

Anna Mae nodded, missing his touch. He was right, and she could get a few things done in the house before they woke up. "Are you hungry? I could fix us something to eat while you are out in the barn."

He grinned. "I'm starving. That bite of cake wasn't nearly enough."

Torn by conflicting emotions, Anna Mae watched him drive the wagon to the barn. She was married to a virtual stranger. What did the future hold for her now? What did the Lord expect her to do from here on out? Would she be a good wife and mother? Girding herself with resolve, Anna Mae forced her lips to part in a curved, stiff smile. She vowed right then that Josiah, Ruby and Rose would never have reason to complain.

Chapter Eight

Josiah wiped his feet before entering the house. Mud and straw caked on the bottom of his boots. He set down the box that held the sleeping girls. They were getting heavier and soon wouldn't be able to sleep in the box or be carried into the house like that.

He took a few minutes to pull the footwear off. Mary had always hated when he'd come home and mucked up her floors. What would she think if she could see him now with a new bride? He set his boots beside the closed door and carried the girls to the sitting room.

Josiah checked that the twins still slept and then made his way into the kitchen. He inhaled deeply. Was that fried chicken he smelled? Anna Mae didn't have time to fry up a hen. Well, that didn't make no never mind; he smelled fried chicken, so if she did cook it, she was the most amazing wife a man could ask for.

Anna Mae stepped out of the bedroom. She had taken off her wedding dress and now wore a light pink housedress. A big white apron covered the front of it.

"Emily Jane left us a wedding present," she said, motioning toward the kitchen stove, where several covered dishes sat.

"Fried chicken?"

"Yes, with a note that says she wanted to make sure I didn't cook on my wedding day. Wasn't that sweet?"

When had Emily Jane had time to do that? He remembered William being late for the service and now knew why. "My sister-in-law never ceases to amaze me," he said, realizing that Anna Mae still waited for some form of answer from him.

She pulled fried chicken, baked beans and big fluffy biscuits from the back of the stove. "It's still warm, too."

"Good, I'm starving." He met her at the table. She'd already set it with four plates, silverware and glasses.

"What about the girls?" she asked, looking toward the box that sat beside the fireplace.

Josiah grinned. "Let them sleep. We can enjoy a rare meal without them demanding to be fed first."

Anna Mae smiled and motioned for him to sit down. "Emily Jane also left us warm apple cider, or you can have coffee if you'd prefer." She paused for him to answer.

"Coffee for me, please." Josiah waited for her to return and sit down. They needed to talk about their marriage, what it would be and what it wouldn't be, but first he'd enjoy their wedding present.

Once she was seated, Josiah said a quick prayer over the food and then dug in. He wasn't sure what to say to his new bride, so they ate in silence. She obviously felt as unsure of him as he did her. It seemed a little awkward, but not intensely so.

After several minutes Anna Mae laid her fork down and sighed. "The service was beautiful, wasn't it?"

"I believe so." Josiah set his fork down also and wiped his mouth. "The women did a fine job."

"Yes, I really do have wonderful friends here. I couldn't have done it without them." She picked up her plate and carried it to the scrap bucket.

"Or without me." Josiah laughed out loud at the shocked expression on her face. "Well, do you think you could have gotten married without a groom?" he teased.

Josiah saw in her face that he'd hit a nerve. She didn't look angry, just hurt. "I'm sorry, Annie. I was only teasing."

She offered a wobbly smile. "You didn't say anything wrong. You're right, a woman can't get married without a groom. No one knows that better than me."

He hurried around the table and hugged her. "Annie, for a moment I forgot about that clod of dirt who left you. It was insensitive of me to say what I did. I really am sorry." Josiah gently squeezed her. The sweet scent of lavender teased his nose. He leaned forward and sniffed her hair.

Anna Mae returned the hug and then stepped out of his embrace. "Really, Josiah. It's all right." She walked to the table and collected the rest of the dirty dishes.

With her back to him she said, "We need to talk about our marriage."

Josiah sat down at the table. He missed the warmth

of her in his arms. "Yes, I've been meaning to talk to you, too."

She poured water into a large pan and set it on the back of the stove. "Do you want to go first?"

"No, you go ahead." He decided the polite thing to do was let her get out whatever she had on her mind.

Anna Mae cleared her throat. "Well, I was thinking that I would like to stay in the room I used last time I was here. If that's all right with you?" The question in her voice made him smile.

"No, I want you with the girls. There will be lots of nights when I won't be home. I'd rather you be close to them. You can have my room and I'll take the smaller room."

"Oh, I hadn't thought of that." She glanced toward the fireplace, where the twins slept peacefully. "But don't you think they are old enough now for their own room?"

Josiah looked at his girls, too. Rose and Ruby would always be his babies. He couldn't imagine them having a room of their own, and yet knew that they were almost old enough now to do so.

"I suppose so," he admitted grudgingly. Then another thought sent his pulse spinning. Maybe Anna Mae didn't want the girls with her. Was that why she'd made that comment? His head swirled with doubts. How well did he actually know her? He'd known plenty of women who acted a certain way until they had a man all hog-tied, then their true colors showed up.

He regarded her thoughtfully for a moment. She

lifted the pan of water from the stove to the counter and filled it with the dirty dishes. She moved quickly from one task to the other, wiping off the table, covering the food, refilling their coffee cups. The apron tied behind her back accentuated her slender waist. There was both delicacy and strength in her face, but did he know much about her character?

He had to find out. He couldn't just sit quietly and let his girls suffer from his poor judgment. He stood and with heavy steps walked to Anna Mae's side. He put his hand on her shoulder and turned her so he could see into her face.

She looked up at him, brows raised with what seemed to be genuine concern. "What is it, Josiah?"

"The statement you made a few minutes ago. Do you not want the girls in the same room with you?"

Her shiny brown eyes widened in surprise. He heard her quick intake of breath, before she placed a hand against his chest. She spoke in a broken whisper. "How can you even ask me that?" Anna Mae dropped her hand.

Didn't she realize they truly were practically strangers? What did she know of him? That he was William's brother-in-law. The father of Rose and Ruby. And that was all. She didn't know what his character was, so how could she expect him to know hers?

"But you must have doubts or you wouldn't have had to ask that. Please—" Anna Mae motioned to the table "—let's sit down and talk a bit more."

When they were seated opposite each other, she

reached out and laced her fingers in his. "I know that we don't actually know each other that well, and I guess I assumed you could tell my character by the company I keep. But you can rest assured in this one thing." Raising fine arched brows, she spoke firmly. "I love Rose and Ruby. I loved them even before you showed up in town. Emily Jane and I took turns watching them while William worked at the store. It was easy to fall in love with them."

Anna Mae's eyes clung to his as she analyzed his reaction. He had no idea what she saw in his expression, but her voice gentled and she squeezed his hands. "Over the last couple of weeks, when I was sick, the twins wound up in bed with me more often than not. I love sleeping with their little bodies cuddled up next to me. But they are getting bigger, and giving them space of their own is the next step. And that is all I meant by the comment."

Josiah felt an indefinable feeling of rightness. He believed her. He stretched out an arm and touched her cheek. "Thank you for not being mad at me. I learned too late in my first marriage that communication was seventy-five percent of what made a partnership work. I hope we always talk things out, and with a marriage like we have, we both need assurances from each other on private subjects that most couples work out during their courting days." He joined their hands again. "Is there anything you would like to ask me? Something that might make you feel better?"

"Well, yes, actually there is." Amusement flickered in the eyes that met his. "Where is your gun?"

* * *

Laughter floated up from her throat as Anna Mae observed the changing expressions that crossed Josiah's face. Clear, observant eyes looked out from his suntanned face, regarding her speculatively before his mouth twitched with amusement. His voice, though quiet, held an ominous quality. Had she not seen the flash of humor, she would have felt like one of his prisoners being interrogated.

"Now why would a sweet little thing like you need a gun?"

"Oh, I didn't say a word about needing a gun."

Josiah untangled their hands, making her wonder if she'd pushed him too far in their teasing. He bent over and pulled a small hand gun out of his boot and laid it on the table. "There's this one. It's a Philadelphia Derringer." He pulled his coat aside and pulled a larger gun from behind his waist. "There is also one here; it's a Colt revolver. And of course when I'm not traveling, the rifle will always be over the fireplace."

He leaned back, sizing her up. "Where's yours?" he asked with an arched eyebrow.

He'd figured her concern was that the guns not be lying around where the twins, or anyone else for that matter, could get hold of them, causing Lord knows what kind of trouble. She gloried briefly in the shared moment. She tipped her cup to her lips and tried to force her expression into all seriousness. "Why, Sheriff, I thought you knew that schoolteachers are not allowed to carry weapons."

Laughter floated up from his throat. It was the first

time Anna Mae had heard him sound so merry. The only problem being his happiness woke the girls.

Two twin heads popped out of the box. "Out," they echoed and then grinned at each other. "Eat," they called.

"Now look what you've done. The monster babies are awake." Josiah turned and collected the two girls.

Anna Mae shook her head. "I'm not the one that was laughing, you were." She turned to the stove and collected the two plates that she'd prepared earlier.

Josiah got the twins seated and then handed each of them a spoon. She returned to the table with cups of warm apple cider. "I wouldn't give this to them until they've eaten their fill," she suggested, "otherwise you won't get them to eat another bite."

"It's that good, huh?"

"Emily Jane made it, what do you think?" she asked.

The two girls stared up at them. Each held a spoon and a piece of bread. Anna Mae realized that neither had taken a bite of their food.

"What are you two waiting for? Eat up," Josiah said, giving them permission to eat.

They shook their heads and closed their eyes before bowing their heads.

Puzzled, Josiah looked from the girls to Anna Mae. She giggled. "They are waiting for you to say grace."

Josiah bowed his head and said a quick prayer of thanks. Anna Mae's heart swelled when he thanked the Lord for bringing her into their lives one stormy night, and then closed by thanking Him for his thoughtful sister-in-law and the food the girls were about to consume. Anna Mae looked up and found it impossible not to return his disarming smile.

While the children ate, Josiah talked to them as he helped them. Anna Mae washed up the few dishes they had dirtied and poured herself a cup of the warm cider. Her life here was going to be pleasant. It didn't have to have the type of love a man and wife shared. She would be happy with the blessing of a family.

Three nights later, Anna Mae sat at the kitchen table and wrote to her parents. She wondered what her mother would think of her quick marriage. The last time she'd written, Anna Mae had bragged on how well school was going and how much she loved teaching. She'd assured her mother that she'd probably never marry. But now, less than a month later, she anxiously tried to figure out how to tell her that not only was she married, she also had two little girls.

The fire crackled and popped. Anna Mae's gaze moved to Josiah. The girls were already in bed sleeping, and he sat reading the Bible that was open in his lap. She had to admit that her feelings of friendship for him were growing. Anna Mae felt certain it wasn't love, because her heart didn't seem to be involved. The Lord knew her heart couldn't take another breaking. And she planned to guard against such things as love.

Anna Mae refocused on the letter.

Dear Mom and Dad,

A lot has happened since I last wrote to you. We have had some really bad weather here and…

Anna Mae chewed on the pencil. And what? And I got married? I was accused of breaking the rules of my contract and was fired as the Granite schoolteacher? Or guess what? You are the grandparents of two very precious girls? How did she tell her parents all the things that had happened over the last few weeks?

Her gaze moved to her kitchen. She'd done a lot of work, cleaning and reorganizing it to fit her style and mood. A new curtain hung at the window over her wash area. She loved the window being there. Come spring, she could look out at her garden in the backyard. She'd also scrubbed all the pots and pans, and Josiah agreed to help her hang them along the back wall. That job they planned to do tomorrow. He'd said something about large hooks packed somewhere in the barn attic.

Outside, the snow drifted down in glistening white flakes. She sighed. Would her mother be interested in hearing about that? Anna Mae wasn't sure. Mother lived in a big house with lots of servants. What would she think of her daughter's three-bedroom farmhouse? What would she think of her sheriff husband and twin daughters?

Did it matter what her mother thought? Not really, since it was already a done deal. Then why should she agonize over it? Anna Mae looked back down at her letter. She picked up where she'd left off.

> And since my last letter, I have gotten married. Josiah Miller is a wonderful man and the sheriff of Granite. He has twin daughters that are almost two years old. They are adorable. Both are small

because they are twins, but they talk more than any girls their age that I've ever met. Not that I've actually met that many others.

We live on a small farm that has a three-bedroom house and an orchard. I'm hoping to have a nice garden next summer. Maybe you can come visit then.

Well, it is getting late and I need to get some rest. I love you both, Anna Mae Miller.

She looked at her name. It was the first time since they'd gotten married that she'd written it out. She whispered, "Anna Mae Miller."

"It has a nice ring to it."

She jumped. When had Josiah come up behind her? Had he read her letter as she wrote? Anna Mae glanced over her shoulder at him. He smiled down on her. A cup of coffee filled his large hands.

"I think so, too," she admitted. "I was just writing my parents to tell them about our marriage." She folded the letter and tucked it inside a homemade envelope.

"I hope they approve of our marrying." He slipped into the chair beside her.

She smiled. Anna Mae hoped so, too, but if they didn't there was nothing they could do about it now. They'd thought Mark Peters was the catch of the season and look where that had gotten her.

Josiah Miller was a good man. She just prayed their marriage could stand the test of time. A flicker of apprehension coursed through her. What if it didn't? Where on earth would she go? Would she be forced to return to her parents' home? Anna Mae didn't think she could face her mother's disappointment in her again.

Chapter Nine

Josiah sipped his coffee. He'd read the letter over Anna Mae's shoulder. Not to be nosy but because he wanted to make sure she was happy. The letter hadn't indicated either sadness or unhappiness. She did seem a little awed when she'd said her married name aloud. He guessed all women had to get used to the name change and possibly enjoyed the sound of their married name. It seemed odd to him but what did he know?

She looked up from the envelope she held. "I'm sure my parents will approve of our marriage." Her hand shook slightly, leading him to believe that maybe she wasn't as sure as she sounded. "After all, what's not to like? You were the catch of the season. Never mind that I had to catch a few other things before I caught you, like pneumonia, high fever..." Her voice contained a strong suggestion of reproach, but her eyes flashed with humor and teasing.

He couldn't help himself as he burst out laughing. On almost every topic they'd discussed, Anna Mae had the best attitude of anyone he'd ever met. "I hope you think you wound up with the best deal of all that catching." He grinned.

"What about you? I noticed a few heads turning in your direction before I allowed you to catch me. One of them being Mrs. Bradshaw's," she teased back.

Josiah frowned. "I refuse to give the woman any more of my thoughts. As the sheriff, I am duty bound to protect her, but as a citizen I think I'll give her a wide berth."

Why had she brought up Mrs. Bradshaw? The woman left a sour taste in his mouth and stomach. He took his coffee to the sink. Or maybe it was the coffee. He might need to stop drinking the stuff for a while if it kept affecting his stomach. Josiah decided to change the subject. "I need to go to town early in the morning. I'll try to be back by midafternoon to help hang those pots and pans." He set the half-empty cup down.

Her gaze moved to the window. "What about the storm?" Was that concern he heard in her voice?

"I'll be fine. It's not supposed to be as bad as the last one, and besides, with my job I have to be out in all kinds of weather."

Anna Mae nodded. "I suppose you do. It will take some getting used to, being married to the town sheriff."

As if to deny his very words, the wind whipped fiercely about the farmhouse windows. Anna Mae noticed it, too, and caught her lower lip between her teeth. He sought for ways to distract her. He'd never asked her about her family. "What does your father do for a living?"

Josiah rinsed his coffee cup, refilled it with cider

and walked back to the table. He enjoyed the feel of the warmth of the cup against his palms. Maybe he was addicted to having something occupy his hands more than actual coffee.

She set back in her chair. "Papa runs a shipping company."

"So I gather that doesn't require him to be away from home in the evenings?"

Her brown hair swayed with the shake of her head. "No, he keeps regular business hours."

"And your mother? Does she work outside the home?"

An amused laugh bubbled out of Anna Mae. "Hardly. She thought I was crazy for wanting to be a teacher. Said a woman's place is in the home."

"What do you think, Annie?" Josiah looked over at her and raised his eyebrows. Did she want to work outside the home or was she content to stay at the house and watch the girls? Perhaps he should have asked her those questions before they got married, Josiah mused.

"I loved being a teacher but I think I'll enjoy staying at home and taking care of things around here." She smiled at him. "Did Mary enjoy staying home or did she want to work?"

"You know, it never occurred to me to ask her." Josiah had just assumed when he'd married his first wife that she wanted to stay home and raise his children. As far as he knew, Mary had never worked.

"Do you have anything against women working?"

"No. Not that I've thought much on the matter. I guess as long as a woman's job didn't interfere with the running of the house or care of her husband and family, it's fine."

"And if it did interfere, how would you feel?"

He couldn't tell from Anna Mae's expression what she was getting at, so he thought carefully about his answer. "Again, to be fair, I don't know how I'd feel. I think the Bible is the final authority and it states that a woman's place is in the home. In other places in God's word, like Proverbs, it speaks of all the work that a woman does and a lot of it is outside the home. So like everything else the Bible teaches, I think moderation is the key."

In neat tight handwriting, Anna Mae wrote her mother's name and address on the envelope. Josiah wondered briefly why she didn't address the letter to both parents. The more he learned about his new wife, the more he realized Anna Mae thought carefully about the decisions she made, never acted flighty or careless, and observed the dictates of society on manners and charity. She made a perfect sheriff's wife. But he guessed correctly, it might take him a lifetime to find out the reasoning going on behind those beautiful eyes.

"Will you mail this for me tomorrow?" She ran a finger over the flap, sealing it tight.

"Be glad to. Do you have a list of things you might need from the dry goods store?"

"No, I haven't checked the larder, but Emily Jane told me there was food in the root cellar that the former owners left."

"Why, yes, there is. I'll bring some of it up tomorrow when I get home. I know there's a lot of beans in a sack down there. I'll get some salt pork from the store and milk from the Smiths' dairy."

Josiah made a mental note to bring other goodies to make their next few weeks a little easier, because from the sound of the storm, they would be closed in for a little while.

"I know it may be a bit uncomfortable for you, but could you bring my book satchel from the school? It has my sight cards…" Her eyes grew round. "Oh, Josiah, those are my writing examples on the walls, and the two red readers are mine. Would it be wrong of me to want to keep them? I could use them to teach the girls when they're older, on snowy days when we can't get to the school. They mean a lot to me. I spent my first paycheck on them."

That was his Annie. She had an inherent kindness and sense of rightness that showed up in her thought processes. He, on the other hand, wouldn't leave anything in the school to help Mrs. Anderson. Let her buy her own books and supplies. *Yes, Lord, I know that's the wrong way to be. I'll try harder.*

"I'll get your things for you. And no, it isn't wrong. If you can think of anything else, let me know before I leave and I'll get it for you."

"Thanks, Josiah." Anna Mae propped the letter against the saltshaker, then stood. "Well, I'll say goodnight. Will you be leaving early in the morning or sometime after breakfast?"

"I'll leave before daylight so no need to get up. I'll let the latch down behind me so you'll be locked in. If all goes as planned I should be back shortly after lunch."

"Be safe, Josiah. 'Night."

Josiah savored the feeling of satisfaction her words left with him. It had been a long time since anyone cared about his safety. It felt good.

"'Night, Annie."

The next morning, Anna Mae heard the latch fall into the slot and jumped from the bed as if it was on fire. She'd awakened at the first sound of Josiah moving in the next room. She'd lain perfectly still, aware that the walls were paper thin, and hoping and praying the twins wouldn't wake just yet. She'd like to get a start on the day while they still slept.

In less than fifteen minutes she'd finished her morning ablutions, dressed and tiptoed into the sitting room. She stood back a ways from the window, but watched as Josiah vanished into the gray dawn. Then she ran and stared, faced pressed against the pane, to see if she could spot him at any other site down the road. Thankfully, it had stopped precipitating, so she could see clearly across the snowy landscape. The road dipped and when he came back up the other side she could barely make him out, but this satisfied one of her many curiosities. If she watched for him at lunch, he wouldn't be able to sneak up on her; for some reason that was important right now.

After all, she planned to move some of his stuff around. Well, she had no idea if the things in the house were his or the former owners, but she knew she could make it look better than it did right now. To her way of thinking it was easier to ask forgiveness than permission. Still, she'd rather not get caught in the act. She was totally bewildered by her mixed emotions, but decided the job before her was more important than analyzing why she felt like a trespasser in her own home. Besides, it would be hers after she put her mark on it.

She looked around the sitting room. It was partially open to the kitchen, but the entrance, which should have permitted one to see all of the kitchen except the pantry and back door, had been blocked off by crates, and Anna Mae could see a shovel and what looked like the girls' wagon that William had used to pull them about in a few months ago.

She quietly lifted the first crate from the top and carried it to the table. Stacks of wanted posters and official looking forms were tossed in haphazardly, so she set it against the wall in the kitchen.

Thirty minutes later, the wagon had been moved to the third bedroom, where Anna Mae nearly fainted. The room looked like the gardener's shed at her parents' estate. Everything from hoes to milk cans filled the space, and even the bed was covered with junk. She closed the door quickly so she wouldn't be tempted to drag everything out and rearrange. If she did that, she'd never be through by the time Josiah arrived home.

Finally, she had the opening cleared and the couch pulled out from the wall. She never had been one to cover windows, and furniture pushed up against one seemed out of place to her. She put a chair on either side of the fireplace and moved the couch in closer. If they sat on the sofa and read to the girls, they could stretch their toes toward the fire. Anna Mae could envision their happy family doing just that and felt deep satisfaction that her thoughts were for their well-being.

She heard the girls stirring, but decided not to rush them. She stepped out on the back porch and pulled bacon from the larder. She did a quick check of the other contents and found quite a bit of meat. There were several packages marked Rabbit and those she had no problem with, but the ones marked Squirrel gave her a moment's pause.

Anna Mae shivered from the cold air whipping at the bottom of her dress, and hurriedly reentered the house. She put bacon in the pan and set it on the stove. Next she whipped up three eggs with a little milk, salt and pepper, and dipped in it three slices of bread from last night's supper. She set another pan on the stove and put in the bread to fry.

The whines and calls from the bedroom had gotten louder and she could barely control her burst of laughter when she peeped around the door. Ruby, with one leg over the rail, could neither get herself over enough to fall to the floor, nor climb back in the crib. Considering she was only about a foot and a half off the floor, the fall would not have hurt her, but her diaper had caught on a decorative wooden knob and she pretty much hung suspended in the air. Rose sat staring at her as if to say, "I told you not to try it, but you wouldn't listen. Now what are we going to do?"

Anna Mae masked her humor and rushed to rescue Ruby. "You naughty girl. What are you doing?" She unhooked the little one and set her on the bed. Then she reached for Rose, who'd stood up with arms raised.

Anna Mae could barely scold for laughing. “What if you had fallen and banged your head, Ruby?”

“Uby bad.” Rose had no intention of taking her sister’s side.

“No bad. Me no bad,” Ruby insisted, as Anna Mae pulled off the soiled diaper and set her on the chamber pot.

By the time she freed Rose of her soiled diaper, Ruby had used the potty and was running happily around the room in her gown, with her backside showing. Giggling as Anna Mae tried to catch her, she screamed with joy to be finally caught, tossed in the air, then pinned on the bed.

Minutes later, with both freshly diapered, Anna Mae carried a girl under each arm into the kitchen. She set them at their respective places and hurried to rescue the bacon and bread. She saw Rose shiver and realized she had let the fire get too low, which had been good for cooking breakfast and her cleaning spree, but bad because the house had gotten chilly.

As she stoked the fire, Anna Mae couldn’t help but worry about Josiah’s reaction to her rearranging his home. Would he like it? Or demand she put things back the way she’d found them?

Chapter Ten

The sound of a wagon coming down the dirt road drew Anna Mae's attention. Rose and Ruby were playing with their pull toys. She looked out the window and saw Mrs. Linker and her daughter draw up in the yard.

The Linkers were their closest neighbors. Josiah had said that they were the first to greet him and the girls when he'd moved in. It looked as if the two ladies were going to be the first to welcome her, too.

She stepped out on the porch to greet them. "Mrs. Linker, Margaret, come on in here and get warmed up."

"Thank you. We thought we'd bring a loaf of Margaret's favorite apple bake bread." Mrs. Linker was a tall woman with gray hair that she kept pulled into a bun on the top of her head. She wore a brown housedress with matching brown shoes and a bulky coat that came a little below her waist.

Margaret climbed down from the wagon. She was dressed much like her mother, only instead of a bun on her head, her hair hung to her waist in a long braid down her slim back. "I hope you like it as much as I do," Mrs. Linker said, hurrying up the icy steps.

"I'm sure I will." Anna Mae held the door open for them to pass. Her gaze swept the room, searching for the twins. Both girls stood beside the couch, eyeing their neighbors.

"Oh, Margaret." Mrs. Linker's voice held a strong suggestion of reproach. "I can't believe we forgot our wedding gifts in the wagon. Will you run out and get them, please?"

"Sure, Mama." The girl left quickly, without a backward glance.

"You didn't have to get us a wedding gift," Anna Mae protested as she took the bread. She inhaled the sweet smell of apple and cinnamon. "This is gift enough. I can't wait to try it."

"Nonsense. Though our gift really won't be much of one until spring."

Now what did that mean? Anna Mae frowned. "I don't understand." She set the bread on the table.

Margaret hurried back through the door carrying a large wooden box much like the one Josiah used in the wagon for the girls. It jostled against her as she hurried to set it down by the fireplace. "Here you go."

A weird yet familiar sound met Anna Mae's ears. Rose and Ruby hurriedly toddled to her, grabbing her skirt in their chubby little hands. Then it dawned on her what she was hearing. Her mouth dropped open. "You brought us chickens?" She turned to the women. Although Mrs. Linker quickly hid her smile, Anna Mae could see it in her eyes.

"Yep, all farms need a mess of chickens. 'Course, I only brought you three, two hens and a rooster to get you started."

Anna Mae worried her lower lip with her teeth. "It's a lovely gift, but I don't have a place to keep them." She didn't want to offend the Linkers, and even though chickens scared her, the idea of having fresh eggs appealed to her. But where would they keep them?

"I'm sure our sheriff will be able to build a chicken coop in no time." Mrs. Linker rubbed her hands together to warm them up. "How about we make a hot pot of coffee to go with that bread and have a nice chat?" she suggested, looking longingly toward the kitchen.

"Of course." Anna Mae nodded, still worried about the chickens. What would Josiah say when he came home? Did he know how to build a chicken coop?

Margaret followed her mother to the kitchen table. "I told you we should have waited." Her gaze moved to Anna Mae, who continued to gnaw her bottom lip.

The older woman waved the statement away. "Nonsense."

Anna Mae dislodged the girls from her dress and Ruby immediately plopped to the floor. Anna Mae hurried to the stove and put on a fresh pot of coffee, while wondering what she should do with the chickens. "I don't suppose you'd want to hang on to them for me until we can get the coop made," she suggested, bringing a knife to cut the bread, and several dessert plates to the table.

"They'll be fine in that box for a couple of days." Mrs. Linker licked her lips in anticipation of eating the bread. "Be sure and tell the sheriff that we clipped their wings, so if he wants to put them in a bigger box until you get that coop done they won't fly off."

Anna Mae didn't even want to think what the inside of that box would look like in a couple days. And just who would take those chickens out in order to clean the coop. She couldn't. Simple as that. To say she was scared out of her wits at the thought of handling the chickens would be putting it mildly. She returned to the cupboard and took down three saucers and cups.

Rose pulled on her skirt. "Eat!" she demanded.

The Linkers had shaken her up so much she'd all but forgotten about the little girls. Her gaze darted about the room, searching for Ruby. She found her still sitting on the floor, staring at the chicken-filled box. Confusion laced her tiny features. Anna Mae felt the same way.

Again the thought rushed through her mind—what was Josiah going to think of the "gift"? And until the coop was built, where were they going to keep the chickens? Surely after a day the box would start to smell, and then what?

Mrs. Linker and Margaret enjoyed their coffee and apple bread. The twins smacked their lips as they ate their share.

"This is a mighty nice place ya got here." Mrs. Linker looked around with interest. Anna Mae felt pride in all she'd accomplished earlier in the day. All the things that didn't belong had been removed and the walls and floor had been scrubbed, swept and mopped. The smell of Dutch Glow furniture polish and the shine of the stone hearth in front of the fireplace caused her confidence to spiral upward.

"Thank you, Mrs. Linker. It's a very nice home for sure." Anna Mae didn't know if it was proper for her to speak so about her own house, but it was the truth and surely one couldn't go wrong talking honestly. "There is still so much to be done. I'm sure there's laundry waiting somewhere, but I haven't found it yet." She laughed self-consciously.

"Oh!" Her neighbor clapped her hands. "Speaking of laundry…" She grabbed a flimsily wrapped present from the counter where Margaret had placed it earlier. "These are for you and Sheriff Miller."

"But I thought the chickens were our gift." Anna Mae unwrapped two striped dishcloths with the letter *M* cross-stitched in the lower right-hand corner. She ran a finger over the monogram. "These are lovely, Mrs. Linker. I don't think I'll ever use them. They're too pretty."

"Pish, now don't go getting no ideas they're special. Just plain cotton, but they make good dish towels. You use them, you hear? The best thanks you can give a person is to put their gifts to good use. Same as with them there chickens. You raise 'em and they will supply you with eggs and baby chicks and then you can have fried chicken for Sunday dinner."

So that's that, Anna Mae thought. *You got chickens as a wedding gift and you can't look a gift horse in the mouth.* "Thank you so much, Mrs. Linker and Margaret."

An hour later, she was no closer to a solution as to

what to do with her new gifts. Mrs. Linker and Margaret waved goodbye and turned their wagon toward home. Anna Mae closed the door and scooped up the girls. "Nap time."

"No nap," they both protested with a yawn.

"Yes, nap. You need to rest and I need to think." She carried them into the bedroom and put them in their bed.

"Tisses!" Rose demanded.

Anna Mae laughed. "Okay, I'll give you kisses, but only if you promise to go right to sleep."

Both girls nodded.

She kissed them each on the cheek and they both lay down with cheeky grins on their faces. "Remember, you promised to go to sleep."

They closed their eyes and pretended to be asleep. Anna Mae returned to the sitting room. She left the door open so she could hear them and then sat down on the couch.

The chickens grumbled low in their throats. At least she thought it was a grumble. Again she shook her head. What was Josiah going to think of having three chickens in the house? She didn't want three chickens in the house. She knew what he'd think. Chickens belonged outside. At this rate he'd think her crazy for keeping them inside and there would go any chance of her finding love with him. Anna Mae sighed her prayer. *Lord, what am I going to do about this?*

The sun was setting when Josiah rode Roy into the yard. He looked to the house, expecting to see Anna Mae in the window or at the door. Disappointment hit him unexpectedly when she didn't appear in either. "Come on, Roy, let's get you settled in the nice warm barn."

He groomed the horse with an air of calm and self-confidence that belied his anxiety to rush in the house and check on things. All day he'd wondered what Anna Mae and the girls were doing. He'd worked in his office, sorting through the mail and new wanted posters. Then he'd checked with all the businesses to make sure everything was running smoothly. It was a habit he'd gotten into when he'd started as sheriff of the small town. Not only was it neighborly but it also assured him that no one had seen any shady characters about town. Then, Emily Jane had run into him and invited him to the bakery for lunch, which he'd gladly accepted. Still, he couldn't seem to get his mind to focus on the job or lunch. His thoughts continually strayed to Anna Mae and the twins.

He finished with Roy and then headed to the house. When he walked in Josiah was surprised to hear the clucking of chickens. He followed the sound and found Anna Mae in the spare bedroom, trying to herd two hens and a rooster into a corner, where she'd piled up furniture to create a pen of sorts. Feathers floated about the room as if the birds had been chased for quite a while. Anna Mae seemed unaware of him standing in the doorway watching her. Every curve of her body spoke defiance.

Her hands trembled as she eyed the chickens. Every time they moved, she jumped. Was she scared of them?

"I've about had it with you three. Either you get into

this pen or so help me, you will be Sunday dinner for sure." She planted her hands on her hips and glared at the unruly animals. Did she really think they'd do what she said?

Her back was to him, but Josiah could see that half her hair was up and the other half down. Feathers stuck out of the locks that hung against her neck, giving him the impression that one of the chickens had decided to make its nest there. A grin teased his lips. Anna Mae's sleeves were pushed up and she had scratches along both arms.

Still unaware of him, she mumbled, "I wonder how one goes about killing two hens and a rooster?"

The rooster squawked and entered the pen. The two hens hurried after him.

"Now that's more like it." She rushed to shut the makeshift door. "You guys aren't as tough as I thought you were."

The rooster changed his mind and ran out of the pen toward her. Anna Mae jumped back and looked as if she might run for the door. When she saw Josiah, she came to an abrupt stop. Her eyes were wide and her breathing quick.

He couldn't contain his merriment any longer. Josiah burst out laughing. He slapped his knees. "You're scared of them? And you let them loose in here?" he asked, still roaring with laughter.

"What was I supposed to do with them? They would have died in that box." Her lip trembled and tears welled in her eyes.

Josiah immediately sobered. He never could stomach

a woman's tears. "Aw, Annie, why didn't you wait until I got home?" He walked across the room and dropped an arm around her shoulders.

"If I'm going to take care of them, I have to overcome my fear. You won't be here all the time," she stated, trying to look brave and failing miserably.

"Where did they come from?" They looked like Rhode Island Reds. The rooster strutted about his new home and the hens followed him dutifully.

"Mrs. Linker gave them to us as a wedding present." Anna Mae smiled up at him, a sheen of purpose in her observant eyes. "Can we keep them? She assured me that come spring the hens will start laying eggs. Just think, we wouldn't have to buy eggs and I might even get enough to be able to sell them at Carolyn's store. Wouldn't that be something?"

Where was the woman who moments before had been scared of the chickens? "You do realize you'll have to feed them? Water them? And collect those eggs, don't you?"

"Of course." She pulled out of his embrace.

She confused him. "But you're afraid of them," he pointed out.

"Well, yes, but I'll just have to overcome that." Determination laced her pretty brown eyes. "If I can face down a roomful of children, I can face three chickens." She looked back at them and shuddered.

"I'm sure you can," he chuckled.

Anna Mae offered him a sweet smile. "Would you like a slice of apple bread and a cup of coffee? Both are still warm."

"I'd love some." He started to follow her through the doorway.

She held her arm out and planted a palm on his chest. "No bread until those chickens are in the pen where they belong."

Josiah watched her turn and head to the kitchen. A grin spread over his face as he called, "Annie, I hate to tell you, but if you're going to sell eggs at the general store, you're going to need more than two chickens and a rooster."

After putting the chickens in her makeshift pen, Josiah entered the sitting room. He stopped. In his rush to discover the chickens, he'd not paid much attention to the rest of the house. She'd rearranged the furniture. The scent of lemon oil reached his nose. The whole house seemed so clean and fresh. Well, all except the spare bedroom where the chickens now resided.

He heard the soft rustle of her skirt as she approached him from behind. "Do you like it?" The uncertainty in her voice had him answering quickly.

"I do. It's different, but I'm sure I'll get used to it." Josiah glanced over his shoulder and offered her a smile. Where had she put the girls' corral?

"The twins are getting too big for that pen you had, so I moved it to the back porch for the moment."

Was she a mind reader? Josiah studied her serious face for a moment. "How will we keep them out of trouble?"

Anna Mae's tinkling laughter would have been endearing if it wasn't pointed at him. "There are two of us now to watch them, and they need to be able to explore and learn what they can and can't do."

Josiah doubted the wisdom of letting them run free, but since she was the one watching them most of the time, he'd let her make that decision. He nodded. "Fair enough."

"Are you hungry for something more hearty than apple bread?" she asked, returning to the kitchen.

He followed. "No. I had lunch with Emily Jane and William. She asked if she could bring the rest of your stuff out and I told her sure. I hope you don't mind, but I also invited them out for dinner."

That smile he'd begun to love graced Anna Mae's face again. "Of course I don't mind. I started a stew earlier; it won't take long to whip up a pan of corn bread to go with it."

"You are amazing, did you know that?" The words came out of his mouth faster than his thoughts.

"For that, sir, you will receive a bigger helping of the apple bread." She sliced off an inch-thick slice, placed it on a small plate and handed it to him.

He teased, "So compliments mean more food?"

She turned to get his coffee. "That depends."

Josiah carried the bread to the table and slid into one of the chairs. "Depends on what?"

Anna Mae carried two cups to the table and set one in front of him. "On my mood." Her eyes twinkled with merriment.

Would he get used to a playful wife? Or would she become bitter at being stuck out on the farm with very few adults to talk to?

Mary had been more of the serious type. She wasn't bitter or playful, she was simply Mary, and he'd loved her. *Lord, don't let me forget how much I loved Mary. I can't allow Anna Mae into my heart. If I should lose her it would hurt even more if I truly loved her.*

Chapter Eleven

How did she do it? Josiah stood out in the cold, hammering boards together to make a chicken coop. Anna Mae had already talked him into hanging pots and pans, and now here he was freezing half to death, making a chicken coop with old boards from the barn. He shook his head.

Josiah heard wheels crunching into the front yard before he ever saw the wagon. He laid the hammer down and walked around the house. *Saved by the Barnses,* he thought happily.

William had just helped Emily Jane down from the wagon. Josiah hurried forward to help them carry Anna Mae's trunk and other things into the house.

"You take the pies in and we'll get the heavy stuff," William was saying as Josiah approached.

"Thank you." Emily Jane grasped two pie pans and turned toward the house.

Anna Mae opened the front door. She stood with a twin on each side of her. "Come on in here and warm up."

"Thanks, I believe I will." With a little giggle Emily Jane hurried up the porch steps.

Josiah noticed his brother-in-law never took his eyes away from his wife. "Be careful. Those steps might be slippery," William called after her.

"Yes, dear." Emily Jane's voice didn't sound as endearing as her words would lead one to believe.

William waited until she and Anna Mae had entered the house before saying, "I do believe that woman is getting tired of me mothering her."

Josiah laughed. "You reckon so?"

William playfully punched him in the shoulder. "I'll have none of that from you. I remember how you hovered about Mary when she was carrying the twins." He pulled a large box from the wagon and thrust it into Josiah's hands.

He had to admit he'd been more than worried about his wife when she carried the girls. Mary's middle had been impossible to ignore as she'd grown larger and larger. Toward the end she'd grown miserable and cranky.

But his girls had come and they were the most beautiful creations he'd ever seen. Briefly he allowed himself to feel sorrow that they would never know their mother.

William pulled another large box from the wagon, the same size as the one he'd given Josiah, and headed toward the house. "What are you waiting for, an invitation?"

Josiah shook his head and grinned. "Don't beat around the bush, tell me how you feel," he answered, following.

William chuckled. "We still have a big trunk to unload and a boxful of books. So no sassing."

Josiah entered the house to find Emily Jane and Anna Mae sitting on the couch, each holding one of the girls and giggling. He heard Emily Jane say, "Seriously, she gave you chickens and hand towels for a wedding gift?"

"Yes."

"But you're afraid of most animals."

He continued walking, but noticed Anna Mae glance his way and whisper, "Shh, I don't want Josiah to know."

Not know? He already knew she feared the chickens. Josiah continued on to the bedroom and set his box beside the one William had just put down. What other animals was Anna Mae afraid of?

"What do you think? Bring the trunk in next?" William asked as they headed back to the sitting room.

Josiah nodded. He'd noticed the trunk and two smaller boxes still in the wagon. "Are both the other boxes Annie's, too?"

William raised his voice for the women to hear. "Yep, between the stuff you brought from the school and the stuff we picked up from the boardinghouse, your Annie has a lot of things to lug around." William pressed his hand playfully against his back as if he were in great pain.

Laughter from the ladies followed his antics. Anna Mae wiggled a finger at them. "As soon as you men get the wagon unloaded, we'll reward you with dinner and pie."

Josiah hurried after William, who acted as if he'd gotten his strength back and part of a child's energy to continue on with what needed to be done. His brother-in-law was a ham, through and through.

As he hefted the trunk and felt the weight of what must be books, Josiah wondered again what other animals Anna Mae feared. Since they didn't have any, besides Roy and the mule, he really didn't have to worry about that, now did he?

Josiah found himself silently praying. *Lord, there is so much I don't know about my new wife. Please help her to overcome her fears. No man or woman should ever be fearful of one of Your creations. And Lord, help me to be a good helpmate to her.*

Anna Mae enjoyed having Emily Jane and William over, but as soon as they left she hurried to her boxes. She left her bedroom door open and listened while Josiah read to the girls from the Bible. She'd made the suggestion earlier, saying it would do the girls good to start putting the word of God in their hearts now, while they were still young enough to teach them how to do so. She explained that the earlier they began to learn about God and His word, the easier it would be for them to turn to Him when times were hard on them later in life. Josiah seemed to have liked the idea, and his reading to them now proved it.

It didn't take long to put her clothes away, but going through the books and things would take a little more time.

Anna Mae pulled out the books and stacked them neatly against the wall. Would Josiah be willing to build her a bookshelf? Or was there one in the room with the sleeping chickens? She'd look tomorrow.

Josiah had seemed tired this evening. Had she worked him too hard? He'd hung the pots and pans and then ventured out into the cold to make the chicken coop. She knew it wasn't finished and thought perhaps she would help him tomorrow. Those chickens had to get out of her house.

She heard Josiah say, "The end." And the sound of the Bible closing assured her he was finished reading to the girls for the night. For a few brief moments Rose and Ruby squealed with joy. Anna Mae wondered what Josiah was doing to bring them so much happiness.

With giggling and heavy footsteps, she heard him bringing them to the bedroom, and Anna Mae sighed. It would have been nice to find her journal before she had to put the girls to bed. One more night of not writing in her diary wouldn't kill her, she guessed. Anna Mae knew she'd find the book in the morning and would record all that had happened since her wedding.

"I think my playful kittens are about ready for bed," Josiah announced, coming into the room. He held a little girl's hand in each of his.

"No bed!" Ruby protested, pulling at his hand.

Rose watched her sister and her lips began to pucker.

He'd said the bed word. Anna Mae shook her head with a grin. It would have been easier to dress them and then put them to bed. "Now, girls, you know the routine. Anna Mae said, read a story and then off to bed." Josiah said, putting blame on her for their routine and newly applied rules.

Her joy quickly turned to sorrow. So that's how it was. If he didn't like her suggestions, he should have said so. They were his daughters. Maybe it was time to remind him of just that.

"Josiah, you know that was only a suggestion, right? I didn't mean to encroach on your rights as their father. They are your children and you must always do as you feel best." There, she'd said it.

His jaw clenched and his eyes narrowed slightly. "Well, that certainly puts a damper on my evening."

What was wrong? She'd only given him the option of setting his own rules. Anna Mae didn't understand and said so. "Why? What do you mean?"

He drew his lips in thoughtfully. "I must have gotten it all wrong, but I thought when you became my wife, you also became their mother." His fingers grasped a hand of each girl.

Anna Mae shook her head in dismay. "No! I mean, yes, I did."

He released their hands and studied her face as if she were an outlaw he hadn't expected to come upon. Josiah ran his hand across the back of his neck.

Anna Mae wanted to scream. This marriage thing was much tougher when you started out with a family, and without the love of your partner.

Josiah sighed heavily as if he were having the same thoughts.

She threw up her hands in surrender. "The way you told the girls it was bedtime made me feel I had taken away your rights to keep them up as long as you wanted.

I feel as if I've crossed some invisible line." She swallowed hard, lifted her chin and boldly met his gaze. "Look, I only meant that I'm a schoolteacher and I'm used to dealing with children, but I would never override your decisions concerning the girls. That's all I wanted to say."

He came close, looking down at her intently. "I'm sorry, Annie. I jumped to the wrong conclusion, again." Josiah reached out and fingered a stray piece of hair that had come out of her ponytail near her cheek. "I'm very much aware of the burden I've placed on you, saddling you with a sheriff and two little girls. It's a huge task, to say the least. I thought perhaps today had proved to be too much and you had changed your mind."

Reaching up, Anna Mae covered his hand with her own. "No, Josiah. I could not love the girls more if they were my own flesh and blood. Still, I have no right—"

He placed a finger across her lips. "Don't say it, Annie girl. I gave you the right the day we got married, and I want you to always do what's best for our children. If you must argue your point with me, do so. That's what parents do. That's what real love is." He paused and then retracted his words. "I mean real love for the girls."

A raw, primitive grief overtook her. He'd just reminded her that she would never have his love or know the joy of bringing new life into the world. Not that Anna Mae would ever love him, either, but having it pressed home like that...well, it just wasn't something that she enjoyed. She dropped her lashes quickly to hide the hurt.

If offer card is missing write to: Reader Service, P.O. Box 1867, Buffalo, NY 14240-1867 or visit www.ReaderService.com
BUSINESS REPLY MAIL
FIRST-CLASS MAIL PERMIT NO. 717 BUFFALO, NY
POSTAGE WILL BE PAID BY ADDRESSEE
READER SERVICE
PO BOX 1867
BUFFALO NY 14240-9952
NO POSTAGE NECESSARY IF MAILED IN THE UNITED STATES

Concern laced his rich voice as he asked, "What is it, Annie? What did I say that was wrong?" He caressed her cheek.

Anna Mae took a step back, breaking his hold on her. "Nothing, Josiah," she hurried to assure him. "Just please have patience with me. I'm new at this, too, and will get it wrong more often than not, but I promise you this. I will give our girls the best care that I can and their health and happiness will always come first."

He didn't seem to want to accept her explanation at first, but thankfully, he let it go. Josiah looked down. "Speaking of our little girls, where did they get to?"

Both adults turned to the bedroom door, to find Rose and Ruby sitting on the floor examining their belly buttons, quietly pointing and touching, seemingly happy that they both had one in the exact same place. Once more laughter sprang from Josiah as he walked over, swept them both into his arms and deposited them in their beds.

Rose and Ruby shrieked and cried for "tisses."

Anna Mae tapped him on the shoulder, aware that he was making them squeal even louder. "Stop riling them up. I'll never get them to sleep if you keep on this way."

He stepped back. "Good night, girls." Josiah offered her a smile and then left the room.

Fifteen minutes later, Anna Mae turned down the covers of her bed and slid between the sheets. She'd wanted to join Josiah in the sitting room, but her emotions had been on a roller coaster all day and she needed time to absorb the things she hadn't understood, and meditate on ways to change or accept her new way of life.

One thing Josiah was dead right about…raising two little girls was a huge task, and with a heavy heart she wondered if she truly was up to it.

Chapter Twelve

Josiah arrived home the following evening, tired and confused. His thoughts had been on Anna Mae all day.

Last night, he'd waited for her to join him after putting the girls to bed, but that hadn't happened. Now that he examined their actions and words from the previous evening, he realized in surprise that they'd both been on the defensive. And why was that? Action and reaction. Interesting. But even more troubling was the look of pure hurt that had entered her eyes when he'd told her the girls were hers.

He felt certain she loved the twins. She'd shown that in more ways than one, so what caused the sadness? Had Anna Mae realized the time-consuming job she'd taken on, and even though she loved the girls, regretted giving up her own life to join his?

He rubbed the back of his neck wearily. What caused women to twist up a man's insides like this? Mary had done the same. It had gotten to where every time he left on sheriff business she'd become quiet and withdrawn. More and more she'd taken to spending time in the bedroom rather than in the sitting room with him. He'd thought maybe it was those woman emotions that took over after giving birth, but now Anna Mae acted the same way.

His communication skills hadn't improved at all. Looking back only brought more confusion and sadness; a feeling of failure.

Instead of going straight to the barn and putting Roy away, Josiah decided to go to the house first. He needed to make sure that Anna Mae was doing all right.

He opened the door slowly and the warm scent of fried potatoes greeted him. The house was unusually quiet. Josiah walked to Anna Mae's and the girls' bedroom. Everything was in its place, but they were nowhere to be found. He hurried to the guest room, where the chickens clucked in low undertones. Again, the room was empty. His heart skipped a beat.

Had she left and taken his girls with her? Where had she gone? And why? He hurried back outside. If Anna Mae had really left, she'd have to have used the mule and wagon.

Roy snorted as Josiah passed by. Josiah's boots squished in the mud and snow as he rushed to the barn. With more strength then he knew he possessed, he jerked the door open.

"Papa!" Rose hurried to him on her short little legs.

Seeing her twin sister and father, Ruby squealed and ran toward him, too.

Josiah's heart leaped with gladness. The girls were safe. His gaze swept the barn and he found Anna Mae kneeling in front of a wooden structure of some type. She had a mouthful of nails and a hammer poised to do some damage.

Both girls grabbed him around the calves and hung on tightly. "Up!" they demanded.

He picked them both up and kissed their little cheeks. His gaze held Anna Mae's as she spit the nails into her hand.

"I wasn't expecting you back so early," she said, once her mouth was empty.

Josiah carried the girls to her. "I'm not early." His gaze moved to whatever it was she was trying so hard to make. "What is that supposed to be?"

"A bookshelf?" Anna Mae turned to look at the wood. With a heavy sigh she said, "Doesn't look much like a bookshelf, does it?"

He didn't want to hurt her feelings. "Well, I'm not a carpenter."

Her delicate laughter took him by surprise. "No, but you are a really sweet man." She looked up at him with joyful eyes. "Come on inside and we'll get everyone fed." She reached up and took Ruby from his arms.

He followed her from the barn. Roy snorted from the front porch. Josiah had completely forgotten about his dear friend.

"I was thinking, Josiah." Anna Mae paused as she reached the front door.

This couldn't be good for him. It seemed every time the woman said "I was thinking," it meant work for him. He started to ask her what she'd been thinking about, dreading what she'd say, when she continued.

"Why don't we put the chicken coop in the barn until spring. That way they would be warm, and all we'd have to do is set up a place for them to sleep." She opened the door and set Ruby down. The little girl immediately started taking off her coat and boots.

Josiah did the same with Rose. "I need to put Roy away for the night. I'll see if I can find space for the chickens."

"The last stall on the right should work well," Anna Mae suggested, as she helped Rose with her buttons.

He headed back to the horse, which nudged him with his nose as if to say "Forgot all about me, didn't you?"

Josiah rubbed his nose. "I didn't forget about you, ole man. It's just now I have a wife and kids to think about, too."

Roy bumped him in the shoulder. Josiah laughed, picked up his reins and led him toward the barn. As he entered the warm building, Josiah had to admit she might have a good idea about keeping the chickens there.

With Roy properly taken care of, he walked back to the stall Anna Mae had said would be good for the chickens. It needed a little repair. Several of the boards looked as if they were going to pop loose.

Josiah shook his head. He'd placed his horse and the mule in the better maintained stalls, thinking he had until spring to repair the rest that needed work. Josiah sighed. Women always wanted something done right away, and Anna Mae was no different.

He gave Roy a final pat on the nose and then headed back to the house. Anna Mae wanted bookshelves, the stall fixed and a nesting box for the chickens. Thankfully, he didn't have anything pressing going on in town and could stay home tomorrow and work on the chores.

When he entered the house Anna Mae had already taken care of getting the girls to the table, and the food smelled wonderful. Rose and Ruby smiled, their freshly scrubbed faces shining. His girls had never looked happier.

"What took so long?" Anna Mae asked, as she set plates before them.

"I checked out the stall you mentioned." He pulled his coat off, hung it on the rack beside the door, then stopped.

When had Anna Mae hung the rack? His gaze roved the house and he saw several other things she'd done to improve the function of his home. He'd been so busy working that he'd neglected noticing the small changes. She'd brought warmth to his home. Would his new wife soon expect him to make changes, too? Would she expect him to express his appreciation with love?

The next afternoon, Anna Mae hummed as she finished wiping down the counters, then hung the dishcloth on the drying rod. Josiah had been called away shortly after breakfast, so she'd found her yarn, and while she knitted two pot holders, the girls played with balls of bright colored yarn. Then she'd started dinner and fixed lunch all at the same time.

Now that the noon dishes were done, she thought about slipping out to the barn and working on the bookshelf while the girls napped. Anna Mae pulled on her gloves, cloak and finally her boots. She'd be out for only an hour and then she'd come back inside.

The sun shone brightly and felt warm on her cheeks. Anna Mae hurried to the barn and pulled the door open; the warm scent of hay and dust filling her lungs. She loved the barn and couldn't wait for Josiah to get the nesting box built for the chickens.

Maybe she could help him do that. She was sick of cleaning up their mess, so something must be done. She walked to the stall and looked about.

From what she could see, all the stall needed was a few boards nailed back into place, and then she could bring the chickens out here and clean up the spare room. With that thought in mind, Anna Mae forgot all about making the bookshelf.

She grabbed the hammer and nails, then hung her cloak on a peg. It took her almost an hour to get the stall secure and in the shape that she thought it should be.

Her hands hurt from hammering and holding boards in place. She'd taken her gloves off and now regretted the action. Anna Mae looked at her swollen, throbbing thumb and sighed. She didn't dare glance at her palms, where she felt confident the blisters were rising.

After spreading fresh hay and sprinkling a few kernels of corn into it, she pulled her cloak back on and headed inside to check on the girls. The wind had picked up and felt colder than when she'd gone out. She opened the door and listened. No sounds came from the bedroom where the twins slept. The chickens were clucking softly in their room.

Anna Mae checked on Rose and Ruby. They were

still sleeping. She smiled. Maybe she could get the chickens out to the barn before they woke.

It was one thing to think she could get them out there. It was another to actually do it. Anna Mae gazed at the birds. How was she going to get them back inside the box she'd taken them out of?

She stared at them and they stared back. Anna Mae didn't know how, but she could tell from their beady eyes that they knew she was up to something. The rooster raised his head, stretching his neck up toward the ceiling, and then strutted about as if daring her to try and catch him.

The hens looked more approachable. Anna Mae shut the bedroom door and then stepped into the pen she'd made. "You can do this, Anna Mae. They are just as afraid of you as you are of them."

She chased the chickens at a walking pace. Just as she reach down to grab one it would dart away. Soon she found herself running about the room, the hens jumping to escape her. They squawked in alarm and feathers flew.

Anna Mae would get ahold of one and it would flap its wings and try to peck her. She'd squeal and let it go. She didn't know how long she'd been trying to catch the hens or how many times she'd let them go when she heard the sound of laughter. She turned to find Josiah leaning against the door frame and laughing as if he couldn't catch his breath. His reaction both annoyed and pleased her.

"How long have you been standing there?" she demanded, out of breath and tired from her day's work.

He tried to compose his features, but failed miserably. "Long enough to see you are no chicken catcher."

"Do you think you can do any better?" she asked, leaning against a wooden chest.

"I didn't say that." He continued to laugh. "You should see yourself."

Anna Mae didn't doubt that she was a sight. Her hair hung about her shoulders and feathers covered her arms. She was sure they were in her hair, as well. "If it's all the same to you, I believe I'll avoid a mirror for a while."

He straightened. "What were you going to do once you caught one?"

"Put it in that box." Anna Mae pointed to the crate Mrs. Linker had brought them in.

He opened his mouth as if to ask another question, but one of the twins interrupted him by yelling from the other room. "Up!"

Anna Mae left the pen and walked toward Josiah. "I'm going to go get the girls up from their nap. If you think you can catch the chickens, by all means do so." She raised her chin and continued past him.

Once she was out the door, Anna Mae headed to the kitchen, where she quickly washed her hands, arms and face. The cool water both stung and felt good as she splashed it over her many scrapes and the broken blisters on her hands. All the while the girls continued to yell, "Up!"

"I'm coming," she called back to them. Anna Mae hurried to the bedroom and found Rose and Ruby clutching the rails and looking unhappy.

When they saw her, their sweet faces broke into

smiles. Anna Mae hurried to get them up, and by the time she had them out of the bed and into dry clothes Josiah stood in the doorway waiting for her.

"They are in the box. Now what?" he asked, his eyes still dancing with merriment.

"Now you can take them to the barn," she answered, setting Rose down and watching as she ran to her papa.

He shook his head. "That stall needs to be repaired before we can put them inside."

Anna Mae ran her fingers through her hair, removing feathers, careful to avoid using her aching thumb and sore palms. "I already fixed it."

Disbelief filled his face. "You did?"

"Sure did." She heard the pride in her voice, but couldn't contain it. "I might not be able to catch chickens, but I can nail boards together." She hoped him seeing that she could get some things done about the place would endear her to him. Maybe what Josiah was looking for in a woman was someone strong who could work alongside him. Maybe he'd see that as a reason to love her. Maybe.

Chapter Thirteen

The woman in front of Josiah never ceased to amaze him. He'd not been able to contain his amusement as he'd watched her chase after that chicken. It was such a small space and no matter how hard she'd tried, Anna Mae couldn't bring herself to just grab the bird and hang on. He felt laughter bubbling up in his chest once more. When was the last time he'd been this happy?

Anna Mae nodded. "Go see for yourself." She tucked her left hand behind her.

What was she hiding? Josiah looked back at her sweet face. Her lips smiled, but something else was going on behind her eyes.

A loud clang in the kitchen had them both rushing out of the bedroom. Josiah knew Rose and Ruby were into something. When had his daughters slipped past him?

Sure enough. There they sat on the kitchen floor, playing in a new puddle of flour.

"Oh, you little scamps." Anna Mae hurried to get

them out of the flour. "You know you aren't supposed to be in here," she scolded, even as she dusted the back side of their dresses.

He chuckled. "You seem to have this situation under control. I'll take the chickens out."

Her gasp stopped him in his tracks. He turned to see Anna Mae clutching her left hand against her chest and grimacing. What in the world?

Rose and Ruby had returned to the flour and were playing happily in the white powder, but Anna Mae seemed to have lost all interest in the little girls.

Josiah set the box of chickens down and hurried to see what she was hiding and what caused the intense look of pain. He took her hand gently in his and examined it. Her thumb had a big blood blister under the nail bed, a sure sign she'd hit it with a hammer. His fingers gently opened her hands to reveal broken blisters.

"Aw, Annie." He rested his forehead against hers. "Why didn't you tell me you were hurt?"

She shook her head. "It's nothing. Just a couple of blisters and a banged up thumb. I'm sure farmer's wives everywhere have to deal with a few blisters. I'll toughen up. I promise." Anna Mae pulled away from him.

Josiah wasn't having that. He gently drew her to the kitchen table and helped her into a chair. Not that she needed help, but he wanted her sitting while he cleaned her hands. "You aren't a farmer's wife. You are a sheriff's wife and most sheriffs live in town and their wives don't have to repair barns." He scooped up his girls and put them in their chairs. "You two stay put. Annie is hurt."

Big blue eyes turned to Anna Mae. "Owie?" Ruby asked, tearing up.

"Oh no," Rose added, her eyes wide.

"It's not so bad," Anna Mae assured them.

Josiah poured water into one of the wash basins. He stepped over the flour and placed the container in front of her. "Here, put your hands in this while I clean up the floor."

He turned stern eyes on his daughters. "Look at this mess you made. If you were older, I'd make you clean it up." Josiah set the flour bucket upright and grabbed Anna Mae's broom.

"Sawee," the girls chorused. Their little faces looked to him for forgiveness.

"Don't tell me, tell Annie. She's the one who has been cleaning up after you this week," Josiah scolded.

The twins each looked to Anna Mae. "Sawee, Awnie."

"Thank you, girls, that's very good that you are sorry." She offered them a sweet smile.

Josiah was glad that she didn't tell them it was all right. The twins needed to learn that they couldn't play in the flour and that they needed to respect their stepmother. He finished cleaning up the mess, put the flour back under the cabinet where Annie had set it and then turned back to check on her hands.

Once he had finished that, he looked at his girls. "You two stay there until I come back in."

"Josiah, you are making too much of this. I'm fine," Anna Mae protested.

He shook his head. "That goes for you, too. I'm going to release these birds into the barn and then I'll be back." Josiah didn't give her a chance to argue. He picked up the chickens and left.

What was he going to do with that woman? Anna Mae was a schoolteacher, and from what he gathered from her, she'd never lived in the country. Between the two of them they had no business living on a farm. She wasn't cut out for hard labor, and if the truth be told, he had no idea how to run a working farm.

The chickens squawked in gratitude as he released them into the stall. He watched as they immediately began scratching in the fresh hay that Anna Mae had spread for them. His gaze moved over the walls, inspecting her handiwork. She'd done a pretty good job.

Josiah grabbed the hammer and finished where she'd left off. It didn't take him more than a couple minutes to reinforce what she'd already done. He left the chickens happily scratching at the ground and clucking softly to one another.

As he started out the door, his gaze landed on the boards that Anna Mae had attempted to create a bookshelf out of. He sighed. If he didn't do it, she would. The woman was determined, he'd give her that.

Josiah stacked the wood into a pile, found the bag of nails and laid his hammer on top. Then he found the wheelbarrow and put it all inside. He pushed it to the house.

Anna Mae had moved to the couch and the girls sat at her feet, looking at some type of picture book. Satisfied his family was resting, Josiah headed back outside and collected the wood, nails and hammer. He set them inside the door and then ran the wheelbarrow back to the barn.

When he returned, Anna Mae had moved to the wood. She was about to pick up a piece when he stopped her. "What do you think you're doing?" Josiah demanded, pulling his coat off and hanging it up.

"I just wanted to help," she answered, standing up straighter and placing her bandaged hands on her hips. "I'm not going to sit around and do nothing because I have a couple of blisters." Her eyes dared him to argue.

The girls looked up at her raised voice, studying the grown-ups' every movement. Aware that his daughters were listening as well as watching, Josiah shook his head.

"Why don't you let me make the bookshelf? You can supervise." He offered her what he hoped was a compromising smile.

Anna Mae nodded. She handed him the board she'd been holding. "All right. I'm guessing this is my new bookshelf?"

"You guessed right."

"Why did you bring it inside?" she asked, gnawing on her bottom lip.

"Three reasons. One, if it's built in the house I won't have to lug it in from the barn when I'm done. Two, I wasn't sure how tall you wanted it, or how many shelves. And three, if I work on it in here we can both be warm and I can keep an eye on you." He knelt down and began sorting the wood, before glancing at his girls, who had regained interest in their book.

"Oh, why didn't I think of that?"

"What? That I want to keep an eye on you?" he teased.

Anna Mae looked troubled. "No, to bring it inside to work on it." She sat down on the arm of the couch. "I guess I'm not as clever as I thought I was."

Josiah laughed. His gaze moved about his home. It felt like a new place since she had arrived. Curtains hung on the windows; blankets and throws draped the furniture. The house smelled clean and fresh, not damp and musty. She'd managed to turn their house into a home in just a matter of days. He hadn't figured out how to do that during the whole time he'd been in Granite. "I wouldn't say you aren't smart. If you hadn't plowed forward and fixed that pen in the barn yourself, I wouldn't have decided to work on the shelves tonight."

She shook her head. "No, I could have saved us both time if I had brought the wood in."

Josiah stood up and walked over to her. He lifted her bandaged hands in his. "Now look here, Annie. This is all new to both of us. I am not a farmer, have never wanted to be a farmer, but here I am, corralling chickens and making bookshelves. You are a schoolteacher, and how often have *you* raised chickens or built furniture?" He didn't give her time to answer. "I'd say never to both. So don't go whipping yourself because you didn't think to bring the wood into the house."

Tears sprang into her eyes. "Do you regret marrying me?"

He shook his head. "Of course not. You are the best thing to happen to this place and my girls. Just look at what you've done to the house." Josiah released her hands. He motioned toward Rose and Ruby. "And look at the girls. I don't think they've ever been this happy and content."

Josiah knew he meant every word he said. What he didn't say was that he cared about her and was happy that she was his wife. He wouldn't say that out loud or even to himself. To do so would suggest that he'd developed feelings for Anna Mae Miller, and that scared him more than any bank robber ever could.

Chapter Fourteen

Anna Mae's hands healed over the next few days. Still amazed by Josiah's tenderness and kind ways, she washed and scrubbed the guest bedroom floor until it shone. The chickens had made a mess of the whole room, but the floor had been the worst part.

A glance at the clock told her she had a little while longer before the twins awoke from their morning nap. She pushed up from the floor and picked up the pail of dirty water. Her plans were to fix ham sandwiches and potato salad for lunch. She'd found a wonderful array of canned vegetables in the root cellar and couldn't wait to open a jar of pickles.

The sound of a wagon pulling into the front yard drew her to the door. The soft lowing of a cow came from the direction of the wagon. Emily Jane and Millie Westland, Levi's wife, waved from the seat.

Happy to see her friends, though a bit puzzled as to why they had a cow tied to the back of the wagon, Anna Mae tossed the dirty water to the right of the porch and hurriedly put the bucket away. She ran her hand over her hair and donned a fresh apron before going back to the door to greet her guests.

"Emily Jane, Millie, I'm so happy to see you both here." Anna Mae rushed down the stairs to stand behind Emily Jane as she disembarked from the wagon. It wouldn't do for her to fall in her condition.

Millie was already tying the horse and wagon to the porch rail. She looped a feed bag over the little mare's head and then walked around to the back of the wagon. "I hope you don't mind us just dropping in like this, but we wanted to get the milk cow out here before it got too late," she offered. "Levi has the baby, so we can't stay long." She started untying the cow from the tailgate.

Emily Jane turned to Anna Mae and grinned. "I brought chocolate cake, enough for now and more for your dessert tonight."

Anna Mae tilted to the right so she could see around Emily Jane to where Millie was undoing the cow's lead. "What is Millie doing with that animal?" she asked, feeling uneasy because she thought she knew the answer to her question.

"She's a wedding present from your neighbor Mr. Green," Millie answered, pulling the cow toward the porch. "The girls will have fresh milk every morning and her milk makes the best butter, according to him."

Should she refuse the cow? Her gaze darted between Emily Jane and Millie. They both looked so happy that she couldn't get her mouth to say what her mind was screaming: *Not another animal!* What was Josiah going to say?

"Where do you want her?" Millie asked, stroking the white streak down the center of the light brown cow's face. Big brown eyes looked up at Anna Mae. The cow let out a low cry.

Afraid she would wake the girls, Anna Mae made a quick decision. "Let's put her in the barn."

"I'll take the cake inside and check on my nieces," Emily Jane said, heading for the door.

Anna Mae shot her a stern look. "If you wake them up, you have to take them home with you." They both knew it was an empty threat.

"I'll be quiet. I just want to look at them and maybe steal a kiss."

Millie laughed. "Come on, Anna Mae. I'm getting cold."

As they walked toward the barn, Anna Mae asked, "Why did Mr. Green send us a cow? I mean, I know he did it for a wedding gift, but why a cow?"

The dismay in her voice prompted Millie to stop. "Mrs. Linker has been telling all your neighbors that you are going to make this a running farm, not just an orchard. Didn't you know?"

Anna Mae shook her head. "No, I can't think what I could have said to her to have given her that impression."

Millie shrugged. "Well, don't be surprised if more of your neighbors show up with other farm animals."

What Josiah would say about the cow didn't bear thinking about. "Did Mr. Green say if she has a name?"

"He called her Jersey. I guess that's her name." Millie pulled on the door to the barn. It opened and a whiff of warm air caressed their skin.

Anna Mae watched as Millie coaxed the animal inside. She'd seen bigger cows and was glad that theirs wasn't as big as those. She felt Millie studying her.

"You have to make friends with her, Anna Mae, or she'll think you don't like her and will probably quit giving milk."

"You're kidding." Anna Mae gazed at the cow. She'd planned on Josiah taking care of her. After all, she took care of the chickens every day. It sounded fair to her.

"Nope." Millie shook her head and pursed her lips.

"How do you become a friend to a cow?" Anna Mae asked, dreading the answer.

Her friend grinned. "Well, first off you need to pet her and talk in a nice voice to her."

"Pet her?" she squeaked.

Millie chuckled. "Yes, she's really gentle. You have nothing to fear from her."

Who ever heard of petting a cow to be friends with it? Anna Mae didn't believe her. For that matter, who ever heard of being friends with a cow in the first place? She eyed the big, brown-eyed animal with distaste. "Then what?"

"Well, Mr. Green said to tell you that she has to be milked at six every morning and evening." Millie looked about. "Where in here do you want her?"

Anna Mae pointed to the only available stall. "In there." Her finger shook. How was she going to befriend a cow? And she knew nothing about milking one. She only prayed Josiah knew how to do both. Anna Mae didn't think she could run a farm. What was she going to do if the neighbors continued to supply her with barnyard animals?

Josiah heard the cow bawling long before he reached the yard. His gaze moved to the house and he thought he saw the curtain fall back into place. He dropped from Roy's back and waited for Anna Mae to join him in the yard.

It was well after eight o'clock and he was sure the twins were already in bed and sleeping. He continued to wait for Anna Mae, but after several long moments he realized that he must have been mistaken and she wasn't coming out.

The sound of an unhappy cow filled his ears. It came from the direction of his barn. "Oh, Lord, please don't let her have gotten another animal."

He pulled the door open. His gaze immediately landed on the cow. She was a Jersey with a white blaze down her nose. From her cries she was a cow who needed to be milked.

Josiah sighed. He put Roy in his stall and promised to return soon to complete their nightly ritual. Then he turned to the bovine.

"Hello, beautiful. What brings you into my barn?" He leaned on the door of her stall and waited until she brought her head closer before extending his hand to touch her velvety nose.

She snorted into his palm.

"Oh, my lovely new wife brought you in here, did

she?" He worked his hand up her face, then gently scratched the stiff hair behind her right ear.

She twitched her tail and stomped a back hoof. He leaned to the side and looked at her swollen udder. "Just as I thought, you need to be milked."

Josiah found a rope and created a loop at one end. Then he approached the stall once more. He patted her nose and face and scratched behind her ear, and at the same time slowly lowered the rope around her neck.

After opening the stall door he gently led the cow out into the center aisle of the barn. He tied her to a sturdy post and grabbed a bucket of oats. Josiah set the bucket at her head and then placed the stool where he could milk her. "This won't take long," he told her, finding another clean bucket. He set it under her udders and slowly began to milk.

The barn door creaked open and a gust of cold air entered the barn. Josiah rested his forehead against the cow to soothe her. "Come inside, Anna Mae, but move very slowly," he instructed, continuing to milk.

She did as he said. Her skirts swished across the dirt floor as she inched closer to him and the cow. "I'm sorry. I didn't know how to do that. But Millie said it had to be done by six and, well, even though I'm late, I came out to try."

"You don't have to whisper. Just don't shout or move suddenly." He looked up at her.

Anna Mae wrung her hands in her apron. Her big eyes took in the animal with renewed anxiety. Why did she keep taking animals that she feared? Instead of asking her that, he asked instead, "Anna Mae, where did this cow come from?"

"Mr. Green gave it to us as a…"

"Wedding present," Josiah finished.

She nodded. "I'm afraid so."

"Why did you accept it?" He heard the frustration in his voice, but didn't know how to hide it from her. Josiah wasn't sure he should even try. She had to know he wouldn't be pleased.

Anna Mae mangled the apron. "Millie and Emily Jane brought it out. I didn't know how to say no and I didn't want to hurt Mr. Green's feelings."

"What about how I would feel about it? I told you I'm no farmer, yet you keep accepting animals that have to be cared for. You are so scared of them you can't possibly help look after them. What are we going to do now with another animal that needs tending? Also, cows aren't cheap to feed, Anna Mae," he barked, not looking at her.

Josiah knew he was overtired from his day at the sheriff's office. Word had it that a gang of bank robbers had moved into the area. He'd spent all afternoon going over wanted posters, memorizing faces and names, just in case they came to Granite.

His town.

The town he'd vowed to protect.

Unless Anna Mae learned how to milk, the cow would have to go. The swish of the door opening and closing again met his ears. She'd left.

Josiah sighed. He finished milking the cow, took care of Roy and pitched fresh hay into all three stalls. By the time he entered the house, Josiah knew he owed Anna Mae an apology. He shouldn't have taken his stress out on her.

Pushing the door open, he found the sitting room and the kitchen empty. A covered plate of food sat at the back of the stove. Anna Mae had retired to her bedroom.

Maybe she would come out while he ate, he thought, pouring himself a cup of warm coffee. He took the plate and moved to the table. Josiah allowed the wood of the chair legs to scrape loudly against the floor.

Had he been too hard on her? He expected his wife would come out any moment, telling him she knew exactly how much a cow cost to keep and that she'd learn to milk, just as she'd learned how to feed the chickens.

He finished his coffee and dinner, but Anna Mae never appeared. Josiah sighed. When he carried his dirty plate to the washbasin, he noticed a large slice of chocolate cake on the sideboard. The thought of eating it left a bitter taste in his mouth.

Josiah walked to the rocking chair by the fireplace and dropped into it. He reached over and picked up his Bible.

Thank God, when a man couldn't commune with his woman, the Lord always proved sufficient. His Bible fell open to Romans 8:25. *But if we hope for what we do not yet have, we wait for it patiently.* He sighed again. Patience was not a virtue he was known for.

He stood and blew out the lamp on the table. At least it would be warm in his room tonight, for Anna Mae had left his door open all day. Last night it had been so cold he could see his breath, and he'd burrowed under the covers like a mole.

She'd thought of him; that was a plus. The minus was that if she kept heating the whole house, he'd run out of firewood long before winter was over.

The bed groaned as it took his weight, and a still small voice from within whispered in his mind: *Tomorrow things will look much brighter.*

Chapter Fifteen

Anna Mae jerked awake. She'd overslept. Sunshine filtered through her window. She sat up quickly and found Rose and Ruby grinning at her from their bed.

She knew without being told that Josiah had gone already. He left every morning long before the sun rose, so why should today be any different? Anna Mae thought about the night before and his harsh words.

It had been childish to hide in her room, but she just couldn't face him. She'd known he wouldn't be happy about Jersey, but he'd never spoken harshly to her before. It had been unexpected but deserved. He could have said what he wanted in a kinder manner, but she couldn't fault him. Who knew what his day had been like before he'd come home to find even more responsibility?

"Good morning, ladies." She smiled at the girls and pushed the covers back. "I overslept. I bet you two are starving."

"Eat?" Rose asked hopefully.

Anna Mae laughed. "Yes, as soon as we're all dressed and ready for our day." She quickly put her words to action and had the girls dressed and walking into the kitchen within ten minutes.

"How about we have pancakes for breakfast this morning?" she asked, looking down at them.

"Sounds really good to me."

Without glancing up, Anna Mae recognized her husband's voice. He hadn't gone to work. Was he sick? She looked up to find him studying her face. What did he hope to find? He didn't appear sick. Had he stayed home to finish what they'd started the night before?

"Then you shall have as many as you like." She offered him a wobbly smile. Why did she feel so close to tears again? Never in all her life had she felt the sting that his disappointment caused in her.

"Papa!" Rose and Ruby toddled as fast as their little legs would carry them, falling against his legs.

He swooped down and picked them both up at the same time. Josiah rubbed his face against theirs, causing more squeals.

The little girls' joy brought a genuine smile to Anna Mae's face. No matter what came their way, Josiah's daughters made it all worthwhile. She'd give up the cow, if that's what he wanted. Even though the previous afternoon she'd dreamed of all the things she could make. Soups, baked custards and cheese were at the top of her future menus.

Just thinking about them gave her renewed bravery. She'd try again to get him to let her keep the cow. He hadn't exactly said they were getting rid of it, just that she'd have to learn not to be afraid of it, and that it would cost more to have.

As she made pancake batter, Anna Mae began to think of ways she could earn a little money to help keep Jersey. Maybe she could make cream or cheese and sell it to Carolyn at the general store.

Lost in thought, she didn't realize Josiah was behind her until his arms snaked around her waist. She gave a little squeal, then tilted her head just as he fitted his face against hers.

"I'm sorry, Annie, for behaving like a raging boar yesterday. Can you forgive me?" Softly his breath fanned her face.

She sighed. How wonderful it felt to have a man apologize. She couldn't recall her father ever apologizing to her mother. And Josiah's arms felt so good around her, as if they were meant to enclose her.

Anna Mae tried hard not to read too much into it, but surely she could enjoy moments like this for what they were. He had hurt her feelings, and he recognized it and wasn't willing to let it pass.

But perhaps he was expecting more. She pushed the thought away. No, Josiah was asking for forgiveness. Even if he was looking for more, she wasn't. Her heart had been broken and still hadn't mended from that embarrassment. Still, that same heart sang with delight that he cared about their friendship and had asked her to forgive him.

She tried to act nonchalant, but her voice broke with huskiness when she spoke. "You are forgiven, with one condition."

He moved back but kept an arm about her waist. "I know, I know. I'll do my best not to ever take my tiredness and frustration out on you again."

Anna Mae shook her head, aware she hadn't put her hair up this morning because she'd thought he was out of the house. "That's not what I meant at all." She poured batter into the heated pan. "I need you to forgive me, too." She set the bowl down and wiped her hands on her apron. "Josiah, I'm so sorry I accepted the cow. A little voice in my head warned me you would be upset, but I was more afraid to offend the giver than I was you."

He gave her waist a little squeeze. "There's nothing to forgive. You did right in not wanting to hurt the old man's feelings. But that still leaves the question, what do you think we should do now?" Josiah released her and rubbed the back of his neck.

Anna Mae knew he was talking about the cow. Was he hoping she'd say to give it back or sell the beast? Had he asked her only out of politeness, and actually planned on selling it regardless of what her answer might be? Or was that just what he did while trying to figure out what to do next? She decided that instead of questioning his motive for asking her, she'd just tell him what she thought they should do now.

"I guess you better teach me how to milk the dreadful animal." Before he could protest, Anna Mae rushed on. "The girls need the fresh milk and I'm sure I can make cream and cheese with the excess and sell it to Carolyn at the store. That will help with the extra cost of hay and oats or whatever cows eat. What do you think?"

She slid fluffy pancakes onto a plate and poured more batter into her hot pan.

Josiah nodded. "That might work." He paused, looked up and grinned wickedly. "But someone has to build a corral and a shed to keep it in. It can't stay in the barn forever."

"Why not? And who would you get to help you?" Anna Mae knew he meant for her to help him, but couldn't stop herself from teasing him back. Yet she really didn't understand why the cow couldn't stay in the barn.

"Cows are leaners. They like to lean against things. And they are heavy. Anything built for use around cattle must be very sturdy." He picked up a couple plates and put a pancake on each one, then carried them to the table.

Rose and Ruby hurried to meet him there. "Up, eat." They waved their arms in anticipation of being served breakfast.

"In a minute," he told them, brushing the tops of their heads with his big hands. Josiah returned and picked up two more plates, one for himself and one for Anna Mae. "As for who is going to help me, I think you have the muscles to do that."

Anna Mae jerked her arm away as he squeezed the upper part, testing her muscles. She giggled as if it had tickled. "So now we are building a lean shed for the cow and a chicken coop for the chickens." With a serious expression she added, "I suppose that's what I get for allowing the beasties on the farm." She carried the pancakes and butter to the table.

Josiah grabbed a jar of blackberry preserves from the icebox and followed her. “Yep.” He set the jar down and proceeded to help the girls into their chairs.

Anna Mae wasn’t sure what to say. Was he teasing again? His tone had sounded very serious.

He straightened, his gaze met hers and he wiggled his eyebrows playfully. “I guess you’ll listen to that small voice next time someone gives us a wedding present. Especially if it’s in the form of some sort of animal, like a pig or a goat.”

She crinkled her nose at the thought of a dirty pig needing care. “I should say so.” She laughed.

Josiah blessed the meal and he and the girls began to eat. He laughed and teased Rose and Ruby as he helped them with their pancakes. Blackberry preserves would have to be washed from their hands and faces and even possibly their hair. Anna Mae didn’t mind. The girls never failed to put a smile on their father’s handsome face, and that made her happy, as well.

Now that she thought about it, Josiah had been serious every time she’d seen him in town. It was only at home that he allowed his softer, fun side to show. A smile touched her lips, because now she was part of his home life, and she liked it and her new husband.

“If you are thinking about getting a pig, stop thinking. I hate taking care of those dirty animals.” He shook his fork in her direction.

Anna Mae held her hands up in surrender. “No, I promise, no more barnyard animals.” She looked to the girls. Purplish-blue goo covered their mouths and cheeks. “Except maybe a dog or a kitten.” She laughed gleefully at the pained expression that covered his face. She could get used to married life if it stayed like this.

Josiah grinned at Anna Mae, enjoying the banter more than he ever expected to. "You know what this means now, don't you?" He wiped the grin from his face and studied her over his coffee.

Confusion laced her pretty features. Her hair hung about her oval-shaped face, giving her a soft, delicate look. "That we have to go dog hunting?"

He shook his head in mock frustration. "No, it means we have to go to town for supplies."

The thought of visiting town brightened her face. "Oh, that's a wonderful idea. I want to buy some fabric. The girls need new dresses. I'd love to make them Christmas dresses and…" Her gaze moved to the kitchen. "We need more sugar, coffee and bacon."

Josiah laughed. He found he laughed more around her than anyone. She brought joy out in him. Even Mary hadn't been able to make him laugh as much as Anna Mae had in the last couple weeks. The thought sobered him.

"You might want to make a list, but I think we also need corn and oats. Not to mention I'm going to have to go to Mr. Green and see if he has extra hay for the cow."

"Oh, that's a great idea." She jumped up and ran to her room.

Rose and Ruby looked at him in confusion. He shrugged. "I guess she went to get paper and pen. Who knows what that woman is doing?"

The little girls nodded as if they agreed. "Go," Ruby said, pushing at the table.

"Oh, no, you don't. You finish those pancakes and then we'll go."

Anna Mae returned with pencil and paper and an open book to make her writing neater. The pencil scraped rapidly across the page as she scribbled out her list. Her head was down and her hair created a curtain that hid her face. "I'd also like to get a few sheets of colored paper, if Carolyn has some." She spoke more to herself than him.

"Annie?"

She looked up. Her brown eyes sparkled with excitement. "Yes?"

Josiah pushed away from the table. "I need to go hitch up the wagon. Do you think you can take care of things in here until I get back?" He looked pointedly at his sticky girls.

"Oh. Sure. I'll give them a quick sponge bath and get them all prettied up." She stopped. "Oh, before we leave I'll need to feed the chickens." Her nose wrinkled in distaste. "And learn how to milk Jersey."

She looked so sweet with her nose all crinkled up and her lips curled. Josiah focused on pulling his boots on before answering. "I'll take care of the animals this morning. This afternoon or tomorrow will be soon enough for you to take over."

Her teeth flashed in a big smile. "Thanks, Josiah."

That smile brightened his outlook on things while he hitched up the horse and checked on the other animals. The mule brayed in her stall. She probably wanted to get out and kick up her heels. Josiah made a mental note to ask Anna Mae if the little mule belonged to her or if they should tie it to the wagon and take it back to the school.

The sounds in the barn had changed in the past month. Once Roy was the only animal in there, but now there was a mule, a cow and three chickens. It was a noisy and warmer place to be. Anna Mae had changed his life in more ways than one since her arrival.

How much more change would she bring to his life? He thought of them as good friends, but would that alter? Could he grow to love her? Josiah shook his head. No, he couldn't allow such thoughts to fill his mind. Mary had been the love of his life, and he could never allow anyone to take her place. Never.

Chapter Sixteen

At the general store, Anna Mae read the proclamation from President Grover Cleveland declaring a designated Thursday, the twenty-fourth of November, as a day of thanksgiving and prayer, to be observed by all the people of the land. She listened to Carolyn as she rushed about the store gathering up their supplies. Anna Mae's gaze moved to the back of the room where the men gathered, talking about the president's latest proclamation.

The Moores had placed several of the newspaper clippings about their store for their customers to read.

Carolyn's voice drew her attention once more. "We can't believe it. Can you imagine how many people will be buying more staples and food supplies here? I placed another order yesterday. I just hope it gets here before the twenty-fourth."

In her excitement, Carolyn didn't really want or need an answer, Anna Mae knew. Her gaze moved to Rose and Ruby, who sat on the floor, playing with a couple other children. The four of them rolled and played with wooden blocks. They would stack them up and knock them down with squeals of laughter.

Anna Mae walked over to the fabric and fingered the softness of the material. Her thoughts were more on Christmas than this new holiday called Thanksgiving. She already planned to make the girls Christmas dresses for the Sunday service and rag dolls with matching dresses. But for Josiah it had to be something special. The quilt on his bed was very worn. Perhaps she could make a new one. Something simple that wouldn't take a lot of time to do. She'd have to hand piece it. Her thoughts raced as she touched each fabric in turn.

A royal blue caught her attention, reminding her of the beauty in Josiah's eyes. She picked up the bolt and carried it to the counter. Then she returned to the fabric table once more. By the time Anna Mae finished her shopping, she had bolts of blue, yellow, white with blue swirls, pink and lavender resting on Carolyn's counter. She'd also picked up a package of needles, plus a few spools of white and black thread.

"You have been busy," Josiah said, coming up behind her.

How did he do that? The man walked more quietly than anyone she knew. She'd have to remember that around Christmastime. It might be hard to conceal his gifts from him.

He ran his hand over the blue fabric. "That's pretty. Are you going to make a dress out of it?"

She hadn't thought of making a dress for herself, but now she would. Anna Mae nodded. "I think so."

"It will look beautiful on you," Carolyn said, pulling the bolt to the side. "How many yards do you want?"

Anna Mae turned to Josiah. "I'm about done here. Would you mind putting those things in the wagon?" She pointed to the box of dry goods Carolyn had gathered for them.

A puzzled look crossed his face but he nodded. "I'll be happy to." He hefted the box and turned to the door.

She quickly turned to Carolyn and gave her the yardage she needed. "Be sure and put the fabric and sewing notions on my bill, Carolyn. It's a Christmas gift for Josiah and the girls."

Carolyn wrote up the bill and said, "Aw, that's why you sent him out of the store. Good thinking." After dropping the money in a drawer, she turned to cut the cloth.

Anna Mae walked over to where Rose and Ruby still played. "Tell your friends goodbye, girls. It's time to go." She waited to see if they would be obedient or throw a fit at having to leave.

Both little girls stood. "Bye-bye."

She took their hands and led them back to the counter. "Pick out a candy stick, girls. Thank you for obeying when I asked you to. Such good girls I have."

"They aren't puppies," Josiah said, coming to stand beside her once more. "You don't have to buy them a treat for behaving." Even though his voice sounded firm, when she looked up at him an unmistakable twinkle filled his eyes.

"No, I don't. But I want to." She picked up Ruby so she could look at the candy jars on the counter.

Josiah did the same with Rose.

As soon as the girls each had candy in their chubby hands, Josiah paid the bill. "We need to stop off at the feed store before heading home. Is there any place else you want to go first?"

"I wouldn't mind stopping in at the bakery and having a treat."

"Sounds good to me." Josiah set Rose up on the seat, took Ruby in turn and then helped Anna Mae up. He pulled himself onto the seat and grinned across at her. "Do you think Emily Jane might have some more of that chocolate cake for sale?"

Anna Mae chuckled. "I hope so. I really need to learn how she makes hers."

It felt as if they were a family as they rode down Main Street. The girls sucked on their candy, making slurping noises and giggling. Josiah sat in the driver's seat looking like a proud papa.

"Sheriff!"

Josiah pulled the wagon to a stop. Wade Cannon, his new young deputy, came running up to them.

Concern laced Josiah's face as he asked, "What is it, Wade?"

The deputy paused to catch his breath. Anna Mae realized he must have run all the way from the edge of town. "Mr. Caldron said to come get you. Someone butchered one of his cows. Took some of the meat and left the rest to rot." He squinted up at Josiah. "Who'd do a fool thing like that, Sheriff?"

"I don't know, Wade. Maybe a stranger was hungry

and thought the cow had no owner. Was it outside the pasture?"

"Why, no, sir. He found it not too far from the barn. I looked about, but you know Mr. Caldron. He insisted you come look."

Anna Mae watched as Levi Westland walked up in time to hear the last of the conversation. He shook his head. "No one local would do something like this, so that can only mean one thing."

Josiah nodded. "Yep." He exhaled loudly. "We've got visitors."

"That could also explain the recent thefts," Levi added, looking studious.

Josiah studied his face. "What thefts? That's the first I've heard of it."

"Well, until right this minute I didn't think of them as anything to worry about, but Millie put two pies on the windowsill to cool and someone took them both. We thought it might be a couple of kids." He rubbed his newly grown mustache. "But then ole Asa, you know, that new fella in town, at the boardinghouse." At Josiah's blank expression, he continued, "Anyway, he hung his wash on the line and two pairs of his pants went missing. Ain't likely no one around here would want Asa's clothes. So again, we wrote it off as kids' pranks."

Anna Mae took the reins Josiah handed her before he swung down from the wagon. "Anything else?"

Levi shook his head. "As far as I know, that's it. Want some company? I assume you're heading over to the livery."

"Can't say as I'd mind a helping hand." He looked up at Anna Mae. "Annie, you take the wagon and go on over to Emily Jane's. Stay there till I come for you."

She looked at him, hoping he'd heed her gentle but firm warning. "You be careful, Josiah Miller." Anna Mae knew Josiah's job was dangerous but seeing him at work caused her heart to flutter with worry. *Lord, please keep him safe,* she silently prayed.

Josiah arrived at William and Emily Jane's house tired and frustrated. He was no closer to finding out who had butchered that cow than he'd been two hours ago when he and Levi had gone to the livery.

No one saw the deed done nor had heard anything. He'd noted two sets of footprints; which meant more than one culprit. The amount of meat they'd taken most likely would have fed four or five men. These thoughts rolled around in his mind, trying to find the right category to be placed in. Evidence or just circumstance?

At Josiah's knock, William opened the door. "Any news?" he asked, stepping back and letting him inside.

"Nope. But I do know it wasn't a random act. Whoever killed that cow knew what he was doing."

Emily Jane walked up behind her husband. "What do you mean?"

"They went for the choice cuts of meat and left the rest." He looked about, expecting his family but not seeing them. "Where are Annie and the girls?"

William coughed and moved back a few steps. "I tried to get her to wait, but she said that there was no telling when you'd return and that Jersey would need to be milked and the chickens put away for the night."

Josiah felt sucker punched. During the investigation, he'd felt a sense of power, as if he could do anything. He'd spotted the evidence clearly and decisively. He knew it was due to Annie's warning for him to be safe. It had lifted him up, made him do a better job, because he felt someone cared for his well-being. It had been a long time since he'd felt like that.

But now the woman had undone all those good feelings. Did she even realize the worry she put on him? Why couldn't that stubborn lady listen to him? She didn't even know how to milk the cow. Josiah took a deep, cleansing breath. "When did she leave?"

"About an hour ago," Emily Jane answered. She wiped flour off her apron, avoiding his eyes.

Josiah shook his head. "Well, that's a fine how do you do." She'd left him in town without a horse. How did she expect him to get home? Walk?

Chapter Seventeen

His temper continued to build as he bounced along in William's wagon. His sweet sister-in-law had insisted on taking him home.

Mary would never have acted so impulsively. She also wasn't quick to smile. Or quick to banter with him. The two women were as different as outlaws and lawmen.

Anna Mae came out of the barn when they rode up. She had one of the twins on her hip and the other by the hand.

As soon as the wagon came to a stop, Josiah jumped to the ground. He started walking toward the barn at a fast clip.

"Papa!" Ruby pulled her hand from Anna Mae's and ran for him as fast as her little legs would carry her. His girls were always happy to see him.

He swooped her up and continued toward his wife. When he got close enough for her to hear him without having to shout, Josiah said, "I thought I told you to stay at Emily Jane's until I returned."

Rose pushed against Anna Mae, trying to get to her Papa.

"You did. But I thought the animals should be taken care of before dark," she countered, as she handed Rose over to him.

Josiah stared into her pretty brown eyes. "How was I supposed to get home?"

She looked at him, confused. "I assumed you'd borrow a horse from William. I really don't understand why you are upset."

Emily Jane and William joined them. They each took a twin in their arms. "We'll take these two inside so you two can talk," Emily Jane said. She gave Anna Mae an apologetic look before turning to the house.

William hurried after her.

Josiah clasped Anna Mae by the arm and turned her toward the barn. He pulled the door open and ushered her inside. "Anna Mae, as my wife you have to do what I ask you to."

"No, I don't." She pulled free from his grasp and placed both her hands on her hips. "I did not stay in town, because I didn't know how long you would be. And whether you like it or not, we now have animals to take care of."

He inhaled deeply. "Those animals can be quickly sold."

"No, they can't." Her eyes took on a fiery glow that told him he would be in for a big fight if he threatened her with the animals.

Maybe he was going about this the wrong way. Josiah walked back to where the cow stood. She mooed in greeting. He heard the hay rustle behind him as Anna Mae followed him. Without turning to face her, he asked, "Did you or did you not promise to 'love, honor and obey' me?"

Silence hung heavily in the air for a few minutes. Josiah didn't dare turn and look at her for fear she might be crying or close to tears at his words.

"I did. But since we took love out of our arrangement, honor and obey shouldn't be there, either." There was a softness to her voice that caused him to turn and look at her. She swallowed hard, then lifted her head and met his gaze head-on.

Josiah felt the fight run out of him. She was right. At no time had they discussed their marriage vows, but both had let the other know that this was no love arrangement. If anything it was more of a business deal. "You're right. You don't have to obey me."

He saw the barely hidden twitch of her lips. "I know."

He grabbed the milking stool and sat down on it, gesturing for her to sit on the bale of hay across from him. "I guess it's time we discussed our arrangement again."

"Do we have to?" The pretend defeat in her tone caused him to grin. She sank onto the hay bale and waited with a heavy sigh.

Josiah mimicked her sigh. "I'm afraid so. You see, when we got married I thought it would be real easy. You would watch the girls and I would work. But, woman, when you take my horse it makes it hard for me to work." He leaned his forearms on his knees and waited for her reaction.

Anna Mae nodded, as if in total agreement. "Yes, I

can see where that might hinder your job. I'm sorry. I shouldn't have taken Roy."

"But that's not all."

Big brown eyes looked up at him. "It isn't?"

"No, ma'am, it isn't. You see, as the sheriff I have to keep law and order. Now, that's going to be hard for me to do if I have to worry about where you and the girls are at the same time. I don't mind telling you, it's a little distracting. Know what happens when a lawman chases outlaws and gets distracted?"

She shook her head. "No, but I'm sure it isn't good."

He sat up straighter. "No, it is not. I could get shot, hanged or worse." Josiah looked her straight in the eyes. He tried to convey that even though they'd been teasing earlier, now wasn't a time to joke or kid around. He needed to know that he could rely on her to keep herself and his girls safe.

Anna Mae knew he was serious, even though he kept his tone light. "I'm really sorry, Josiah. I don't want you getting shot, hanged or worse. I'll try to do as you ask in the future."

"That's all I'm asking," he said, standing. "Now, I think you need a lesson in milking a cow."

She curled her nose. "I suppose so. I fed the chickens and gave them fresh water. But, well, after I got here I realized I have no idea how to go about milking Jersey."

He nodded. "Well, first off we need to pull her out here so she's easier to manage."

Anna Mae watched him put a rope through one of the loops in the new halter she wore. He handed over the rope. "Now open the door and gently pull her out into the aisle."

Anna Mae nodded, a flicker of apprehension coursed through her as the big animal took a step toward her. *Jersey is just a cow, Jersey is just a cow. She will not bite you. Or step on you.* The encouraging yet fearful thoughts kept her backing up.

"Whoa, Annie." Josiah stopped her by standing behind her. "The cow's not trying to get you. She's just coming out to be milked."

He placed his hands on her arms and gently rubbed them up and down in what she assumed was his way of trying to comfort her. Anna Mae knew it was silly to fear the cow, and she had no real basis for doing so other than she'd never been allowed around animals before. Well, horses didn't count, because they weren't farm animals—at least that's what her father always said. Anna Mae tried to halt her runaway thoughts and listen to Josiah.

"Tie the rope around that pole." He indicated a post that was part of the stall beside them.

When she'd done that, he continued, "Now, give her these oats." He put the bucket in her hands and watched.

Anna Mae closed her eyes. Could she get close enough to the cow's mouth to set the bucket down? What if it decided to bite her with those big teeth? She opened her eyes and looked to Josiah. "Maybe we should sell her. I don't know that I can do this."

He turned her to face him. "Think of the cow as one of the older, bigger boys in your classroom. Would you not teach him because he's bigger and older than the rest?"

"Of course I would teach him, but he isn't a cow!" Her voice and frustration rose with each word. Josiah simply didn't understand her fear. And how could he? She didn't even understand it.

"No, she's a dumb animal who is hurting because her bag is full of milk. By milking her, you are helping her. Just like you helped the bigger boys in your classroom get an education. Try thinking of her as an oversize dog that doesn't bite," Josiah suggested with a grin.

A big dog. Anna Mae turned back to the cow. She looked into her beautiful brown eyes and tried to imagine her as a dog. Then Anna Mae squared her shoulders, took two steps forward and set the bucket down within reach of the cow's head.

"See? That wasn't so bad." Josiah praised her from behind.

"For you," she murmured. Then she turned to face him with a nervous smile. "Now what?"

He shrugged. "Now we milk the cow." Josiah picked up the stool and a milk bucket and sat down. "It's really easy once you get the hang of it." He reached out, took a teat in his big hand and gave it a tug and a squeeze. Milk spurted into the bucket. "See? Nothing to it. And look, Jersey isn't paying us no never mind because she's happily eating."

Anna Mae nodded. She knew she had to try to milk the cow. Deep inside she told herself she wanted to, but her feet wouldn't move. "I seem to be stuck here, Josiah. Why don't you show me again how it's done?"

A grin split his handsome face. "All right." He demonstrated again. "Now it's your turn." He stood and moved aside so she could sit on the stool.

It took all Anna Mae's willpower to walk forward and sit down.

"Now reach out and do what I did."

She closed her eyes. *Lord, please help me.* That was as far as she got with her prayer. Big warm hands wrapped around hers. Heat from Josiah seeped into her back. He'd come up behind her and was guiding her hands toward Jersey.

Without another word, together they milked the cow. When the job was done, Josiah eased away from her. She turned around and faced him. Anna Mae whispered, "I did it."

He grinned. "Yes, you did. Now grab the milk and put it on the hay bale over there." He looked a little flustered and Anna Mae wondered if he felt all right.

She did as he said. The warm milk sloshed as she walked it over. She couldn't believe she'd milked a cow. The cow hadn't seemed to mind and she'd done it, with Josiah's help of course.

He set the stool off to the side and then instructed, "Untie Jersey and then take the feed bucket and hold it in front of her while pulling on the lead rope. Turn her around and lead her back into her stall."

Anna Mae looked at him. Was he nuts? A twinkle filled his eyes. He knew she couldn't do that. Was he making fun of her? Or was it a challenge? Tomorrow she'd try, but for today Anna Mae thought she'd come a long way. She smiled sweetly at him. "How about we make that a part of my lessons tomorrow and you do all that right now?"

Josiah walked over to her and leaned toward her. He kissed her on the cheek. "All right. I'm proud of you. You did good, but tomorrow you have to do it all."

The warmth of his lips lingered on her skin and it was all she could do not to reach up and touch where he'd kissed. Anna Mae sighed, telling herself it was only because she was happy not to have to put the animal away. It had nothing to do with the sweet kiss he'd just delivered.

She watched as he and Jersey entered the stall. New fear pushed romantic thoughts away. Would she be able to milk the cow tomorrow morning? Or would Josiah have to help her again?

The thought of them milking together sent a shiver down her back. Maybe she really should try to do it on her own. Getting too close to him wasn't good for her mending heart.

By the end of the following week, Anna Mae had a handle on the milking thing; in fact, she felt accomplished about most everything she put her hand to these days. She could walk among the chickens to feed them, and though it took her much longer than Josiah to milk Jersey, she still got the job done. She'd even petted the brown-spotted cow a time or two.

Day by day the house took on more of her personality, and Josiah and the girls seemed pleased. While thoroughly cleaning one day she discovered that the bed in the third bedroom was broken. As fast as the girls were growing they'd soon be moving into the bedroom. Anna Mae decided she'd start working on it now.

She tried to repair the bed but couldn't, so she took it apart. She carried the frame piece by piece to the barn, then emptied the straw tick mattress and washed the covering. While working on this, she ran through different ideas of what to do with the room. The girls were too young to sleep in there still but maybe they could use it as a playroom.

There was an old table in the barn that had only three legs. She toyed with the idea of nailing a board in place of the missing leg. She could use it as a sewing table; a place to cut out material and quilt pieces. Then she thought about an office for Josiah. With the same plan, she could shorten the legs and make him a desk. Or maybe she should make something for the girls.

Anna Mae made her way back to the house to look the room over. It was a corner room with windows on both outside walls. The natural lighting was wonderful.

She stood looking at the room with fresh eyes, worrying her lower lip between her teeth. Excitement threatened to overwhelm her good sense from time to time, so she examined her new idea with extreme caution. It would work. After a long pause, she checked to make sure the girls still slept, and then she headed for the barn. In less than an hour the table was clean and a forth leg was nailed into place. She dragged the table onto the porch. All she needed was for the girls to wake so she could finish her plans.

Quietly she carried, from other parts of the house, things that were needed to make the room perfect. She made a little more noise each time she entered the room where the twins slept. Surely by now they were ready to get up. Finally Ruby wiggled around to peer through the slats in her crib, and Anna Mae ran back to the porch and in a few minutes had dragged the heavy table to its new home. By the time she finished, both girls stood in their cribs yelling "Out."

With happy expectation she set them on the floor and led them to see what she'd been doing. Their squeals of delight caused her smile to broaden in relentless joy. They ran from the table to the dolls on the lower shelf of a small bookshelf, back to the table, then back to the higher shelf to get a book. They carried it to the table and sat to read, then were up again. Anna Mae watched with complete pleasure.

She'd chopped the three legs off the table and made it the exact height for the girls. The shelves also were within hand reach for them. It left a large part of the room unoccupied, but maybe she could make a rug for them to play upon. All in all, it had been a morning of hard work that had paid off for her little ones.

She left them playing and went to the kitchen to see what else she could tackle. Anna Mae felt an indefinable feeling of rightness. Who knew she could be so creative? Just the thought sent her confidence level soaring.

All this time, she'd thought teaching was all she had a talent for. Now Anna Mae saw that she could accomplish whatever she set her hand to. Philippians 4:13 immediately came to mind. *I can do all things through Christ which strengtheneth me.*

She looked at the churn Josiah had brought up from

the cellar. His instructions were "You just mash this thing up and down till the milk turns hard. Then you have butter."

However, Anna Mae had helped her mother make butter a few times so she knew that wasn't all. Making butter had been one of the chores that her mother enjoyed as a child and so had continued to do, even though she hadn't needed to. A smile touched her lips at the memory.

Anna Mae washed the churn thoroughly and the paddle board, too. Then she packed snow into the churn to get it good and cold inside. She took the fat off the top of the milk Josiah had left covered and sitting on the porch this morning, and carried it back into the warm house. As she was churning the noise brought the girls to the kitchen, but they soon lost interest and went back to their room.

The whole process took about forty-five minutes, and then Anna Mae poured the butter onto a cold slab. She salted it, then rolled it into round balls. When finished, she had fifteen beautiful balls of butter, which she placed in a dish and put in the larder outside. She quickly cleaned up the kitchen, humming, with a dance in her steps.

Anna Mae played with the girls for a few minutes, then went to put on supper. She salted a slab of rabbit meat and put it on to fry. When it was almost done, she dropped a pat of butter in the pan and her mouth began to water. Biscuit dough rose in the side oven of the wood stove. It would taste wonderful tonight with fresh butter tucked between the flaky bread.

As she peeled potatoes, something kept niggling at her brain, something she'd forgotten to do. Or maybe it was something she'd promised to do. Anna Mae thought and thought, but nothing rang a bell. Maybe if she focused on something else, it would come to her. She washed the potatoes, intent on concentrating on dinner.

Finally she heard Josiah ride into the yard. Anna Mae felt giddy with excitement. She had accomplished so much today and knew he would be so pleased. Why, she might even get another hug. To be quite frank, she had enjoyed their hug from last week. Thoughts of it had occupied a lot of her time.

Ten minutes later, the back door swung open and hit the wall with a thud. "Anna Mae!" To say he roared would be putting it mildly.

She rushed from the kitchen. "Yes, Josiah. What is it?"

She watched him struggle for composure. "Did you use the turpentine today?"

A feeling of dread shook her from head to toe. "Yes, I mixed it with beeswax and polished a table for—"

He interrupted her. "And did you seal it up and put it back where you found it?"

She sank down into a chair, her legs too weak to hold her. "No, I—"

"No, you didn't. And the chickens turned it over and it's all over the barn floor. One strike of a match could burn our barn down right now, and Lord only knows how much the chickens have ingested."

Anna Mae's hands flew to her cheeks in dismay. "Oh, Josiah, are they dead?"

His lips puckered with annoyance, but his voice became calmer. “Not yet, but they are wobbling around like they’re drunk. My main concern is getting the spill clean before an accident or fire breaks out. I carry the lantern out in the mornings to milk by. If it turned over, God forbid, the entire thing would go up in smoke.”

“I’m so sorry. You stay with the girls and I’ll go clean it up.” She stood and reached for her coat.

“No, put the girls’ coats on and we’ll both clean it up.” He paused, then turned back to her. “That won’t work. The smell might overpower them. I’ll do it. Hold supper, this will take a while.”

He was gone before Anna Mae could even respond. Tears welled in her eyes and ran down her face. Josiah had seemed so disappointed in her. Smothering a sob, she checked the biscuits.

She’d had such a great day. Now this. Her joy in all she’d accomplished suddenly left her and she sat down at the table and wept. Why did it always seem she took two steps forward and three backward? Would Josiah ever see her as a suitable wife and mother?

Chapter Eighteen

Josiah pulled Roy to a stop. He searched for tracks in the mud. His prey were slicker than foxes when it came to hiding. They'd evaded him so many times over the past few weeks that he'd began to doubt his tracking ability.

With a heavy sigh, he turned the horse back toward town. It wasn't helping that his thoughts continued to dwell on Annie and the girls. His heart had leaped out of his chest at the turpentine on the barn floor and he'd snapped at Annie. To say things between them had been strained over the past few weeks would have been an understatement.

Now they'd been invited to William and Emily Jane's tonight to celebrate with a big meal, thanks to the new holiday that everyone was so excited about. He understood the need to be thankful to the Lord in all things, but wondered if this new holiday wasn't really just an excuse to get together and call off a day of work.

Josiah knew he was simply irritated that he'd lost the

communication he'd begun to enjoy with Anna Mae, his Annie. It ate at him and he hated that he'd hurt her with the harshness of his words. Maybe he'd overreacted. No, she needed to understand the severity of what could have happened to the barn and the animals that lived inside it. Thankfully, the chickens had recovered.

He rubbed the back of his neck. Worry ate at him. Would she behave the same tonight as she had earlier in the day? They'd gone to church that morning and he'd endured her silence during the service. It was the first time they'd had to sit so closely since the turpentine incident weeks ago. The church had been packed due to it being Thanksgiving Day.

He'd been aware of the tension in her body. It felt as if she strained to get away from him. He might be sorry that he'd snapped at her, but Josiah wouldn't apologize.

When he arrived at the bakery, Roy snorted a greeting to the other horses in William's barn. Josiah patted his faithful companion on the neck. "We'll be heading home soon, ole boy."

William stepped out of a stall he'd been mucking. "Any news?"

Josiah grew so tired of that question. "No, just when I think I'm on the trail, I lose it."

"Are you even sure you're trailing the right men?" William asked, picking up a pitchfork and jabbing it into the hay.

"Yep, one of the horses has lost a shoe. Makes it easy to follow until they do something like cross the river, and then I lose them." Josiah helped William spread the hay in the stall. "What are you doing out here?"

"The women were all quiet and Emily Jane gave me 'the look' so I hightailed it out of there with the excuse I needed to tend to these critters." He indicated the two mares and gelding that stood in stalls.

Josiah felt his ears turning red. Anna Mae was probably telling Emily Jane what a clod he'd been to her.

William leaned against the pitchfork and eyed him. "Yep, that's what I figured. What did you say or do? Maybe I can help you get back in her good graces."

He shook his head.

"Might as well tell me. You know Emily Jane will later, anyway." William grinned, knowing he was right.

"I didn't do anything but clean up her mess." He jerked the pitchfork from William's hands and stabbed it into the hay.

Catching his balance, William asked, "Before or after you scolded her?"

"What makes you think I scolded her?" Josiah wondered if he were truly that predictable.

William chuckled. "Let me guess. You came home, and she'd either left something out, burned dinner or done something even more ghastly. Your first instinct was to find her and tell her what she'd done wrong." Sensing he was on the right track, William continued with a dramatic flair. "Or if it was something dangerous that she did, you told her how foolish she was and then proceeded to condemn her for it, not out of spite but so that she'd learn her lesson and not do it again. And when she apologized, you didn't except it graciously but told her that now you had to fix whatever it was that she'd messed up."

Josiah sank onto a hay bale. "Now how do you know all that?" he asked, baffled. He was sure that Anna Mae would not confide in William, and she hadn't had time to convey to Emily Jane all the sordid details William had just supplied.

William joined him on the hay bale and slapped him on the back. "I'm married now, too, remember?"

"You've done that, too?" At William's questioning look, he clarified, "Accused her of all she did wrong? And all the other stuff you said?" Josiah dropped his head into his hands.

"Sure, a couple of months after we were married, I did just that. Emily Jane forgot about the bread and it burned to a crisp in the oven. I felt it was my place to tell her how dangerous, foolish and wasteful that was. I wasn't very smart back then, either."

"Well, burning bread isn't the same as leaving turpentine open in the barn and having the chickens tip it over and spill it on the floor." Josiah looked up, hoping for support.

William shook his head. "Doesn't matter. Did you hurt her feelings?"

He sighed. "I reckon so."

"So let me enlighten you, brother-in-law. She probably tried to do something nice for you, which was why she had the turpentine out in the first place. Did you ask why she used it?" When Josiah shook his head, William continued. "Trust me, when you find out, you'll feel like a dirt clod. When you yelled at her, you undermined her confidence, so now she's afraid to tell you. You can either eat crow now or eat it later, but it's for sure you're gonna eat crow." William shook his head as if in sad commiseration.

Josiah already felt the noose about his neck. "So what should I do?" He was a doomed man. He picked up a piece of straw and began shredding it.

"Well, if it were me, I'd at least apologize for hurting her feelings. Especially if she's already said she was sorry." William stood and put the pitchfork away. He pulled one of his mares into the clean stall.

Low-down snakes couldn't get any lower than Josiah felt. Yes, she had apologized, even offered to clean up the mess, and he'd still left her feeling like the stupidest woman in the whole of Texas. And now he had to go in the house and face her. And by now Emily Jane knew what a sorry excuse he was. He heaved a sigh, tossed away the straw that he'd managed to destroy in a matter of seconds. "Might as well get this over with."

William clapped him on the back. "Wise move, my man. Face the music. Just remember to give her a hug and whisper in her ear that you're very sorry."

"I've been married before, too. I think I know how to make up." Josiah said the words, but did he really believe them? His and Anna Mae's relationship wasn't a true marriage. He just prayed he'd find the right words when the time came.

Inside the house, Anna Mae had just finished telling Emily Jane about the tension in her marriage. She couldn't believe how quickly her friend had figured out there was problem between herself and Josiah. She hadn't wanted to tell her, but seemingly Emily Jane already knew, and understood what was going on.

"Look, men sometimes react over the least things. It is our job as women to keep them grounded. It's obvious you didn't mean to do whatever it was that you did, so just let it go. In time, he'll come around and say he's sorry, too." Emily Jane pulled the roasted chicken out of the oven.

Even as she said it, Anna Mae felt foolish, but she wanted to be truthful with her friend. "I know, but he hurt my feelings."

Emily Jane placed the chicken on the side board. "And he will again."

Anna Mae poured hot green beans into a big bowl. "Just pretend it didn't happen? He practically called me stupid."

"If you want him to apologize, then yes." Emily Jane looked her straight in the eyes. "Do you want to continue the way it's been lately? Or go back to being happily married to your best friend?"

How little Emily Jane truly knew. Anna Mae and Josiah were far from happily married. They didn't even have a real marriage. As for them being best friends, well, that was a good description of their relationship from her viewpoint, but she doubted Josiah saw her that way. Still, if it would bring peace to their home once more… "I'll try."

Emily Jane hugged her. "That's all you can do." She released her. "Now, would you mind setting the table while I spread the rolls with this wonderful butter you brought? I can't wait to sample it."

Anna Mae nodded, then looked to the twins. They were content to peer at the picture book that she'd brought to entertain them. They pointed at pictures and communicated with each other in both English and baby talk. For the girls' sake, she'd try to forget that Josiah had hurt her feelings and made her cry. Lord willing, they'd be back to normal in no time.

The sound of the men stomping their boots on the porch alerted the women and children that they were coming in. "The table's ready," Anna Mae said, just as they entered the kitchen.

"Good, let's set this on the sideboard and eat buffet-style." Emily Jane handed Anna Mae two plates. "Why don't you go ahead and fix the girls' supper while I get them seated."

Anna Mae took the plates, very aware of Josiah walking toward her. She turned toward the food to avoid his gaze. *Lord, it's going to be hard acting as if my feelings aren't still hurt.*

"Here, let me help you with those." He placed a hand on her shoulder.

She nodded and handed him one of the plates. Together they chose green beans, mashed potatoes with gravy, a roll and a chicken leg for each of the girls.

William and Emily Jane talked to Rose and Ruby. The twins laughed as they squirmed in their chairs, trying to see around their aunt and uncle at the plates they knew were for them.

Anna Mae placed hers in front of Rose and Josiah did the same for Ruby. "Girls, wait for the rest of us," he instructed, joining William back at the sideboard.

Anna Mae filled the girls' milk glasses while Emily Jane poured coffee for William and Josiah. "Tell me more about the girls' room."

Josiah looked at her with a question in his eyes as he took his place at the table. Emily Jane set a steaming cup in front of him. Anna Mae looked away.

She didn't want to talk about the room she'd created for the girls. She hadn't shown it to him. As soon as Josiah had left to clean up her mess in the barn, she had taken the girls from their room and shut the door. Since they never used that third room, he hadn't had any reason to see it.

After the way he'd acted, Anna Mae was afraid to tell him what she'd used the turpentine for. She feared he'd think her foolish and the desk she'd created foolish, too.

Why had Emily Jane brought up the room when she knew it was a sore spot? Anna Mae wanted to kick her friend, but instead answered, "Oh, well. It's really nothing special, not even worth mentioning." She picked up a plate and turned her back to the table.

Emily Jane joined her. "I love the idea of them having a desk for reading and drawing. That was really smart of you to create such a space for the twins."

Anna Mae shot her a "hush up now" look. "Thank you," she answered, for the men's benefit.

Both she and Emily Jane returned to the table. After sitting down, William offered a grace of thanksgiving. While he prayed, Anna Mae felt Josiah's hand reach under the table and clasp hers.

Warmth spread up her arm and threatened to melt her reserve. When William said "amen," Josiah gave her hand a gentle squeeze before releasing it. She looked up to find him smiling at her. It seemed as if he looked straight into her soul.

Josiah leaned over and whispered for her ears only, "I'm sorry I hurt your feelings. I really didn't mean to." Then he sat back up and turned to help Rose with her chicken.

At that moment, Anna Mae knew he was forgiven. Would she regret forgiving him? She hoped not. She told herself it was time to let old hurts go. But a question plagued her. What did it mean that she could forgive him with one softly whispered sentence? What would letting it go cost her in the long run?

Chapter Nineteen

Life on the Miller farm fell into a routine over the next three weeks. Josiah went to work each morning after a hearty breakfast. While he was gone, Anna Mae cleaned, cooked and created Christmas gifts for her family.

While the girls napped she worked on Josiah's gifts. She had managed to crochet him a scarf and was in the process of piecing the blue-and-white nine-patch quilt together for his bed. While she worked, Anna Mae imagined his surprise at the gifts.

In the evenings, while Josiah read to them all from the Bible, she worked on the little girls' dresses. They were so small that she was sure they didn't realize what she was doing, but still kept the rag dolls and clothes a secret from them, working on them only after everyone went to bed. It felt good to have a family to create Christmas gifts for.

It saddened Anna Mae that her mother and father hadn't written back to her. She'd hoped to have their blessings on her marriage, but wasn't really surprised. Father was busy with his business and Mother her social life. Time passed fast when you were busy, and her parents stayed busy.

A glance at the clock told her Josiah would be home soon. She went to the kitchen and stirred the stew she'd had simmering on the stove all day. Corn bread sat at the back, warming. She scooped out stew for each of the girls and set their bowls off to the side to cool. A sense of pride burst forth as she put fresh butter on the table.

She heard him stomping up the porch steps, and hurried to finish setting the table. "Rose! Ruby! Papa's home!"

The sound of the little girls scrambling from their room caused her to smile. They loved the room she'd created for them and spent most of the day playing in it.

Josiah had praised her on the job she'd done and suggested a way to finish the room. He'd asked Levi Westland to build the girls each a small bed that they would receive Christmas morning. Rose's would have tiny butterflies along the headboard and Ruby's little birds. Anna Mae couldn't wait to see them up and ready for the girls to sleep in.

"Papa! Papa!" they squealed, stumbling over themselves and each other as they attempted to race for their father.

Emily Jane had told her that the girls were small for their age. Anna Mae remembered laughing and responding, "Yes, but what they lack in size they more than make up for with their vocabulary." They'd developed so much since that fateful snowstorm.

Living out on the farm was lonely sometimes. She missed seeing Emily Jane every day, but the little girls were plenty of company when they weren't napping.

Anna Mae set the last spoon on the table just as squeals of laughter burst from the front door. Without looking she knew Josiah had grabbed up his girls and was kissing their faces. She smiled at him as he entered the kitchen.

"Something sure smells good in here," Josiah said, coming over and giving her a hug.

Anna Mae pretended the hug didn't make her feel shaky inside. "It's rabbit stew. I hope you like it." She hurried to help Rose up into her chair.

"I'm sure I will. I'm as hungry as a starving coyote." He lifted Ruby into her chair and patted the girls on the head. "Were you two good today?"

The twins nodded and grinned at each other. From the mischievous expressions on their faces, Anna Mae wondered what their room looked like.

Within a few minutes, she had the stew, corn bread and their drinks on the table. As soon as she took her seat, Josiah said grace. The sounds of Rose and Ruby smacking their lips while they waited for him to finish made her smile.

"Amen." Josiah looked at the girls. "The way you two were smacking those lips, I'm not sure the good Lord even heard my prayer." He placed their bowls in front of them and inhaled. "From the smell of this, I really can't blame you."

The girls immediately began to eat. Anna Mae wondered if they were about to hit a growth spurt. Their appetites indicated they probably were. She made a mental note to add lace to the bottom of their Christmas dresses. More than likely they would need it to help cover their little knees.

She turned her attention to Josiah. "How was your day?"

He blew on his spoonful of stew. "Worrisome." He sighed. "Caldron found another dead cow today."

Anna Mae buttered a slab of corn bread and passed it over to him. "Oh, I'm sorry to hear that." She thought about Jersey out in the barn and worried that she might be in danger. Although it seemed the cows closer to town were more at risk than Jersey.

"Yeah, me, too. I had hoped since there hadn't been any incidents in over a week that the thieves had moved on, but now I know they haven't." He spooned the stew into his mouth and his eyes opened wide. Once he'd chewed and swallowed Josiah smiled. "That rabbit is so tender."

She couldn't hide her pleased expression. "Good, that's what I had hoped for."

He took a large bite of the corn bread and chewed with gusto. It did her heart good to see him enjoying her cooking. She nibbled at the edge of her corn bread, savoring the sweetness. Emily Jane had told her that adding a little sugar would make the best corn bread and she'd been right.

"You really are a good cook, Annie. I'm blessed to have you for a wife. Truly blessed."

Anna Mae looked up and found him looking down on his plate. Did he really mean that? Was he happy to have her as his wife? Her heart raced at the thought. She quickly tried to subdue it. *Don't read more into his words than what he said,* she mentally warned herself.

The next day, Josiah stomped his feet before entering the general store. The snow had all melted, but mud remained and seemed to coat everything in sight. Especially his boots. The sole had worn thin on the right one and he'd soon have to buy a new pair.

But not today. Today he was Christmas shopping for Annie and the girls. The smells of cinnamon, leather and pipe tobacco warred for his attention.

"Hello, Sheriff. Are you out of coffee over at the jail already?" Wilson Moore asked. He held a broom in his hand and wore a green apron.

Josiah shook his head. "Not today. I'm looking for gifts for Annie and the girls." He saw Carolyn come out of the side door and into the store. Josiah walked over to the counter where she stood pulling an apron over her head. "I'm glad you're here, Carolyn. Has Annie mentioned anything to you about what she'd like for Christmas?"

Carolyn's forehead crinkled and then cleared. "Oh, you're talking about Anna Mae. Took me a second to make the connection. Annie, that's cute."

He raised an eyebrow and waited for her to answer. Josiah leaned his hip on the counter and looked at the penny candy. The girls wouldn't mind having some of that, he felt sure.

"Well, she bought a lot of that blue fabric. She might like a blue ribbon to go in her hair that would match it." Carolyn moved around the counter and headed to where the ribbon was located.

Josiah followed. "I'll take some of that, but I thought something a little more..."

She picked up a spool of the ribbon and turned to face him. "Personal?"

He had the impression she fully enjoyed his discomfort. "Yes, but not anything frilly."

Carolyn laughed. "We just got some new necklaces in. Would you like to see those?"

Josiah leaped at the idea of a necklace. "Yes, please."

She continued to chuckle as they walked back to the counter. Carolyn moved behind it to where a glass case sat at the far end. "Here they are." She pointed down through the glass.

His gaze swept the necklaces. What he had in mind wasn't there. He wanted something that would suit her delicate beauty. Something good, wholesome and sweet. These were big flowers. Flowers were nice, but they just weren't what he wanted.

"Not what you had in mind, huh?"

Josiah straightened. "No, they are a little too big."

"Well, we also have these. No two are the same." She pulled out a small tray of rings.

They were simple gold bands, each with a different swirl or pattern on it. Josiah's gaze immediately fell on one that had an intricately woven vine engraved in the gold. He pointed to it. "How about that one?"

Carolyn pulled it from the tray and handed it to him. He slipped it on his little finger. "Do you think this will fit her?"

"Let me see it." She held out her hand.

He dropped it into her palm and watched her slip it onto her ring finger. "It's a little snug, but I think her hand is just a bit smaller than mine, so it will probably fit." Carolyn smiled up at him.

"I'll take it." *Surely it will fit one of her fingers,* he thought.

"Good. I'll find a pretty box to put it in while you decide what you want for the girls."

Josiah turned to the toy section. He'd already gotten the twins stuffed animals, so he eyed the other items. What else could he get Rose and Ruby? Anna Mae had shown him the rag dolls she worked on each night, so he wouldn't get them a doll. They had blocks and pull toys. Each of them had a favorite blanket. He sighed.

Maybe he'd choose something more practical, like a new pair of shoes for each of them. He walked to that section of the store and found little black shoes, but then realized he had no idea what size the girls wore. Mary had always taken care of their clothes and shoes, not him.

His thoughts turned to Mary. This would be his and the girls' first Christmas without her. She had enjoyed Christmas, but not in the same way Anna Mae seemed to.

Anna Mae went about the house humming Christmas hymns and talking about Christmas gifts. He was surprised she hadn't asked for a Christmas tree. Josiah realized he was grinning and frowned. How had his thoughts moved from Mary to Anna Mae?

He ran a hand around his collar. It was natural, he told himself. Anna Mae was his wife now. She was with him every day. They were friends. He nodded. Yep, that was it.

They were friends, only friends. A new and unexpected warmth surged through him as it slowly dawned on Josiah that Anna Mae had become his best friend. The one he shared his day with over the supper table each evening. Who helped him get the girls ready for bed every night. He thought of things during the day he wanted to tell her; things he knew would bring a smile to her face or cause the little crease in her forehead when she puckered her face into a frown.

Wilson walked up beside him. "What's wrong with the shoes, Sheriff?"

"Huh?"

"You're staring at them as if perplexed. I just wondered what was wrong," Wilson answered.

Josiah shook his head. "There's nothing wrong with them. I just realized a few moments ago that I don't know what size to get the girls."

"Would you like for me to call Carolyn over here? She might know," he offered.

"No, I think I'll just wait and ask Annie if she thinks I should get them anything else for Christmas," Josiah answered, wishing he was out on the trail of an outlaw right now instead of in a store thinking about the women in his life.

"All right. Is there anything else I can help you find?" Wilson swept a clump of dirt out from under the shelf.

Josiah shook his head. "Naw, I think I'm about done for the day." He walked back to the counter, where Carolyn waited. He paid for the ring and the ribbon and slipped them into his pocket.

The cold air felt good against his warm cheeks as he stepped outside. He walked back to the jailhouse. The air tasted of snow and sent a shiver down his spine. Josiah decided to check in with Wade, and if everything was fine, he'd head home before the snow hit.

"Glad to see you back, Sheriff." The young deputy stood by the stove warming his hands.

"Why's that?"

He poured a cup of coffee and handed it to Josiah, then poured a second cup for himself. His boots clomped across the wood floor as he walked over to the desk. "These just arrived in the mail. Thought you might like to take them home and study them." He handed Josiah two wanted posters.

Josiah read them. "Looks like these're the fellas suspected of holdin' up the banks in these parts."

"That's what I got from reading them, too, but I don't think they're right," Wade said, leaning against the bars of the only cell.

Josiah moved to his desk and sat down. "No?"

The young man shook his head. "I think the cattle butchers and the bank robbers might be one and the same. And if that's the case, then we're looking for four or maybe even six men, instead of just two."

"What makes you think that?" Josiah leaned back in his chair and propped his feet up on the desk.

Wade sipped his coffee. "Well, it seems to me that a couple of days go by and during that time a bank gets robbed, thankfully not ours." He paused as if considering his words. Josiah had learned to just wait him out. "Then the next day we find a dead cow someplace."

Josiah had to agree that that was the way it seemed, but that still didn't mean they were the same men. He studied the wanted posters and waited. Wade would continue as soon as he got his thoughts together.

"If I was a robbin' them banks and I didn't want people to think it was me, I'd do something else to throw them off the scent. I think that's what the robbers are doing. They rob the bank and then butcher a cow to confuse the law." He took another sip of his coffee, then stood up straight. "'Course, I could be wrong. It might be different men, but my gut says I'm right, even if I ain't makin' a lick of sense." Wade finished his coffee and set the cup down.

Josiah pondered what the young man had said, then nodded. "Well, you could be right. I've learned to listen to my gut and if yours is saying they might be the same, well, they might just be." He folded the wanted papers and placed them on the desk. "We'll continue to keep our noses to the ground. They're sure to slip up somewhere along the way."

Josiah dropped his feet back down on the floor, took

the ring box from his coat pocket and dropped it into the lap drawer of his desk. "When they do, we'll be there to get 'em." He tucked the blue ribbon deeper into his pocket to take out at home.

Wade nodded. "That sounds good to me, boss."

"Don't call me boss," Josiah scolded as he stood. He picked up the wanted papers and stuck them in his front coat pocket. "You ready to take over the town?" he asked, walking toward the door.

"Just for the night, Sheriff. She's all yours come morning." Wade pushed away from the bars and followed Josiah to the door.

"I'll see you then." Roy snorted as Josiah climbed up.

"Sheriff?"

Josiah turned to see what his deputy wanted now. "Yes?"

The young man ran his hand along the back of his neck. Josiah grinned. The lad was picking up his bad habits. Wade looked him straight in the eyes. "You be careful heading home. No tellin' where those mangy thieves are hiding out."

Josiah nodded. It pleased him that Wade cared enough to offer a warning. "Will do. You watch yourself, too." He turned the horse toward home. "Let's head home, boy. If I know Annie, she's got dinner on the stove and a fire in the fireplace."

Roy knew the way to his warm barn, oats and hay. The gelding wasted no time getting there.

For the next half hour, Josiah let Roy have his head while he thought about the robbers, the butchers and Wade's comparison of the two. Was it possible they were one and the same? If so, was his little family in danger out on the farm alone every day?

A bitter thought entered his mind. He hadn't been able to protect Mary in town. What made him think he could protect Annie and the girls out on the farm?

Chapter Twenty

Snowflakes, big and fluffy, cascaded gracefully to the ground at a fast pace. Anna Mae and the girls laughed and looked up into the gray sky. "I love this time of the year, don't you, girls?"

"Me wuv no," Rose answered, and stooped down to touch it.

"Uby wuv no, too." Ruby knelt beside her sister to examine the freshly fallen flakes. They giggled and shivered, all the while poking holes in the snow with their little gloved fingers.

Anna Mae set the bucket of warm milk beside the barn and then danced about in the snow. Thankfully, it hadn't gotten deep enough to keep her from her fun movements.

The girls jumped and leaped about also, laughing and trying to catch snowflakes on their tongues. Both fell and giggled, then pushed themselves up from the frozen ground, only to fall back down again.

"It's wet enough that we might be able to build a

snowman tomorrow, if it keeps snowing," Anna Mae told them as they squealed and rolled about on the ground, looking like bundled-up snow babies.

She laughed at their antics. According to the locals, this winter was the harshest they'd had in many years. Anna Mae loved the snow and was glad to see it, even if the townspeople weren't thrilled. Still, the cold started seeping into her body, and sleet mixed into the snow, which began to fall faster. "Come along, girls. Time to go inside and warm up."

Anna Mae grinned as Rose and Ruby pushed themselves up from the frozen ground. They were a pair and a sweet pair at that. Once on their feet, they toddled after her.

She'd just gotten them out of their coats and into their high chairs when a knock sounded at the door. Anna Mae hurried to answer it, thinking that perhaps Josiah had his hands full and couldn't open it himself. She was surprised to see a large man with a big heavy coat standing in her doorway.

"I hate to disturb you, ma'am. My name is John Meeker and my horse has thrown a shoe. I'm afraid to ride him much farther. Would it be all right with you, if I put him up in the barn for the night?" He tilted back a flat brown hat, and green eyes the color of summer grass looked into hers.

Anna Mae swallowed hard. She should have called out to make sure that whoever was at the door was Josiah. Now here she stood, facing a mountain of a man and having to make a decision that only Josiah should be making. Cold air blew in and caused her to shiver.

If the man was telling the truth she couldn't leave him and his horse out in the cold. Anna Mae nodded. "You and your horse are welcome to spend the night in the barn." She thought about adding that Josiah would be home soon, but decided it was better not to alert the stranger that she and the girls were alone.

He tipped his hat toward her. "Much obliged." John Meeker stomped as he went off the porch.

Was he angry that she'd said he and his horse could stay in the barn? Had the big man expected to be invited into the house for the night? Anna Mae didn't care what his expectations were, she would not endanger the twins by inviting a stranger into their home.

Her gaze went to the road. Darkness was falling almost as fast as the snow. Anna Mae closed the door and dropped the heavy bar over it. *Lord, please hurry Josiah home.*

Josiah followed the hoofprints and realized they were headed to his place. Like before, the prints were that of a horse with only three shoes. This horse usually seemed to trail the other outlaws, but this time the hoofprints were alone. Josiah's heartbeat picked up two paces. He kneed Roy. "Hurry, boy, he can't be that far ahead of us."

The night was quickly descending and so was the sleet and snow. Those prints had almost been filled in when he'd noticed them. Now Josiah was afraid he'd lose the man again in the snow and dark.

A few minutes from the house, he lost the tracks. Snow created a white blanket with no blemishes. Fear crawled up his spine and chilled him to the bone. He shivered both from the cold and the worry that the stranger would get to his place before he did.

Roy thundered into the front yard, kicking up snow as if driven by a need to spread the white stuff himself. Josiah was off and running up the porch steps before the horse came to a complete stop. Josiah pushed the door, only to find himself barred from the house. "Annie!"

He heard someone fumbling with the heavy piece of wood and then the door flew open. Anna Mae grabbed the front of his coat, pulling him through the opening, her eyes filled with a curious intensity. "I'm sorry it was locked, Josiah, but we have a visitor in the barn and I wasn't taking any chances."

He shut the door behind him and dropped the safety board into the slots. "Tell me about this visitor. Did he introduce himself? Or just head for the barn?"

His gaze darted to the girls, who quietly sat at the table in their high chairs. Their little bodies seemed poised for action, as if they knew something was up, but were uncertain if it would prove good for them or bad. He winked and they visibly relaxed, grinning at him around mouthfuls of bread.

Anna Mae answered, "He said his name is John Meeker and his horse is missing a shoe. I told him that he and his horse could stay in the barn tonight."

"What time did he arrive?" Josiah returned his attention to her. Her hair was down, giving her a soft, vulnerable look. He shouldn't have left her and the girls out on the farm alone. What had he been thinking?

She brushed her hair back. "About fifteen minutes ago."

Josiah placed his palm on her warm shoulder. "Did he threaten you or the girls in any way?"

"No, he was very polite. Just asked if the horse could stay the night in our barn." She laid her hand on Josiah's and sighed. "I'm glad you're home."

He raised his fingers and touched her soft cheek. "Me, too."

"Papa!" Rose called from the table. She was bouncing in her chair, wanting attention from him, too.

Ruby swallowed her bread and echoed her sister's excited cry.

Josiah dropped his hand and turned to the twins. "Hello, girls. Papa has to go check on something in the barn. You be good for Annie. I'll be right back." He turned to Anna Mae. "Bar the door behind me. I'm going to go check on our visitor and put Roy away for the night." He could have mentioned that he speculated that they had a thief in their barn, but didn't want to alarm her more than she already was. Josiah reached for the bar.

Anna Mae put a light, restraining hand on his arm. "Josiah, please be careful. He's a big man."

For the second time in one day, someone had warned him to use caution. Josiah heeded both of them. "I will be. You just stay inside until I come back." He removed the bar.

At her nod, Josiah stepped out the door. He waited until he heard the bar fall into place before grabbing Roy's reins and heading out to the barn. What would he find there? He felt sure that this man was the same who had given him a merry chase all week.

Mentally, Josiah brought every wanted poster into his mind. He traced each face, checked that it was in his memory and then slowly pulled the barn door open. He intended to slip inside quietly.

"'Bout time you got home." The gravelly voice sounded familiar. Josiah ducked just as a beefy fist plowed into the door frame. And another punch knocked the gun from his hand.

Josiah turned and connected his fist with the big man's right rib cage. A grunt from his opponent gave him some satisfaction. He grinned.

"Faster than you used to be, too."

The sound of a rifle being cocked stopped both men in their tracks. "Take another step and I'll blow your big brains out." The threat was as cold as a rattlesnake's eyes and just as deadly.

Josiah recognized that voice, as well. Although he'd never heard it sound so lethal. He slowly turned to his bride. "Annie, put the gun down," he said, cautiously moving toward her.

She held the weapon steady as a rock, pointed dead center at the green eyes of the man she had in her sights. "I don't take kindly to anyone trying to kill my husband," Anna Mae threatened through clenched teeth, as if she hadn't heard him.

If the circumstances hadn't been so dire, Josiah would have grinned proudly, but right now he feared for Meeker's life. "Annie, we were just horse playing.

I'd like you to meet Grady Meeker. Remember? I told you about him?"

Her gaze swept to Josiah, confusion in their beautiful brown depths. "Sheriff Grady?"

"One and the same," the big booming voice confirmed.

Anna Mae lowered the rifle. She handed it to Josiah, turned, and with stiff dignity stomped back to the house. At the porch she yelled back at them, "Since you forgot to mention that you know my husband, you'll definitely be staying in the barn." She sized up Josiah's grin. "You know what? You can both stay out here tonight." Her skirts swished as she slammed the front door.

Josiah watched her go. She'd followed him. Put herself in danger, put Grady in danger, and now she was mad at him. Josiah couldn't help but wonder if he wasn't the one in the most danger.

Booming laughter filled the barn and a hard hand slapped him on the back. "Well, I'll be. She's a little spitfire, isn't she?" Grady picked up the gun he'd knocked from Josiah's hand.

"It would seem so," Josiah answered, taking his gun and sliding it into his waistband.

"You didn't know she was a spitfire? How long you two been married? I saw a couple of young'uns in there that says you should have known her for at least three years. I declare, son, I thought you was smarter than that." Grady returned to the stall where his horse was stabled.

Josiah shook his head. "Annie is my second wife. We've only been married about six weeks."

"Looks like we've got a lot of catchin' up to do." Grady sat down on a bale of hay. "Why don't you start at the beginning and tell me what all you've been up to since last we met."

He nodded. That had been over three years ago. Maybe by the time he finished catching Grady up, Anna Mae would have cooled off some. Josiah knew he'd have to go into the house sooner or later, and decided later might be better. Anna Mae probably wasn't ready to hear that he'd had no idea Grady Meeker was in the area or going by the name John Meeker. Plus, he needed to find out what his old mentor was doing in Granite.

Two hours later, Josiah slipped into the house. He heard Anna Mae saying good-night prayers with the girls, and went into his room to consider what he should say to her.

Once she heard that Grady was on the trail of the bank robbers that were in the area, and that Josiah hadn't known about him being here, she'd understand. At least he prayed she would. He lit the lamp. The room had been cleared of his things. What had the woman done? Thrown them out the back door? Even his Bible was missing off the nightstand. This didn't bode well at all.

"I moved your things into our room." He jumped at the sound of her voice.

"Why?"

Anna Mae's brows drew together in an incredulous squint. "Because I assumed you wouldn't want your friend to freeze in the barn tonight." She walked out the door and into the kitchen.

Josiah followed like a dog with his tail tucked between his legs. She poured a cup of coffee and took a sip. Now why had he thought she was getting it for him? "Look, Annie. I didn't know Grady was in town or that he'd started using his given name when out on the hunt. He's a lawman, like me. After the same thieves as I am." Josiah paused. She still stared at him with steely brown eyes.

"Well, you both scared the living daylights out of me," she said, looking over her cup at him.

"How do you think I felt? There you stood, pointing a gun like you were willing to kill a man." He could no more stop the grin that crossed his face than he could stop breathing. "I sure hadn't expected you to come and protect me. But I'm glad you did. Thank you."

She sighed and let her shoulders drop. Anna Mae slipped into a chair at the table, as if her legs would no longer hold her up. "Why don't men just say hello like normal people?" She set the cup down and sighed again.

He shrugged. "No idea."

Picking up a clean cup and the coffeepot, he poured himself coffee, too. Josiah leaned his hip against the warm stove. "Now what's this about sharing a room?"

"I figured you didn't want him to guess that this is a marriage of convenience, so I moved you into mine and the girls' room. That way he won't know and no one else will find out, either." She traced a pine knot in the table.

He chuckled. "You told him he has to stay in the barn."

"I told you to stay there, too," she reminded him with a cheeky grin.

Josiah laughed, glad to see his good-humored wife back. "I don't think a woman's ever made Grady Meeker sleep in the barn."

She carried her cup to the sink. "Well, then, I don't want to be the first to make him, either. It's too cold out there for him, anyway. You go out and tell him to come inside. I'm going to bed."

"What about me? Am I to sleep on the couch tonight because you're angry with me? After all, I did disobey and come inside." Josiah followed her to the sink.

She turned to face him. "I'm not angry with you. And no, you can sleep in our room. On the floor." Anna Mae left him standing in the kitchen.

The woman never ceased to amaze him. She'd thought of his reputation as a husband by moving him into her room, but also put him in his place by making him sleep on the floor. A proud grin slipped across his face. Anna Mae Miller was quite the woman. She was his Annie and tonight she'd proved she could hold her own against him or anyone who threatened him or the girls.

Anna Mae quietly cleaned the breakfast crumbs from the table, her mind on the conversation in the front room. She could see Josiah from where she worked, but Grady sat opposite him, hidden by the fireplace that partially divided the two rooms.

So, trouble had found its way to their little town. Not just mischievous pranks, but ugly, serious trouble that threatened their very livelihood. Someone might be robbed, or even worse, killed. It began to sink into her heart just how dangerous her husband's job could be.

It seemed Grady had turned into some kind of a bounty hunter. The older man had been trailing the outlaws for some time. He'd explained earlier that his horse had lost a shoe before he'd arrived in the Granite area and that he'd left it off to make the outlaws think he was just a drifter.

"So, you don't think the cow killing is a decoy to throw us off track?"

Josiah had explained Wade's theory earlier and Anna Mae felt pretty impressed with the young man's reasoning. At least Josiah had someone to help him figure things out. But as she listened to Grady, she realized her husband had been trained by one of the best.

Grady answered as though he'd really given the question some thought. "No, not to my way of thinking. Not a decoy, a weakness. They're never spotted in town till the day of the robbery and then they have their faces covered. They stake out the area thoroughly, get to know the comings and goings of the locals before they even strike."

Anna Mae heard the rocker creak as he set the chair in motion and then continued, "Killing cattle is a slipup, and the thing that's going to get them caught is their appetite."

Josiah nodded. "They like fresh meat." He ran a hand around the back of his neck.

"Yep." Grady answered matter-of-factly. "They're spoiled, too lazy to hunt, and have no shame at killing or stealing another man's possessions."

Josiah sat quietly for a moment. "I wonder when they will have enough money and quit robbing."

Grady barked a laugh. "Never. They will lose their lives over this."

Her husband sighed. "Why a man would sell his soul like that beats me."

Anna Mae stood looking out the kitchen window toward the barn. She'd been thinking the same thing. What would cause a man to continue a life of destruction?

"Well, I best be going. Going to get to the boardinghouse early so few people see me." Grady pushed himself up from the chair, straightened his shoulders and cleared his throat loudly. "Remember the protocol."

"Got it." Josiah followed him to the door.

"Thank you, Mrs. Miller, for the hearty breakfast." He patted his stomach. "Nothing like a good meal to start a man's day."

She stepped into the sitting room. "Please, call me Anna Mae."

He nodded, then opened the door. Anna Mae watched from the front window as the two men walked to the barn. When Josiah returned to the house she still hadn't moved.

"Brrr, it's cold out there." He held his hands out to the warmth of the fireplace. "Come away from the window, Annie. The air seeps through and you'll catch your death of cold."

She walked to the couch and settled into the fluffy pillows and quilt, her mind in turmoil as she worked through the morning's activities. "Josiah, do robbers ever straighten up? You know, get out of that lifestyle?"

"Sometimes. Depending on the circumstances that got them involved in the first place." He turned to allow the fire to warm his back.

"What do you mean?"

He shrugged out of his coat and hung it by the door. "Some men are just mean and too lazy to work. They see what another man has and they decide it should be theirs, so they take it." Josiah sat down on the rocker across from her. "Then you have the young men that fall on hard times and see no other way out. They steal to stay alive. They get sick of it, but once you sign your soul over to the first type of men, the evil ones, you never get it back. They won't let you stop."

Anna Mae felt bad for the young men. Surely some of them got away from that lifestyle. She looked up at Josiah. "But some do, right?"

He seemed to know what she wanted to hear. "Yes, on occasion one may take the higher road and straighten up his life."

She heard the skepticism in his voice. "You think it's few and far between?"

"Like I said, it does happen on occasion, but like Grady said, once they get an appetite for the lifestyle—drinking and gambling, women and traveling from town to town—it's hard to get them to turn away from it."

Josiah stood. He walked to the kitchen and put a pot on the stove. She watched as he poured cider into it. "It's sin, Anna Mae. Sin drags a man down, turns him into a person he never wanted to be. And sin doesn't stop until it has wrecked and ruined his life. There's only one thing that can rescue him and pull him up from the muck and the mire."

Anna Mae nodded. Her gaze moved to Josiah's large Bible. "The Lord."

He pulled two mugs down from the cabinet. "That's right. The saving grace of Jesus. It's a beautiful thing when that happens."

He poured them both a steaming mug of cider. Josiah returned to the sitting room and handed her one. Anna Mae wrapped her hands around the warm cup, impressed by her husband's thoughtfulness.

They sipped their drinks, each lost in thought. Anna Mae knew that Josiah hoped to catch the outlaws before they could do more harm. She worried about their souls.

Josiah suddenly snapped his fingers. "I almost forgot. We've been invited to a taffy pull at the boardinghouse Saturday evening. Sounds like there will be all kinds of activities and food."

Thankful for something else to think about, Anna Mae smiled. "Oh, good. I bet everyone's excited. When I lived in town and we planned something, the excitement was almost tangible. It lifted everyone's spirits and made life fulfilling."

"Do you miss living in town?" He set his cider on the floor and studied her intently.

"Some, but..." She knew that he watched her with curious intensity. "My life is completely fulfilled right here with my girls, my animals and my home."

"And what about your husband?" His intense blue eyes continued to study her face.

Anna Mae's heart pounded in an erratic rhythm. He seemed unsure of his place in her life. She hoped to ease his worry. "Oh, Josiah, when you explain things to me like you just did, I think I'm married to the smartest man in the world. You have such wisdom. And you keep getting me out of scrapes. You're kind and thoughtful, and I'm so thankful to be married to you. I just hope you aren't ashamed to be married to me." She set her cider on the side table and offered him a sweet smile.

Josiah reached over and took her hands in his. He rubbed the backs with his thumbs. "Don't ever let me hear you say those words again. I couldn't be more proud of you."

"But I keep messing up." When his eyebrows rose in question, she continued. "With the turpentine, and then I chopped the table legs off and you had to saw them to make them even and smooth."

His jaw dropped and his thumbs stopped moving against her skin.

"What? You didn't think I'd notice the difference? How smooth and even the legs suddenly appeared? So I no longer had to worry about the girls getting splinters from my mess."

He burst out laughing and released her. "Now who's the wise one?"

Anna Mae missed the warmth of his hands holding hers, and picked her drink back up. "You gave me this beautiful life, Josiah, and I love it. I just wanted you to know that."

His eyes were gentle and contemplative. He'd just started to speak when a scream brought them both to their feet and racing to the girls' room.

Anna Mae didn't know whether to laugh or be serious. Ruby's head was stuck between the rungs of her crib.

Anna Mae held the bed as Josiah extricated the child, then listened as he softly scolded her, cautioning her to be more careful. Anna Mae took Rose from her crib and set her on the floor.

Ruby's lip pushed out and she glanced at her twin to see her reaction. Rose stood, hand on her hip, observing the situation. Then she walked over to her sister. She patted Ruby on the shoulder. "You o'tay, you alwite." That pronouncement did the trick, for both girls immediately began to play as if nothing had happened.

Anna Mae brought her hand up to stifle the giggles. She looked up to find teasing laughter in Josiah's beautiful eyes.

He shook his head. "That one reminds me of someone else I know. You may not be her birth mother, but we'd never prove it to anyone else."

She smacked him playfully on the shoulder. Ruby was a bit of a daredevil. If the child could get into trouble, she did. Did Josiah really see Anna Mae that way, too? She grinned.

"At least Rose is like me. The voice of mighty wisdom." He placed his hand on his hip in mock Rose pose and repeated, "You o'tay, you alwite."

He and Anna Mae fell against each other, laughing; his arms went around her as hers closed around his waist. He looked down into her face, his eyes alight with pleasure, then fitted her head snugly under his chin. Anna Mae experienced happiness like never before.

"Annie?" His voice rumbled against her ear.

"Yes, Josiah?"

"There's one other thing we need to fix, if you're willing."

"What would that be?" Intrigued, she leaned back in his arms to see his face.

"The girls have a mother now. Don't you think it's time they called you that?"

Anna Mae pulled out of his grasp. For a brief moment she'd started to think of them as a family, but at the reminder of Mary, the idea seemed to evaporate like fog on a sunny morning. "No, they have a real mother. Her name is Mary. I know that I can't replace her in your heart, and I shouldn't try to replace her in theirs." Anna Mae returned to the cup of cider he'd poured for her, and sat down on the couch. So much for the fun, loving feelings they'd been sharing. Now she just felt deflated.

As if she'd ruined the moment for him, too, Josiah walked to the door and pulled his coat on. He turned to her and she saw in his eyes that he knew she spoke the truth. "Well, should you change your mind, you're welcome to allow them to call you Ma." The door slammed behind him.

So much for being wise. Anna Mae knew she'd handled that wrong, but she wasn't delusional enough to think he loved her and had replaced Mary in his heart with her. She should remember that next time she started feeling all mushy inside.

Telling herself to remember and being able to do so were two very different things. How much longer would she be able to protect herself from heartbreak? Josiah had said nothing about loving her and she'd do well to remember that.

Chapter Twenty-One

Saturday arrived with overcast skies, but the road was clear enough for them to drive to town and attend the taffy pull.

"I'm so glad you all could attend. You must stay with us tonight," Emily Jane said, smiling at Anna Mae with pleasure.

"Are you sure you don't mind us spending the night?" she asked, uncomfortable with the idea of staying at Emily Jane and William's overnight.

"Of course I'm sure," her friend answered. "It will be late when the fun is over and I'd hate to think of you all on the road home. Especially as cold as it is."

Beth Winters stood at the stove, making the taffy that would be pulled later. She'd already set several batches in bowls on the counter beside her. Hot water steamed under them to keep the taffy soft and manageable.

It was just the three of them standing in the kitchen. "Is it supposed to snow again?" Beth asked, measuring sugar, corn syrup, water and salt into a saucepan.

She blended it with a wooden spoon while the other two women watched.

"I hope not," Emily Jane answered, "I'm sick of snow and cold." She shivered.

Anna Mae smiled. She loved the snow, but not the cold so much. "I wouldn't mind having a white Christmas."

"That reminds me, William wanted me to ask if you and Josiah would mind coming into town Christmas Day instead of us going out there. He's concerned about the baby." Emily Jane rubbed her swollen belly.

Beth continued to stir the sugar concoction. "Men are always worried about the first baby."

"I'll have to ask Josiah, but I'm sure it won't be a problem." Anna Mae watched Beth's every movement. She loved taffy but had never gotten the knack of how to make it. If she learned today, maybe she could teach Rose and Ruby when they got older. Hers always came out crystalized. Crystalized candy wasn't bad, but it wasn't taffy.

"Ask me what?"

Anna Mae recognized her husband's voice and her heart greeted him. She turned with a smile. "If we'd come to town Christmas Day and save William and Emily Jane the hassle of coming out to our place."

"I don't see why not. Unless we get a white Christmas, and then it will depend on how much and how wet it is." He walked over and poured himself another cup of coffee. "Beth, is that first batch about ready to pull? We have some young'uns in there who are getting restless."

Beth touched the taffy she'd made. "I think it's cool

enough for little hands to pull. Anna Mae, would you get the butter and start greasing palms? Emily Jane, will you make sure the kids stay on the floured sheet out there? I'd really rather not clean up a sticky floor when this party is over."

Both women nodded.

"Here, Josiah, you take the taffy and instruct the children to use only their fingertips to lift the edges of the warm, flowing candy, and then to pull it out about twelve inches from each other. As quick as possible they will need to fold the taffy and then pull it again."

Josiah took the big bowl and nodded. "How much should I give each pair of children?" he asked, looking puzzled and as if he regretted coming into the kitchen.

Anna Mae grabbed up the butter and grinned at him as she walked by. She'd expected the past few days with him to feel strained, but they hadn't. They'd both acted as if he'd never told her to ask the girls to call her Mother. It was easier to pretend it never happened and continue on with their friendship.

"Just give them a big hunk of it and let the pulling begin." Beth waved them all out the door.

"Line up, everyone. Time to grease your hands so you can pull taffy," Anna Mae said, as she hurried into the room. Several of her students were present and smiled at her in greeting.

Sometimes Anna Mae wished she were back in the classroom, but when they started pushing and arguing the way they were now, she didn't miss it a bit. "If you children don't settle down I'm not going to give you any butter, and that means no taffy pulling."

Immediately the kids formed a nice straight line. She smiled at each of them as she scooped out a little bit of butter and told them, "Rub that all over your hands."

As soon as they were ready, Emily Jane called them over to the sheet that had been covered in white flour.

Anna Mae watched with pleasure as Josiah divided the children into teams of two and began giving them taffy to pull. Laughter immediately rang out as the kids began to tug at the sticky candy. The longer they pulled the harder it became to do so.

"Adults, time to get your hands dirty," Beth called as she came from the kitchen carrying another big bowl. "Husbands find your wives. Singles find a partner."

Levi and Millie stood with Josiah and William. Levi raised his voice for all to hear. "Better do as she says, or no candy for you to take home."

Several of the men grunted and the women giggled. It was amusing to watch those same grunting men hurry across the room to their wives. Anna Mae smiled as Josiah came to stand before her. She coated his big hands with butter, very aware of the callused skin that set her fingertips to tingling as she smeared it on.

She took a glob of butter for herself and then passed the bowl to the woman closest to her. Anna Mae tried to ignore Josiah's waiting eyes as she applied the butter to her hands as she would lotion.

Beth came by and gave them a large glob of candy. Together they followed her earlier directions, working the candy between them and laughing as they tried to keep it from oozing to the floor.

"This is really fun. I'm glad I told Levi we'd come,"

Josiah said, glancing at the twins, who sat on the sidelines in high chairs with other children around their age. They all had taffy and were eating it faster than it could harden. "The girls are having a grand ole time."

"Yes, and the added sugar will keep them up most of the night, too." Anna Mae felt the taffy becoming harder. She grunted as they pulled again. When they came together once more she said, "Emily Jane has invited us to spend the night." She pulled away again.

They came back together. "No can do. We have a cow to milk and she's not going to be happy to be getting milked late as it is."

Anna Mae stopped and looked at him. She'd forgotten all about Jersey. She should be grateful for an excuse not to have to sleep in the same room with Josiah, but she found herself feeling a little disappointed. The one night they had to share a room she hadn't slept a wink. Josiah had tossed and turned on the floor so much that she was sure Mr. Meeker had heard him through the wall.

"Let's see if this is ready to cut," Josiah said, pulling her and the taffy as he made his way to the table.

They found an empty platter and laid their candy down. Beth walked past and thrust a pair of scissors into Anna Mae's hand. "Get to cutting. I'll have one of the older boys come get it to wrap."

Anna Mae laughed. Beth Winters could be very bossy. She watched as the older woman walked about the room, praising the children on their wrapping and rushing the adults to hurry and get the candy cut.

Josiah's warm breath tickled her ear. "You might

want to get started. I believe if you don't have that cut by the time her boy comes by for it, Mrs. Miller, we'll be in big trouble and get no candy."

A giggle eased from her throat. "While I'm cutting what will you be doing?" she asked, looking up into his bright blue eyes.

"Supervising, of course." His face was only a few inches from her.

If she wanted to, Anna Mae could easily lean forward and kiss him. She ducked her head. Now where had that thought come from?

She snipped the candy into small pieces, aware that Josiah watched her every move. Why? Why was he studying her as if he'd never seen her before? Had he thought about kissing her, too?

Josiah knew he had to get away from his sweet wife. She smelled of candy and he'd felt the urge to kiss her just now. Kiss her right in front of everyone, something he was sure she wouldn't appreciate. "I'm going to go let Emily Jane and William know that we won't be able to spend the night."

As he approached his brother-in-law and wife, he heard their teasing remarks. "I can't remember the last time I had this much fun making candy." William winked at his wife, who was busy cutting their candy into bite-size pieces.

Emily Jane giggled and her cheeks flushed a pretty shade of pink. "Probably when you were a little boy."

"Probably so." He hugged her growing waist. "But I bet it wasn't nearly as much fun as this."

Josiah shook his head. Even though they'd been married several months now, they still behaved as newlyweds. For a few short moments he'd shared similar happiness with Anna Mae. Not like "in love" newlyweds, but fun just the same.

He cleared his throat. When they both looked at him expectantly, Josiah said, "Can you help me with something outside?" He motioned for William to follow him.

Emily Jane frowned. "Josiah, are you sure? It's pretty cold out there." Her brow furrowed with worry.

"This won't take long, Emily Jane."

William didn't seem to want to leave his wife any more than she wanted him to leave. "I'll be right there, Josiah."

"All right. I'm heading out for some fresh air." Josiah crossed the room and then reached for the front door handle.

"Pssst."

As natural as breathing, Josiah's hand lowered slowly to his holster. He turned to face the stairs behind him.

Grady leaned over the rails and whispered, "Come here, Josiah."

His shoulders sagged in relief and he removed his hand from his gun. Josiah took the stairs two at a time.

"Where you headed?" Grady asked in a low voice, as soon as he was close enough to talk.

"I invited William to meet me outside. I planned to tell him me and Annie can't spend the night at his place." He didn't add that the desire to kiss his wife had him hankering for much needed fresh air.

Grady frowned. "Why not?"

Not used to having to answer to another man, Josiah all but snapped, "We have animals to take care of."

It wasn't lost on Josiah that his friend had slipped into the shadows to avoid being seen below.

"Why are you living in the country, Josiah? You're not a farmer, you're a lawman. Shouldn't you be near the town you swore to protect?"

Irritation rose in him again. Josiah had no intention of discussing his situation with anyone at the moment, so he shrugged casually. "It works right now."

Grady shook his head and probably would have argued if Josiah hadn't changed the subject. "You find out anything?"

That did the trick. Grady growled. "Yes, no thanks to that bumbling deputy of yours."

Weariness settled between Josiah's shoulder blades. "What happened?"

"Had a situation back of the stable the other night about an hour after you went home. Saw two fellows ride up the back alley, so I hid in the loft. It's not good, Josiah."

Unease joined the weariness. "Did you know them?"

"One of them. It's Jose Garza."

Josiah's misgivings increased by the minute. "Jose Garza of the James gang?"

"The one and only."

"But why would a notorious gang want to mess with a little town like this? We're not even on the map. Our bank won't have enough money in it to make it worth their while." His head was beginning to pound at the seriousness of their situation.

"Not sure. They could be looking for a town to make their home. They may check out Granite and decide there's not enough law here to keep them from taking over." Grady grimaced. "Or they could be looking for towns with newspapers so the tales of their actions can be recorded."

Josiah resented the first remark, but knew it was true. "But our newspaper is just local stuff. Probably not more than fifty copies per week."

"Doesn't matter. Newspapermen, like your Mr. Lupan, tend to write about all these shenanigans. Other newspapermen will take what your Mr. Lupan wrote back to their syndicated presses and make heroes of criminals. The story could go all over the United States."

"You met Mr. Lupan, our newspaper editor?"

Grady nodded. "You might want to deputize him. He's a much better tracker than the one you've got. I've been dodging him for days. He knows I'm staying here at the boardinghouse. He plans to find out who I am and why."

Josiah couldn't help but smile at Grady's description of Mr. Lupan, who wasn't above spreading a little bit of gossip, since he'd learned it sold more papers than the news. "Speaking of plans, did you overhear the James gang plans?"

"Enough to know they're waiting on someone else to arrive on the stage. I'd have learned more but your deputy came down the alley and heard voices. He cocked his pistol, Josiah." Grady's voice reflected his scorn at the error. "Gave his position away before they ever saw him. They would have ambushed him had they not been waiting on this other feller to arrive. He'd be a dead man right now."

"I'll have a talk with him." Josiah felt momentary panic when he thought of young Wade trying to protect the town by himself.

Steely green eyes stared into his. "He needs to be trained, Josiah, not talked to. And who's going to train him when he's out on patrol at night and you're thirty minutes away on the farm?"

He didn't need a lecture from his mentor. What he needed was to move to town. But how to approach Anna Mae about the sensitive subject? She liked living on their farm and taking care of the animals. "I'll see to it, Grady."

An hour and a half later, Josiah handed the twins down to Anna Mae. Neither awoke and he knew she would have them tucked in for the night before he ever finished with the chores.

He turned Roy and the wagon toward the barn. Once the horse was unhitched, Josiah started the dreaded process. He looked at the chickens. He didn't much care if he ever saw one again. Unless it appeared on his Sunday plate. He led Jersey out of the stall and reached for the stool.

What was the James gang doing in his town? He should have been the one to learn of them, not Grady. And then there was the training of Wade. If the James gang shot the boy, there'd be no reason to train him. Josiah leaned his head against the cow's side. He couldn't afford to let his deputy make mistakes like cocking his gun before he even knew what he'd be shooting at.

"What's on your mind, Josiah?"

Warning spasms jolted him around. Lost in thought, he hadn't heard her approach. Had she opened the barn door? He must not have closed it, which was even worse. He was losing his touch. And any good lawman knew that was a dangerous thing.

Pretending her sudden appearance hadn't shaken him up, Josiah asked, "What do you mean, Annie? And what are you doing out here? You'll catch your death of cold."

"I came to help with the chores so you wouldn't have to be out here so long." She pulled her cloak tighter around her. "You didn't say a word all the way home."

Josiah raised his head but continued to milk the cow. "Neither did you."

"But I was reliving the excitement of the day, and I would have shared with you except that you seemed so withdrawn." She placed a palm on his arm.

He stared at her fingers while some illusive thought tugged at his memory. She jerked her hand away and clasped it against her chest. "I'm sorry. I didn't mean to be forward. And I don't deliberately try to intrude. I just wanted to help if something is troubling you."

He recovered her hand. "Oh, Annie. You could never be any of those things." Suddenly the chores didn't look so dreadful, and fresh eggs, butter and milk sure did make a man's stomach feel good. He saw the uncertainty in her eyes and felt strongly compelled to convince her of her worth. "Annie, you make things look so much better, easier. When I feel things are impossible, you challenge me to rethink. I feel like I can accomplish anything if I work hard enough."

She made a slight gesture with her right hand. "That's exactly how I feel, Josiah. I make a mess of things, but you don't treat me like I'm hopeless. You help me without making me think I'm an idiot."

He lifted an eyebrow inquiringly.

"Like with the legs on the girls' table. Or your patience teaching me to tend these animals," she reminded him.

He couldn't contain the grin that overtook his face. "Well, I need your help out here."

"Exactly, and you trust me to help." She shifted from foot to foot. "What I'm trying to say is that I love my life with you. We're connected somehow."

He finished milking the cow and moved the bucket off to the side. He stood and pulled her close for a hug. "I agree."

Carried away by emotions they both seemed to feel, he watched as she straightened the lapels of his coat. He felt the shy yet eager affection coming from her. Anna Mae looked down as if focused on the material under her fingertips.

Josiah couldn't have stopped his reaction to her if the barn had been on fire. He placed a hand on either side of her face and tilted her head. He touched her lips with his like a whisper. She closed her eyes, waiting, and he kissed her again, tender and light as a summer breeze.

She opened her eyes, then bumped awkwardly against him. He barely managed to keep them from falling. His kisses had never had that effect on Mary. Josiah searched Anna Mae's startled face.

"Jersey pushed me!" Anna Mae accused, pointing at

the cow. "Can you believe that? She knocked me against you." Her eyes widened in understanding. "She's jealous."

Josiah laughed out loud. "Most likely she wants to be back in her warm stall. She figures you need to quit lollygagging and get to work."

He dodged Anna Mae's friendly slap against his arm and set about putting the cow back in her stall. Farmer Miller to the rescue. How long would he be able to keep this up?

Grady was right. Josiah did belong in town, but how would he tell Anna Mae? Could he tell her? So many unanswered questions plagued his mind as he added fresh hay to the stall. And any good sheriff knew that the sooner you solved a case the quicker your mind could rest. But if he continued to kiss his wife, his mind would continue to remain mush and the case would never get solved. He sighed, knowing he'd enjoyed the kiss more than he should have. Now what? Had their relationship just changed again? And if so, what did the future hold for them?

Chapter Twenty-Two

A few days later, Anna Mae gathered all her scraps of fabric and carried them in a basket to the sitting room. "Rose, Ruby, come help me please."

The twins entered the room with big grins. They spotted the basket and hurried over. Each grabbed the colorful strips and started pulling them out.

"Pitty," Ruby said, grinning as if she'd just had another piece of taffy.

Rose nodded. "Pitty."

Anna Mae touched their soft curls. "Would you like to help me make pretty decorations for Christmas?"

They looked at each other and then nodded.

"Good." Anna Mae pulled her scissors out and began cutting the strips into smaller pieces. "We're going to make Christmas garlands so that we can decorate our house. Won't that be fun?"

They nodded and giggled. For the next hour Anna Mae worked with the girls tying the fabric strips into loops and then tying the loops together.

The little girls played with the cloth and took turns helping her string their homemade garland about the house. The brightly colored fabric brightened the room.

"Pitty," Rose said, pointing at the garland Anna Mae had hung about the bedroom door.

Ruby clapped her hands together and grabbed the next string. She hurried to the playroom, tripping on her little legs and hurriedly picking herself up. Rose, hot on her trail, picked up the tail of the string and followed her sister, laughing and chattering a mile a minute. Some of the words were intelligible, most were not. They both were doing much better in that department.

Anna Mae adored the little girls. They were such sweet babies and they loved to laugh. She grinned and followed them inside. They stood in the middle of the room, looking about.

"How about we hang that one above the window?" she asked, walking toward it and pulling a chair over as she went.

Again the girls nodded in agreement, so Anna Mae climbed on the chair, then reached down for the string of bright fabric.

As she hung it, she recognized the blue from her dress and the quilt she'd made for Josiah's bed, the pink and yellow from the little girls' dresses, and green, purple and red that she'd used to make doll clothes. The scraps represented their first Christmas together and the many hours she'd worked to create gifts for her family.

Once garlands hung from every available space about the house, Anna Mae turned to the twins. Their eyes darted back and forth as they admired the decorations they'd put up. "Would you like a warm glass of milk?" she asked them, heading to the kitchen.

The sound of little feet following caused her smile to broaden in approval. It seemed these days she smiled a lot.

It took only a few minutes to get the girls in their chairs and the milk on the stove warming.

Josiah came through the door, stomping his feet. "Boy, it's cold out there." He took his coat off and hung it up, then walked to where the girls sat. It was sweet the way he kissed the tops of their heads.

He looked at Anna Mae, eyebrows raised inquiringly. "So what have you ladies been up to?"

"Pitty!" Rose squealed, pointing at the garland.

Anna Mae laughed, amazed he hadn't noticed the many colorful swags that decorated his home. "Getting ready for Christmas."

Josiah looked about at the various strings of looped fabric. "It is very pretty."

"Yep, pitty," Ruby agreed, with a nod at her father.

"We're having warm milk and cookies. Would you like some?" Anna Mae asked, stirring the milk to make sure it didn't scorch.

He pulled out a chair and sat down. "I was hoping for something a little heavier. I've not had lunch yet."

She poured the warm milk and grabbed four cookies from the cookie jar. "How about a couple of ham biscuits and a pickle?" She handed the twins their cookies, then set their glasses of milk just a little out of their reach.

"Sounds wonderful. Do you have any cold milk

left?" He snatched up one of Ruby's cookies from her chubby hand and pretended to take a bite from it.

When the little girl sent her a wide-eyed look, Anna Mae hid her smile. "I do." She turned around so that Ruby wouldn't see her pleasure at Josiah's teasing.

While she made Josiah's lunch, Anna Mae listened to him talk to his daughters, his voice filled with love and warmth. What would it be like if he spoke to her like that? Anna Mae pushed the thought away and finished fixing his food. She hadn't expected him to come home for lunch. She'd hoped to be able to go to town and finish her Christmas shopping.

She set Josiah's plate in front of him. "You're home early."

He looked up at her. "I decided to come home this afternoon and after dinner return to town. Would you like to go Christmas tree hunting after I finish this sandwich?"

Anna Mae couldn't contain her excitement. "You mean it?"

"Why not? It will be a fun outing for the girls." He bowed his head and quietly thanked the Lord for his meal.

When he finished Anna Mae pulled four more cookies from the cookie jar and poured herself a glass of milk. She placed two of the cookies on his plate before sitting down. "They will need to go down for a nap before it gets too late."

"No nap!" the girls said in unison.

Josiah laughed. "See? They don't want to nap." He

tipped his glass up and drank about half his milk in one big gulp.

Anna Mae shook her head. "You are not helping me keep their schedule, but today, it's all right. I'm looking forward to getting a tree." Joy bubbled within her. Her husband had been paying attention. He'd noticed how much the tree would mean to her. Did she dare hope that he was finding something to love about her?

Josiah pulled a sled behind him as he and Anna Mae made their way into the woods. Rose and Ruby sat on the toboggan, giggling. The breeze was cold as it blew against his cheeks.

"Do you think they will be all right? It's a little chilly out here," Anna Mae said, looking over her shoulder at the twins.

"They will be fine. It won't take long to chop down a tree and get them back to the house. We might even have time to get them down for—" he lowered his voice "—that nap you mentioned earlier."

Her pink cheeks and the soft tendrils about her face gave her a youthful look. Anna Mae's eyes sparkled as she turned to face him. "That would be good."

He pushed on through the light snow. She didn't know it but he'd already found the perfect tree. He just hoped Anna Mae thought it was perfect, too.

"Did you have a Christmas tree when you were a kid?" she asked, looking at all the evergreens around them.

Josiah sighed. "No, Grady didn't think Christmas trees were safe. He didn't allow one."

"That's too bad. What about before you went to work for him?" she pressed, again checking on the girls.

"My dad enjoyed his bottle more than he did Christmas trees." How could Josiah change the subject? He searched his mind and then it dawned on him to just ask her the same question. "Did you?"

Her gaze swept back to him. Big brown eyes studied his face knowingly. "Yes, my parents threw a big party every year, so we had a large tree in the entry."

Josiah arrived at the tree he'd picked out. "What do you think of this one?"

Anna Mae walked around it and studied its branches. "It's not very tall." She touched the vibrant green pine needles.

"I don't know that we want it too tall." Josiah ran his hand around the back of his neck.

She turned with a smile. "You're right. I think it will work fine." She glanced at the girls again. "Uh-oh."

Josiah spun around to see what she was looking at. His sweet daughters were curled up like little foxes on the sled. "Well, you got your wish. They are napping now." He leaned down and tucked the blanket tighter around them.

Anna Mae sighed. "Yes, but I kind of hoped they'd wait until we got home."

He gently turned the sled back toward home. "I'll take you home and then come back for the tree."

Her shoulders slumped as she walked along beside him. His girls often interfered in things Anna Mae wanted to do. Feeling bad, Josiah draped his arm around her. "I know you wanted to be there when I cut it. I'm sorry."

"It's all right. I'll get them down for their nap, then start looking for things to decorate the tree with."

The brave smile she gave him melted a small part of his heart. Josiah leaned over and kissed her temple. "You are some woman, Annie Miller." He'd been looking for a reason to get this close to her since he'd seen her stirring milk at his cookstove. He only wished she'd offered her lips for his kiss and not just her temple. He could get used to kissing Anna Mae and deep down he knew his feelings for her were growing stronger every day.

Chapter Twenty-Three

The next morning, Anna Mae walked up Main Street. Many of the houses sported Christmas decorations and store windows displayed the best of their goods. In some shop entryways Anna Mae spotted mistletoe.

She grinned and blushed at the same time, remembering the kiss Josiah had given her in the barn. How many times would she relive that sweet kiss? Yesterday, she'd enjoyed his lips on her temple. Heat fill her face as she remembered, wishing it were another true kiss on the lips. She pushed the thoughts away and focused on the reason she was in town.

She'd dropped the twins off at Emily Jane's, with plans for a little time to herself. It felt odd not to have the girls with her. Over the past two months she'd grown used to having them around at all times.

What would Josiah think of her sneaking off with the girls so that she could buy a pair of boots for him? His looked worn and needed to be replaced. She knew he didn't like not knowing where she was, but for Christmas Anna Mae wanted to buy him new boots, and the twins ribbons and penny candy.

Anna Mae knew Josiah wasn't in Granite. Wade had come by the house earlier in the morning to tell her that Grady wanted Josiah to meet him on the edge of town. Later the deputy had returned, saying Josiah would be gone for the rest of the day.

Anna Mae had seen it as the perfect time to come into town, do her last-minute Christmas shopping and then get back home. He would never even know she'd left the farm.

She made her way to the bank. It wouldn't do to buy Josiah's Christmas boots with his money. Anna Mae had saved her teaching salary, and along with the money she'd earned selling eggs and butter to Carolyn at the general store, she would have just enough to take care of Christmas.

Pulling the bank door open, she stepped inside. Its interior seemed dim after the brilliant sunshine she'd just left. Anna Mae waited until her eyes adjusted and then made her way toward the tellers.

An older woman, a younger one and two children stood in line ahead of her. The children were too young to attend school, so she didn't know them. Even so, Anna Mae smiled at them.

As she waited she glanced about the bank's interior. There were two offices, but both were empty. Heavy dark furniture filled the rooms. A chair was positioned beside the main entry to the bank. She wondered if a guard sat there.

Turning her attention back to the line, she noted that

the teller was a middle-aged man who had a bald spot on top of his head. He seemed focused on the papers that the older woman had handed him.

Anna Mae glanced over as the bank clock chimed the hour. It was probably the largest clock she'd ever seen, shaped like the sun, with big numbers on its face. She realized that she'd already been gone from the girls for over thirty minutes. She'd promised Emily Jane that she would be back in an hour.

Wishing she hadn't dawdled, Anna Mae turned back to see what was taking so long. The woman was arguing with the teller in a low voice and pointing at the papers in question.

The younger woman held on to her children's hands and tapped her toe. Anna Mae thought about telling her that as long as they were waiting in line, at least nothing was expected of them. But she, too, felt her impatience growing as the big clock ticked loudly.

Sunlight briefly filtered into the room as two sets of heavy boots clomped into the bank. Anna Mae turned to look at their owners, and her blood froze. The lower halves of the men's faces were covered by bandannas and they both held guns pointed at the bank occupants. One of them stopped and locked the door, while the other continued walking toward them as if he owned the place.

The other two women and the bank teller paid the men no mind. Anna Mae wasn't sure what to do. If she alerted them to the danger they were in, would they overreact and get shot?

Two seconds later the decision was taken out of her

hands. "Put your hands in the air, keep your mouths shut and we won't have any trouble," the bank robber closest to them growled.

The two women immediately did exactly what he'd just told them not to do. The younger one started to cry out, and the older one argued, "Why, you good-for-nothing scoundrels, how dare you threaten us?"

Anna Mae watched in horror as the man shoved the old woman to the floor, effectively silencing her. He grabbed one of the kids and raised his eyebrows menacingly at the mother. "Your choice, woman. Either close your mouth or lose your kid." The child, a little boy of about five, reached for his mom, his lips trembling and his face crumpling.

The woman shook her head quickly. Not another sound issued from her and she caught her son tightly against her as he was shoved into her arms.

Fear knotted inside Anna Mae's chest. Why had Josiah chosen today of all days to go out of town? Wade had pulled the second night patrol, so he most likely had returned to the jailhouse to sleep for a few hours.

As Anna Mae studied the scene in front of her, reality sank in. She might never see Josiah or the girls again. Now she wished she'd told them that she loved them. Would she ever get the chance?

Would Josiah ever know that his wife cared for him as a wife should?

Josiah's stomach tightened once again, a sure sign something wasn't quite right. One of the first things Grady had taught him was to follow his instincts, and his instincts today shouted that he was headed in the wrong direction. From the moment they'd left Granite for Hancock, that little warning voice had whispered in his head.

Hancock was a small town with a bank about the size of Granite's. Grady had said he'd overheard a couple men saying that the Hancock bank was in for a surprise. Feeling sure it was going to be the location of the next bank robbery, Grady had asked Josiah to help him capture the James gang.

Josiah looked across at his mentor. "How many men do you suppose are in the gang?"

The older man pulled his horse to a walk. "Rumor has it that they are up to six strong, but I'm not real sure on the numbers. I've only seen the two scouts hanging out in Granite. Why do you ask?"

"The night before Mary was killed, I had been stalking a couple of men who I suspected were bank robbers. While they sat around their campfire, I hid in the bushes. They plotted their next robbery, and because I had to catch them in the act, I listened. Sure 'nuff, the next morning I hightailed it to the bank I thought they'd be at, only they never showed up. Instead, they robbed the town I was sworn to protect, and killed my wife." He paused.

"Son, that wasn't your fault," Grady said, before setting his horse into an easy gallop.

Josiah caught up to him. "In a way it was. I learned later that they had planted a false trail for me to follow." The knot in his stomach tightened. "They knew, Grady. They knew that I was listening." He pulled on

Roy's reins. "They caught on to the fact that I was trailing them and they set me up."

Grady slowed in turn. "What are you trying to say, son? That you want to turn back?"

"I'm trying to tell you that this situation feels the same, Grady. What if they split up and are hitting two banks on the same day?" Josiah rubbed the hairs that stood up on the back of his neck. "They could have caught on that you were on their trail and deliberately set you up, just like they did me."

Grady's hand rested on his gun. "It's possible, I suppose."

The two lawmen studied each other, both knowing that if they split up they could possibly be facing several bank robbers alone.

Josiah had friends and family in Granite. He couldn't leave them vulnerable to a gang of thieves. Wade wasn't experienced enough to know what to do should the men come out with guns blazing. Plus if Josiah knew his deputy, Wade was probably asleep on one of the jail bunks. "You taught me to trust my gut. My gut says to go back."

The old man nodded. "Go on," Grady said. "Take care of your town. I'd do the same thing, if I was you."

Josiah sighed. "What if I'm wrong? You'll be facing the gang by yourself."

"Naw, I won't. I'll scout out the situation. If there are too many of them for me to handle, I'll wait and capture them another day." Grady edged his horse up close to Josiah's and clasped him on the shoulder. "And if I have to track them down again, you can be sure you're going with me."

That was all he needed to hear. Josiah nodded once and then spun Roy around. The wind tore at his hat as they raced back to town. The closer he got the more apprehensive he felt. *Thank you, God, that Annie and the girls are home safe.*

His horse's sides heaved and white foam sprayed against his sleek coat as they finally arrived in town. When Josiah reached the bank, Levi was pulling at the door, but it didn't open. Josiah looked at the sun. By now, the bank should be open for business. As casually as he could manage, he slid off Roy's back and called Levi's name. He looped Roy's reins over the hitching post and patted his nose.

His friend strolled toward him. "What's up with the bank being closed, Josiah? It's not a holiday." Levi didn't try to hide his irritation.

When he got close enough to hear him, Josiah answered in a soft voice, priding himself on sounding calm. "Levi, I figure the bank is being robbed. Go home and keep your wife and family safe. Let me handle this."

To his credit, Levi never reacted, just turned and walked down the street. Josiah crept around to the back of the bank, cocked his gun and eased open the door. Mr. Anderson should know better than to keep this door unlocked. However, up until today, the town had never had reason for caution.

Silent as a church mouse, Josiah passed the safe and stepped into the main part of the bank. Bitter, cold despair twisted inside him. Just as he'd figured, the place was being robbed.

He took in the situation swiftly. There were only two

outlaws visible, one standing by the door with his gun aimed at the customers, and one holding his weapon on the teller, who trembled so badly he had trouble putting the money into a bag.

Then Josiah's gaze moved to the customers. His heart stopped. Anna Mae stood between the robber and the small group of distraught women and children.

Just as Josiah stepped out to confront the robbers, the sound of keys jingling in the lock of the front door drew everyone's attention. Mr. Anderson and Levi burst through the door. The bank president shot the man closest to him.

The young woman screamed. Anna Mae and the other woman dropped to the floor. His Annie grabbed the child closest to her and pulled her down, too. When the young woman saw them on the floor, she dropped, too.

The other robber turned to run out the back door, and saw Josiah. Shock held the man immobile for a few seconds, then the assailant aimed and fired. Pain ripped through Josiah's shoulder as the outlaw's bullet found its mark.

Josiah fired off a shot as he went down. Two things registered at once: the outlaw falling forward into the hardwood floor, and the look of horror that crossed Anna Mae's face when she saw the blood spreading across Josiah's chest.

Searing pain took his breath away as his legs gave out under him. With extreme effort, he fought off the beckoning darkness. Everything seemed to move in slow motion, especially Anna Mae rising to her feet and struggling to get to him.

Why was she here? Why did she have to see him get shot? She should have been home taking care of the kids. She could have been killed, like Mary. Anger that his job had once more put someone he loved in danger, filled him.

Chapter Twenty-Four

Anna Mae watched the events unfold before her like a bad dream. A raw groan of despair erupted from her throat as she saw Josiah stagger backward, then slump to the floor. She pushed herself up, untangled her skirt and ran to him. Anna Mae collapsed beside him, reaching to touch his chest.

For a brief moment she clung to him, but within seconds Josiah shoved her behind him. "Stay down," he growled. His gun arm raised and he kept it on the robber who lay a few feet away from them.

Why? Both robbers had been shot. Anna Mae didn't care about them or herself. All she wanted was to make sure that Josiah wasn't going to die from his wound. "You're hurt," she protested.

"I am very aware of that, Anna Mae."

Anna Mae. He'd called her by her given name, not Annie. Anger poured from him like hot butter. She felt it scorch her heart, and the withering look stopped her from attempting to touch him again.

Levi pushed the robber over and shook his head. “This one is dead,” he said.

“This one’s not,” the bank president called from across the room. “But he’s not going anywhere.” He pointed his gun at the man’s head and growled, “Get up.”

Moisture began to flow down Anna Mae’s face. She swiped at it with her hands. One man was dead, two were injured and Josiah was angry with her. Disconcerted, she crossed her arms and looked away.

Josiah lowered his head and looked down at his shoulder, where blood seeped into his shirt. “Levi, would you escort these people out of here and help Mr. Anderson get that man over to the jail?” He waved his hand toward the injured robber.

“What about you?” Levi asked, coming to stand beside him. “You’ve been shot.”

A harsh laugh echoed in Anna Mae’s ears and then Josiah stopped laughing and looked up at Levi. “I’m very aware I’ve been shot, Levi. My wife has already pointed that out to me.”

“Come along, folks.” Anna Mae watched as the women and children practically ran from the bank at Mr. Anderson’s command.

“Anderson, do you need help getting that man to jail?” Levi asked, holding Josiah’s gaze.

“Nope, Mr. Sheridan can help me.” He motioned for the bank teller to join him. Together they lifted the injured man and then pushed him out the door.

When he was outside, Anna Mae heard the bank president say, “There’s nothing to see here, folks. The sheriff has stopped an attempted bank robbery. Go on home. Mr. Lupan, if you will come with me, I'll give you the whole story for your paper."

Her husband's voice pulled her attention back inside. "Anna Mae, where are the girls?" Josiah still didn't look at her.

"With Emily Jane."

Speaking between gritted teeth, he commanded, "Get them and go home."

"You need to go to the doctor," she protested, wanting to pull him into her arms and give him comfort from the pain.

"Do as I say!" he growled.

Levi knelt down to look into her tearstained face. "I'll make sure he goes, Anna Mae. Please, do as he says."

She jerked awkwardly to her feet, then spoke in a suffocated whisper. "But how will I know you are all right?"

His voice softened. "Annie, it's only a shoulder wound. I'm fine. Please, get out of town. I don't know where the rest of the James gang is and I want you and the girls home safe." Pain-filled blue eyes slowly rose and met hers. "Please."

Anna Mae nodded. She stumbled and a desperate sob escaped before she managed to walk away with stiff dignity. She paused just inside the door and looked back. Josiah stared after her, an unusual play of emotions on his face.

Thankfully, everyone had followed Mr. Anderson's orders and left. She turned in the direction of the general store and ducked around the building. Holding her breath, Anna Mae waited for her husband and Levi to come out of the bank. She wanted to make sure Josiah could walk on his own.

Both men exited the bank, and though Josiah bent forward slightly, he walked without assistance. His face appeared pale in the bright sunlight. He pulled his hat down low and turned in the opposite direction from Anna Mae, straight toward the doctor's office. When they were out of sight, she returned to the boardwalk and headed to the general store.

She'd come to get the girls hair ribbons and penny candy for Christmas, and that's what she planned to do. The boots would have to wait for another time. Anna Mae still refused to buy Josiah's Christmas gift with his own money.

The pleasure of the morning had been poisoned by ugly events. She ached with an inner pain.

As soon as she walked inside, Carolyn exclaimed, "Please tell me you weren't in the bank."

Anna Mae couldn't speak for the lump in her throat, so she nodded.

"Is everyone all right?"

A small crowd of men stood at the back of the store. They inched forward, waiting for her answer. "One of the bank robbers was killed and the other was injured. Mr. Lupan is with Mr. Anderson, who's giving him a full report. You'll all get to read it in this week's paper, I'm sure."

She didn't want to talk about the attempted robbery. Anna Mae hurried to the ribbons, chose two spools that matched Rose's and Ruby's dresses, and carried it to the counter.

"Praise the Lord," Carolyn said, taking the ribbon.

"I'd like half a yard of both of those." Anna Mae tried to smile, but knew her lips wobbled too much for a genuine one.

Carolyn nodded. "Are you all right?" she asked as she cut the ribbon.

"Yes, just a little shaken up. Can I also get three peppermint sticks, a small bag of lemon drops, three apples, three oranges and three of those sweet potatoes?" She'd make a sweet potato pie for Christmas. The potatoes were huge and knobbed, and might even be enough for two pies. Anna Mae kept her mind on mundane things in an effort not to break down.

She paid for her purchases, left the store and ran to the side of the building. Her stomach roiled and she lost her breakfast. With one arm clasping the bag and the other hand propped securely against the wall she stumbled along till she found the steps at the back of the store and sank down wearily.

Anna Mae rocked back and forth, weeping hot cleansing tears until she captured her composure. She saw with abrupt clarity that she had fallen in love with Josiah Miller. She thought she should feel sorry about that, but instead it felt right.

A sense of strength came to her and serene peace wove its way into her heart. Her husband lived. God had protected him. She was grateful.

She gathered her purchases and walked calmly

to Emily Jane's house. Her friend pulled her quickly through the door, exclaiming with fear, "You're hurt."

Anna Mae looked at the front of her dress and saw spots of Josiah's blood where she'd held him close for those few seconds before he'd shoved her behind him. She wrung her hands. "I'm not hurt. That's Josiah's blood." Why hadn't Carolyn mentioned the blood? Maybe she hadn't noticed.

Emily Jane's hands went to her cheeks. "Oh, no."

Anna Mae held up her trembling palm. "He's alive. He was shot in the shoulder by a bank robber. He will be fine." *Lord, please let him be fine.*

She managed to give Emily Jane the shortened version of the robbery. Remembering her promise to leave town, Anna Mae announced, "We have to go." She started gathering the girls' coats, blankets and toys. "Thank you, Emily Jane, for watching them this morning. I was able to get their Christmas gifts bought and a few groceries for special holiday dishes."

They said their goodbyes and she headed out of town.

"Mrs. Miller!"

Anna Mae pulled the wagon to a stop and looked over her shoulder. Amos, the delivery boy for Carolyn, came running up to the wagon.

Breathlessly, he panted, "Mrs. Moore asked me to give this to you." He handed her a letter.

"Oh, thank you, Amos."

"You're welcome." He turned and ran back the way he'd come.

Anna Mae turned the envelope over and immediately

recognized her mother's penmanship. She tucked the letter into her bag and continued on home.

When she pulled into the yard a cry of relief broke from her lips. She'd never before been so glad to see the place. Rose and Ruby clapped their little hands and laughed. They, too, seemed to be glad to be home.

Once the girls were down for their afternoon nap, Anna Mae pulled the letter out of her bag and opened it. For weeks she'd wondered what her mother thought about her marriage, and now she'd find out. With trembling fingers, she pulled the letter out and began to read.

> My dear, sweet Anna Mae,
> I know you say you recently got married, and I respect that. Your father and I have to wonder why you married so quickly. We know how devastated you were when Mark left and then when that dreadful Mr. Westland chose another over you. We hope you didn't get married for the mere sake of being married. But I fear the worse.
>
> I spoke with my dear friend Grace Hardy, and she tells me that a teaching position has come up at the school and she'd love to have you back. You were one of her best teachers, after all. I told her I'd let you know as soon as possible. She would like for you to be here to start after the Christmas break.
>
> Honey, I know you are married, but are you happy? If not, this is the perfect opportunity for you to come home and start anew. No one has to know you were married.

Please write me back as soon as possible so that I can give Grace your answer.

We love you,

Mother and Father

So that was it. After months of humiliation, now the school board wanted her to return to her old job as if nothing had happened. As if they hadn't rejected her when she'd asked for her job back after Mark had left her standing at the altar. She laid the letter down and began making a fresh pot of coffee.

Anna Mae knew she'd never be able to leave Josiah and the girls. She no longer thought about Mark and even wondered if she'd ever really loved him. Her feelings for Josiah were so much stronger than they'd ever been for her old fiancé. Anna Mae closed her eyes and tried to pull up Mark's handsome image. For a moment she felt confused. She remembered him, but his face no longer appealed to her.

Josiah's laughing blue eyes and handsome features eased forward in her mind's eye. She loved him. She'd never loved like this before. And if he didn't ever return those feelings, at least she knew what it meant to be head over heels. She exhaled a long sigh of contentment.

In comparison, Josiah was the better man. He treated her like an equal, not a thing that belonged to him. Her opinions mattered to Josiah; Mark had never consulted her on anything. Josiah never talked of money and Mark lived for the almighty dollar. The more she compared the two men, the more Anna Mae realized that she'd never loved Mark, and it really hadn't been her heart that had been broken, but her pride.

Josiah had given her back her self-esteem without either of them realizing it. He might never love her as he had Mary, but Anna Mae knew that she loved him. Her husband was a good man and he'd made her feel worthy and confident.

Although, at the bank he'd been angry. Angrier than she'd ever seen a man. Was that anger at her? The robbers? Maybe after the robbery he'd want her to leave.

A knock sounded on the door, pulling Anna Mae from her thoughts. Her heart soaring with her newfound knowledge, she swung the door wide, then fought to keep the disappointment from showing on her face.

For the second time in less than a month, Grady filled the entryway. "Woman, have you lost your mind? What if I'd been one of the James gang?" He growled down at her like a concerned father.

Anna Mae gasped. He was right. She should have realized that the gang might come after Josiah's family. But then again, Josiah wouldn't have sent her and the girls to the farm if he hadn't thought it was safe.

"Are you going to let me in or continue staring at me as if I've grown horns on my head?" The lawman placed both large arms on the door frame.

A feminine voice sounded and two small hands pushed him from behind. "John Grady Meeker, get out of the way. Can't you tell she's in shock?"

"Susanna?"

"Yep, it's me." She poked her head under Grady's

arm and smiled. "Do me a favor and invite this mountain of a man in so I can give you a hug."

Anna Mae opened the door wider. "Of course, come in. Both of you."

Grady cleared the doorway and Susanna shot around him. She grabbed Anna Mae in a tight hug. The sweet scent of roses filled her nostrils.

"When I heard from Carolyn what had happened and that you had blood on your dress, I just had to come. You poor dear. Are you hurt anywhere?" Susanna pulled back and searched Anna Mae for injuries.

"No, I'm fine. The blood Carolyn saw is Josiah's, but he's all right, too."

"Oh, good." Susanna pulled her toward the couch. "Sit down and tell me all about it."

"Sure, you do that. I'll shut the door," Grady said in a disgruntled tone.

Anna Mae turned to him. "I'm sorry, Mr. Meeker. Did Josiah send you out? Is he all right?"

"Nobody sends me anyplace, young lady," he grumped, and then sat in Josiah's rocker. "But yes."

Susanna continued to rub Anna Mae's back as one would a small child. "You really should change dresses so we can try to get the blood out of that one."

Anna Mae inched away from her friend. "I will, Susanna, but let me find out about Josiah first." She turned her attention back to Grady. "Have you seen him? What did the doctor say?"

The big man leaned forward and rested his arms on his knees. "Yes, I saw him. Josiah's shoulder is going to hurt for a while, but the doctor says he'll heal."

She heaved a sigh of relief. It had pained Anna Mae to leave him in town, but she'd seen for herself that he could walk to the doctor. "I'm glad." If he was fine, then why had he asked Grady to come out to the farm?

Susanna sat forward. "So if Josiah didn't send you out here, what are you doing here?" she asked in her no-nonsense way.

The lawman leaned back in his chair. "Young lady, there are still four bank robbers running loose. I came to check on Anna Mae and the girls. Josiah wasn't thinking straight when he sent them out here alone."

Grady propped his fingers in a steeple and stared at her with steely green eyes. "I'd thought to persuade Anna Mae into returning to town, where she belongs."

Anna Mae shook her head. "I'm sorry, Mr. Meeker, but I have animals out here that need tending to. I appreciate your concern, but I'll be fine."

Grady stood. "He said you'd say something like that. Mrs. Marsh, are you going to stay out here for a while?"

For the first time ever, Anna Mae saw a serious, determined side of Susanna. "I brought a bag with me. I didn't like the idea of them being alone out here, either."

The two exchanged a look of understanding and respect. Anna Mae stared at her friend.

Susanna Marsh had been one of four mail-order brides who had arrived to marry Levi Westland months ago. She was the oldest and the only one who had been married before. When they'd arrived, Susanna had seemed the most determined to marry Levi, but was also the first to give up on him. She had seemed bossy, arrogant and a little flighty.

But the woman sitting beside her now seemed more mature, in control and caring. Anna Mae realized at that moment that she had developed close friendships here in Granite, another reason not to return to her parents.

"Well, then, I'll be going. We still have four men to catch." Grady walked to the door.

Anna Mae hurried to catch up with him. "Mr. Meeker, is Josiah heading home?" She didn't like the idea of him being injured and out chasing outlaws.

"No, ma'am. He's planning on catching those other men. When I left town, he was in the process of questioning the prisoner to find the location of their hideout. If I know Josiah, he won't rest until he has all five of them behind bars." Grady looked down at her with kind eyes.

She nodded. Tears felt close to the surface once more.

He walked back to her and turned her to face him. "Josiah is a good lawman. He knows how to take care of himself."

Through a tight throat she managed to say, "And yet today he got shot."

"Yes, ma'am, he did." Grady lifted her face to look up at him. "But I believe he was distracted by a pretty lady. That won't happen again." Grady winked at her and then turned to leave.

As soon as the door closed, Susanna said, "You know, I'd like for a man to find me distracting." She sighed dramatically and patted her lips with her pointer finger. "I think I'm going to do some advertising of my own."

Anna Mae turned to face her. "What?"

A comical expression crossed Susanna's face. "Wouldn't it be fun to place an ad in Mr. Lupan's paper? Something like 'Husband wanted: See Mrs. Marsh for details.'"

Anna Mae giggled. Now there was the friend she recognized. She felt grateful for the company, but she knew she wouldn't relax until her husband was home safe.

Josiah slid from his horse but hung on to the saddle horn while he gained his balance. His body felt too weary to stand, let alone walk the distance from the barn to the house. His shoulder felt as if it were on fire. It had been two days since he'd been home and the relief he felt walking up to the porch knew no bounds. How he had missed Anna Mae and the girls, but thanks to the help of Grady and Wade, all the remaining James gang members were in the paddy wagon headed to Austin.

Grady would travel with the prisoners there and then return to Denver. Saying goodbye had been hard, but he knew his old friend and mentor needed to get home to his own community. Before he'd left, Grady had pressed him once more to move his family to town.

Josiah twisted the door handle and pushed lightly. To his utter surprise the door swung open. He quietly closed it behind him. The fact that Anna Mae hadn't dropped the bar into place across it proved Grady was correct. Josiah shook his head in disbelief. It was way past the midnight hour and she'd left the door open. What was wrong with her? Anyone could have come in.

The click of a hammer being cocked froze him in his tracks. He raised his hands out to the side and slowly turned to face his attacker. The glint of metal eased from the shadows. The scent of roses wafted toward him, and had he not been about to crumble to the floor he would have laughed.

"Either shoot me or lower the gun, Mrs. Marsh."

"Sheriff?" Her voice sounded sleepy.

"Yes, it's me." He moved into the light from the fireplace so that she could see him better.

Susanna eased the hammer off, lowered the gun and joined him in the firelight. "I'm glad you're home." She yawned.

"Where is Annie?" He looked about the room for his wife.

"Sleeping." Susanna sat on the couch and yawned again. "Midnight to six is my night-watch time. Hers is bedtime to midnight. It works better that way, since she has to get up with the girls in the mornings."

"Whose idea was this?" he asked, as he sank into his rocker. What a blessed relief to be off his feet.

"Anna Mae's. She didn't want to lock you out and she didn't want to invite outlaws in." Susanna pushed herself up from the couch. "Since you're home, I'm going to bed." Just before she walked away, she whispered, "Did you catch them all?"

He grinned. "Yes, they are on their way to Austin."

"Good, a body can rest now. Night, Josiah." Susanna walked to the girls' playroom.

Josiah leaned back and closed his eyes. So his Annie hadn't been foolish. She'd thought of a way to keep them safe and also make sure that he felt welcomed home. Which surprised him, considering the treatment she'd received at his hand the day of the robbery. He'd been downright mean to her. He figured he had a lot of explaining to do.

One thing he was certain of—he'd died a slow death when he saw Annie with her arms spread wide, trying to protect the other bank customers. He'd felt gutted. Weak. He began to shake as his mind spiraled to what could have happened. Could have happened, but didn't. His mouth suddenly felt dry.

Josiah walked to the kitchen for a sip of water. He was bone tired. Drinking from the dipper, he sat down at the table, happy to be home.

His gaze fell upon a piece of paper. It was open for anyone to read, so he did. His heart clinched in his chest as he read Anna Mae's mother's words. Just to be certain of what he'd read, Josiah went through it again.

They wanted her to come home. To a teaching job. Would she go? After the way he'd treated her he wouldn't be surprised if she did leave. Just the thought of it caused his heart to contract in a way that almost took his breath away. Josiah silently prayed that God would supply a way for him to explain to Anna Mae that he loved her. And a chance to ask her not to leave.

Chapter Twenty-Five

Anna Mae paced from window to window, waiting for Josiah to arrive home. This was the third day, and still no word came from town, saying whether he was safe or not.

Over the past few days she'd worried about Josiah, and yet she also wondered if he wanted her to leave. He'd been so angry, and now that she'd had more time to reflect on it, Anna Mae knew he was upset with her. Was he angry enough to ask her to leave once he'd captured the outlaws and secured his girls' safety?

Thoughts of the twins had her looking over her shoulder at them. She'd brought them into the kitchen so they wouldn't awaken Susanna, but it proved harder each moment to keep them occupied. They wanted to go to their playroom. She'd let them help mash the sweet potatoes she'd cooked earlier, then they'd helped pat out cookies. Now they ran their hands through the dried beans she'd poured on the table in a desperate attempt to silence their whining.

"Papa."

Anna Mae whirled around to shush or comfort the girls, whichever was needed, and her senses leaped to life. Josiah stood in the doorway to his bedroom, hair tousled. He had a big white bandage covering one shoulder and wrapped around his chest and back.

"Josiah." She could barely get his name past the lump in her throat. She moved toward him, compelled by an unseen force. He stepped forward and clasped her body tightly to his. She buried her face against the corded muscles of his neck, her heart bursting with love and anguish at the same time. She could no more stop the tears than she could stop breathing.

She felt him swallow and then he kissed her forehead.

"Shh, Annie girl. I'm fine."

She refused to budge from his arms, her face against his unhurt shoulder. He murmured words of encouragement and sweetness. "Seeing you in danger..." He paused and swallowed again. "You are so brave." His hand softly brushed the hair flowing down her back. "I'm sorry."

"I'm so thankful you're alive." Her voice was a weak, tremulous whisper. She leaned back to look up into his face.

He started to answer her then gave her a gentle squeeze, a grin the size of Texas tilting the corners of his mouth. Josiah looked down.

She had no problem identifying the source of his amusement as the twin now climbing his leg was almost to her waist, fingers digging into the fabric of her dress. She stepped back to give the child more room.

Once Anna Mae was out of his arms, Josiah lifted Ruby on up to his shoulder as Anna Mae clasped Rose in front of her.

"I guess all her climbing has made her strong." She laughed.

He nuzzled his two-day bearded chin into Ruby's neck, making her shriek and giggle, then leaned forward to snuggle Rose, as well. Rose patted his face, then buried her head against Anna Mae as if she might cry.

"What's wrong, Rose?" Anna Mae had a notion she knew what troubled the child. "Does Papa's hurt scare you?"

Ruby gingerly touched her father's bandage, then looked him in the eyes. "You falled?"

"Something like that." Anna Mae saw the uncertainty that crept into his expression even as tears welled up in his beautiful blue eyes. That was all it took for Rose's soft heart and she launched herself from Anna Mae's arms to Josiah's, effectively pushing her twin to the side. Anna Mae's frantic grab was all that saved Ruby from landing on the floor.

It lightened the situation and Anna Mae laughed happily. Rose's little arms tightened around her papa's neck until he walked to the table and sat down. Only then did she lean back and look into his face. There was no sign of tears. Instead, Rose's beaming smile melted Anna Mae's heart, and from the look of love in Josiah's eyes, it did the same to him.

Anna Mae also saw pain in the depths of his gaze.

It was time to get his arms free and to fix her husband some much needed breakfast. He was starting to look a little thin to her.

"What's going on in here? A person can't sleep with all this caterwauling." Susanna took Ruby from Anna Mae and swung her round and round. Anna Mae wondered how long Susanna had been watching. The rims of her eyes appeared a little red and puffy, as if she'd been crying. Had her friend been listening in on her small family and been touched by the sweetness of it all?

Anna Mae took Rose from Josiah and put her in her high chair. "I'll start breakfast and we can eat in a jiffy."

"If you don't mind, Anna Mae, I'd rather get on back to town." Susanna set Ruby in her high chair as well and cleared her throat. "I've been gone three days and I figure work has piled up."

"I'll saddle your horse. Just give me a few minutes to get dressed." Josiah turned to go into his bedroom. Only then did Anna Mae notice the bare parts of his chest, back and shoulder.

"I've been saddling my horse for as long as I remember, Josiah Miller, and I'll not have you insulting me. I'll be gone before you get your boots on." She pointedly looked down at his bare feet, pulled on her scarf, then her coat, and picked up her valise.

Josiah shook his head and went to his room. His door closed softly and Anna Mae rushed to hug Susanna, who hugged her back, then released her. "You have a wonderful family now, Anna Mae. I'm happy for you." She turned and blew kisses to the twins.

Anna Mae wasn't quite ready to let her go just yet. She caught Susanna's sleeve. "Thank you for staying with us. I don't know if I would be sane now if it hadn't been for you and your assurances that Josiah was fine."

Susanna smiled. "It was my pleasure. I'll see you Sunday." The door closed behind her.

Anna Mae turned to find three sets of eyes on her. Josiah's were gentle and contemplative and held a gleam of interest she returned wholeheartedly. The other two identical sets said, "You mentioned breakfast, so what's the holdup?"

She clapped her hands together. "So, what shall we do?"

"Eat."

Ruby echoed Rose and then grinned as if she'd just been offered a prize at the fair.

Josiah and Anna Mae exchanged open looks of amusement.

She nodded and walked to the stove. "Then breakfast it is." Anna Mae noticed the letter from her mother still lying on the table where she'd left it the night before. She'd read it every night since its arrival, and she still felt her place was here with Josiah and the twins. Anna Mae stopped and picked it up, folded it and stuffed it into her apron pocket.

That letter, along with worrying about Josiah, had kept her awake most of the nights he'd been gone. At times she knew she'd be writing her mother back saying she was happily married and not coming home. Other times she thought about her unrequited love for

Josiah, who could never love her like a true wife should be loved. It was all just too confusing.

"Annie, if it wouldn't be too much trouble, would you mind rustling up a batch of biscuits and gravy?" Josiah asked. He sounded sad, as if he thought she wouldn't be making them for him again soon.

She looked over at him. Had he read her letter? And if so, what was he thinking? That she was going home? Or that she should go on home? "I'll be happy to."

"Egg," Rose called. Josiah handed her a cloth ball to play with.

"All right, one egg for Rose." Anna Mae looked to Ruby. "Ruby, would you like an egg, too?"

The child shook her head and took the picture book Josiah was handing to her. "Bikit."

Josiah eased into a chair at the kitchen table. "I hope you don't mind, but I read your letter."

Anna Mae turned to the counter and began mixing dough for the biscuits. "I don't mind." She poured milk into the dry ingredients.

"Have you given any thought to what your mother told you?" He paused, waited, then continued. "About the teaching job?" His voice sounded pained.

She stirred the batter. "I've done nothing but think about it." She folded the batter over with her hands, adding a little more flour each time till the mixture was stiffer. Then she pinched off a little section, rolled it in her palms and patted it flat in the pan.

He waited until she'd finished making the biscuits and had put them in the oven before asking, "And?"

Anna Mae wiped her hands and came to sit at the

table. "I guess that depends on you." She held up a palm to stop him from interrupting her. "I've prayed about that letter for three days. I don't believe God wants me to leave you and the girls. But if you truly feel you don't need me or that you want me to go—" she swallowed hard "—I'll go."

There. She heaved a sigh. *I said it.* Silent prayers began flying heavenward. Anna Mae didn't want to leave Josiah. It would break her heart. She loved him and the girls with everything that was in her, but she also knew it wouldn't be fair to keep him in a marriage where he felt no husbandly love for his wife. *Lord, it's in Your hands now.*

Josiah felt as if a big piece of the puzzle finally fell into place. Love shone from her eyes. He'd been afraid Anna Mae would reject him after he'd treated her so poorly at the bank, but now he knew she cared for him as much as he did her. He patted his front pocket to make sure that Anna Mae's ring was still there.

He reached across the table and took her hands in his. "I never want you to leave me, Anna Mae Miller." He searched her face, her eyes, noted the trembling in her fingers, all evidence that her emotions were involved. That was a positive. But would they return to the advance-and-retreat actions of the past? Could he allow her to see what was in his heart?

Now was the time. He'd spent the past three days studying his heart and he knew Anna Mae held it as surely as he knew anything. He could hold back no longer. She had to know that he loved her.

Josiah pulled the ring box from his pocket and set it on the table. "Things have changed, Annie. Three days ago I walked into a bank and my wife stood between a gunslinger and banking customers. My heart leaped into my throat. I died a slow death. I knew right then and there that if we lived through that bank robbery, I would never let you go. It just took my heart three days to convince my head it was true." He prayed she'd see all that he felt for her in his smile and eyes.

A lone tear escaped the corner of her eye and slowly trickled down her face. Josiah used his thumb to wipe it away. He continued, "I've been an idiot, Annie. I realize that now. I thought I could only ever love one woman. I thought that to love you, I'd have to forget Mary and the relationship we had together. But that was wrong, too."

"I never want you and the girls to forget Mary," she protested.

He scooted his chair around the table so that he could wrap his good arm around her shoulder. "Thank you. I'm glad you feel that way." She rested her head on his chest and it felt good. It felt right. "I need to explain something, so hear me out."

She leaned back to look up at him. The trust he saw in the depths of her eyes gave him the assurance that Anna Mae was listening to him.

"I grew up without a mother. When I married Mary, she'd run a hand over my hair or touch my arm and I'd feel special, and it fed something that had been missing in my life. The softness of a woman's touch and the desire to matter to someone. But over time, she was as happy to see me leave on the trail as I was to get away.

Neither of us minded being apart for weeks, sometimes even months."

Josiah kissed Anna Mae's cheek and smiled secretly to himself when her face reddened. "With you, my precious Annie, I hate leaving you to go to work in the mornings. I'm dying to run home for a bite of lunch, and I really resent the thirty minutes it takes to come home. That's half an hour I could be spending loving my family."

"Oh, Josiah, I feel exactly the same." She snuggled against his side. "When I was engaged to Mark, it felt scary and like I had to do what was required. But when I am with you, I feel safe and happy. It comes naturally to try and make you happy. I search for things that will please you."

Josiah laughed joyfully. "Don't look now, Annie, but I think we are in love." He reached for the ring box and opened it. "Merry Christmas, my sweet Annie."

She giggled and raised her face. "I love you, too, Josiah. I have for a long time, just was too afraid to admit it to myself and to you."

All he had to do was lower his head and he could kiss her. Josiah did just that. His lips touched hers and he knew he'd finally found where he belonged. Kissing Anna Mae was as necessary as breathing.

He would have been perfectly content to sit and kiss her all day, but a tugging on his shirt interrupted him. "Tisses!" Rose demanded. "Div me tisses, Papa."

"Me tisses, too." Ruby joined in, pushing at her sister to get closer to their papa.

Reluctantly he released his wife. “In the very near future we have to teach them to wait their turn.”

Anna Mae laughed and slipped out of his arms. “I better check on the biscuits while you give these babies their kisses.”

Josiah grabbed her hand and slipped his gift upon it. The ring fit perfectly on her finger. He held her hand for several more seconds. Leaned over and kissed the back of it.

“Peases, tisses,” Ruby begged.

Josiah laughed. He looked up at Anna Mae. Her eyes, as she moved away, promised she wouldn’t be gone long. If she didn’t return soon enough to suit him, he’d just go after her. Simple.

Josiah turned to his girls and gave their little faces kisses. One of the Psalms suddenly came to mind and his heart blessed the Lord. *Delight thyself also in the Lord, and He shall give thee the desires of thine heart.*

Josiah hadn’t even known what those desires were, but his Father had, and had given him his heart’s desire. His soul sang as he realized that he was loved not just by his little girls, but his Annie loved him, too.

Chapter Twenty-Six

The next day was Christmas. The night before, Josiah had enjoyed watching Annie and the girls open their gifts. They'd read the Christmas story from the Bible and sang hymns.

He sighed, almost hating to share them with Emily Jane and William. He finished hitching Roy to the wagon and smiled. But it was Christmas Day and everything was perfect. He wanted to climb up on the highest peak of the barn and crow like an old rooster.

Annie and the girls stood on the front porch waiting when he led Roy toward them. Annie's eyes sparkled and her hair fell in beautiful waves about her shoulders. She wore her blue Christmas dress, with matching cloak.

Anna Mae lit up the morning. His stomach clenched tight. He wondered if she truly knew how desperately he needed her in his life. The gold ring caught the light and he smiled.

Rose and Ruby clutched their Christmas babies to

their chests and wore big smiles on their little faces. Rose wore a new green dress with a matching ribbon in her hair, while Ruby sported a new red dress and ribbon. They both looked cute and happy.

Anna Mae held a large package in her arms. "What's that?"

"Emily Jane and William's Christmas gift," she answered, handing it to him.

"Oh." He took the present. "I thought it might be for me," he teased. "After all, I do have a surprise for you."

"You do?" She stepped back up on the porch to retrieve something else.

"Yes, and I'll show you when the time is right."

Josiah put the gift in the wagon and then swung each of the girls up. When he turned back around, Anna handed him a box filled with dishes. "What's all this?" he asked, placing it carefully in the back.

"Part of our Christmas dinner." She propped both hands on her hips. "What did you think I was doing in the kitchen all morning?"

"Reading a book." He laughed at the expression on her face. "It wouldn't be the first time I've caught you in there reading when you were supposed to be cooking," he teased.

She playfully slapped him on the arm. "That may be true, but not today. Today I cooked up a feast." Anna Mae pulled herself up onto the wagon. "Scoot over, girls," she said.

"Alwite, Mama." Rose answered with a grin.

"Mama?" Her eyes grew round.

Ruby pulled at Rose's coat. "Me sits wif Mama."

The girls scrabbled back and forth till Josiah raised his voice. "If that don't beat all. No one wants to sit with me?" He faked a pout and Rose patted him on top of his head.

"Me will, me will." She immediately climbed into her place beside Ruby, both girls unaware that they had made their new mother the happiest woman in the world.

Josiah watched his Annie surreptitiously wipe at her eyes. Then she gathered both girls as close as she could and kissed them soundly.

Truth be told, he was just as surprised as Anna Mae appeared. He'd never heard them call her Mama, or anything, for that matter. Carolyn at the general store referred to Annie as their mama so maybe that's where they got it from.

"Thank you, my sweet girls. I think that's the best Christmas gift I have ever received." She couldn't seem to let them go until they squirmed, wanting out of her arms.

Josiah pulled himself up into the wagon. He looked at Anna Mae. She'd once told him that she didn't want them to call her Mother. Looking into her eyes now, he knew she was ready. More than ready.

"They called me Mama." She reached across and squeezed his arm. Her eyes flashed with happiness like silver lightning. "Did you hear that?"

"I sure did. It's about time, too." He tickled Rose until she scooted over.

He slapped the reins on Roy's back and clicked his tongue. Then Josiah's eyes drifted right back to his wife.

He couldn't seem to quit looking at her. The satisfied expression on her face spoke volumes about what was in her heart. He should know; it was a reflection of his own.

He ignored the little twinge in his gut. If he'd learned anything the past few days, it was that his gut instincts about Annie were not always right. But he had also learned something important from his marriage that would work equally well on his job. Communication was the key to success.

That's why he knew he'd better start talking. They had thirty minutes tops for him to present an idea to his wife and pray she'd like it. He drew a deep breath.

"Josiah, I've been thinking hard about something these last couple of days."

He closed his mouth with a snap and all but groaned. He'd missed his chance. His gaze moved to hers and he forgot that he'd wanted to talk first. "What is it, Annie?"

She played with the folds on her cloak. "Well, the things you mentioned the other day about coming home for lunch and not caring for the long drive home." She paused, waited until he nodded and then continued. "I've been thinking how much I would love seeing you at different times during the day."

He gave her a sidelong glance of utter disbelief. Had she read his mind?

"Would you be very upset if we sold the farm and moved to town?"

Joy filled him. Josiah pulled Roy to a stop and twisted sideways on the wagon bench. "Annie, that's my surprise." At her look of confusion, he clarified, "Remember the house that wasn't destroyed by the storm? That sat about four down from yours and Emily Jane's?"

"You mean Mr. Parker's place?"

"Yes, that's the one. Mr. Parker passed away and Mrs. Parker plans to move back East to live with her children, just as soon as she sells her home. I wanted to show it to you today to see if you'd consider moving back to town and living there."

She bounced on the seat in her excitement. "Oh, Josiah, I love that place. It has a wraparound porch and three fireplaces."

He nodded. A smile the size of the Rio Grande split his face. "Right, and a huge fenced in backyard. The girls can play without us worrying about them wandering off."

"You wouldn't miss the farm?"

He studied her intently. Then decided honesty was the best policy. He squinted, but kept eye contact. "No?"

She giggled. "That's a question, Josiah, not an answer." She picked Ruby up and slid into her place on the seat, then plopped her on the other side of her. Depositing Rose right next to her sister, Anna Mae effectively closed the space between herself and Josiah. She was near enough to kiss with the barest of movement from him. From the look in her eyes, that's exactly what she planned.

"Will you miss the farm, Annie?"

"Like the plague."

He threw back his head and let out a great peal of laughter. His Annie was a minx. She brought her hand up to stifle her giggles, but he caught it and kissed her.

As though his kiss drove her, she wrapped her arms around his waist. When he released her, Anna Mae laid her head against his shoulder.

The sound of whispered "tisses, tisses" echoed from the girls' side of the wagon. But it seemed they understood that these were special kisses, and didn't demand they be included this time.

Josiah had never felt happier in all his born days. He silently began to thank the Lord above for all his blessings.

For the birth of Christ that they celebrated on this special day; for coming to earth to die for the sins of mankind, and last but most certainly not least, for sending Anna Mae into his life on a cold winter night. Josiah had never dreamed he could feel this happy and loved.

Her soft voice drifted up to him. "Merry Christmas, Josiah. I love you."

Those were words he'd never get tired of hearing. His wife loved him.

"Wuv you, Papa." Rose and Ruby chimed in.

"I wuv *you*, too." He placed his lips against Anna Mae's brow. His Annie. He hoped she felt the depth of his love. Thanks to her they were a family. A family full of love.

* * * * *

Dear Reader,

This is Josiah Miller's story. He stepped on the page in *The Texan's Twin Blessings* bigger than life to me. Being a lawman in the 1800s was a dangerous job. Josiah's family meant the world to him and when he lost his wife, he really thought he would never find someone he would love that much again. It got me to thinking about God's love and how when we lose a loved one God steps in and loves us even more than He ever did, much like Anna Mae stepped into Josiah and the girls' lives and offered them a new love. It is my prayer that, if you have lost a spouse, you have allowed God to step in and wrap His loving arms around you.

I hope you enjoyed this book.

Warmly,
Rhonda Gibson

COMING NEXT MONTH FROM

Love Inspired® Historical

Available January 5, 2016

INSTANT FRONTIER FAMILY

Frontier Bachelors

by Regina Scott

Maddie O'Rourke is in for a surprise when handsome Michael Haggerty replaces the woman she hired to escort her orphaned siblings to Seattle—and insists on helping her care for the children he adores.

THE BOUNTY HUNTER'S REDEMPTION

by Janet Dean

When bounty hunter Nate Sergeant shows up and claims her shop belongs to his sister, widowed seamstress Carly Richards never expects a newfound love—or a father figure for her son.

THE TEXAS RANGER'S SECRET

by DeWanna Pace

Advice columnist Willow McMurtry needs to learn to shoot, ride and lasso for her fictional persona, and undercover Texas Ranger Gage Newcomb agrees to teach her. But as the cowboy lessons draw them closer, will they trust each other with their secrets?

THE BABY BARTER

by Patty Smith Hall

With their hearts set on adopting the same baby, can sheriff Mack Worthington and army nurse Thea Miller agree to a marriage of convenience to give the little girl both a mommy and a daddy?

LOOK FOR THESE AND OTHER LOVE INSPIRED BOOKS WHEREVER BOOKS ARE SOLD, INCLUDING MOST BOOKSTORES, SUPERMARKETS, DISCOUNT STORES AND DRUGSTORES.

LIHCNM1215

Maddie O'Rourke is in for a surprise when handsome Michael Haggerty replaces the woman she hired to escort her orphaned siblings to Seattle—and insists on helping her care for the children he adores.

Read on for a sneak preview of INSTANT FRONTIER FAMILY by Regina Scott, *available in January 2016 from Love Inspired Historical!*

The children streamed past her into the school.

Maddie heaved a sigh.

Michael put a hand on her shoulder. "They'll be fine."

"They will," she said with conviction. By the height of her head, Michael thought one part of her burden had lifted. For some reason, so did his.

Thank You, Lord. The Good Word says You've a soft spot for widows and orphans. I know You'll watch over Ciara and Aiden today, and Maddie, too. Show me how I fit into this new picture You're painting.

"I'll keep looking for employment today," he told Maddie as they walked back to the bakery. "And I'll be working at Kelloggs' tonight. With the robbery yesterday, I hate to ask you to leave the door unlocked."

"I'll likely be up anyway," she said.

Most likely she would, because he had come to Seattle instead of the woman who was to help her. He still wondered how she could keep up this pace.

You could stay here, work beside her.

LIHEXP1215R

As soon as the thought entered his mind he dismissed it. She'd made it plain she saw his help as interference. Besides, though his friend Patrick might tease him about being a laundress, Michael felt as if he was meant for something more than hard, unthinking work. Maddie baked; the results of her work fed people, satisfied a need. She made a difference in people's lives whether she knew it or not. That was what he wanted for himself. There had to be work in Seattle that applied.

Yet something told him he'd already found the work most important to him—making Maddie, Ciara and Aiden his family.

Don't miss
INSTANT FRONTIER FAMILY
by Regina Scott,
available January 2016 wherever
Love Inspired® Historical books and ebooks are sold.

LIHEXP1215R